DRUMTA...
And The Guardians ...
Roberts

R.J.GREER

This book is dedicated to my children

Mary Jane Roberts was only 19 years old, today 13th Oct 1902 was the saddest day of her life. Today was the day she buried her late husband who had contracted measles and sadly passed away. Mary Jane had been married to John Roberts for less than a year however, John was her childhood sweetheart they had dreamed of the day they would marry and start a family.

That sad day was also the strangest day of Mary Jane's life. The sun had just started to fade along the western woods close to Mary Jane's little thatched roof farmhouse. Hog Hill Farm was bought on the week John and Mary Jane married, on the agreement of the payment of a silver crown each month to their neighbour, farmer William Giles. Mary Jane and John had talked for hours about buying Hog Hill Farm, the animals they would keep and the vegetables and fruit they would grow.

That evening was drawing cold as Mary Jane closed the door to the chicken coop. The night sky was clear, as Mary Jane looked up, she could see the brightness of the stars. As the tears ran down her face she thought, *'how lonely life was going to be without John, how am I going to manage the farm and the cost. How am I going to afford a crown payment each month?'* Just before John had passed away, Mary Jane made a promise to him, that she would never give up on Hog Hill Farm and she would keep their dream alive.

Mary Jane turned towards the house, she wipes her tears and spoke out loud, *"Grow up woman, what would John Roberts think if he saw you now,"* Mary Jane started to walk towards the house, when a warm wind passed over her, this warm wind swirled hard and fast around Mary Jane, it tore the shawl off her head, which she had just wrapped herself up in to keep the chill off her bones, her long dark brown hair blow frantically in the wind covering her face and obscuring her vision. Her whole body had been twisted in the opposite direction as if someone had grabbed her by the shoulder and physically turned her around. She found herself facing the opposite direction in which she meant to walk.

As Mary Jane composed herself, she felt the coldness of the winter night on her skin. While swiping her hair away from her

1

eyes, Mary Jane looked up she could see the wind that had swept past her. In front of her were dust, dirt, and winter leaves swirling in this strange breeze as she looked into the swirl, she could see what looked like the outline of a man. *"John!"* Mary Jane called out. *"John is that you?"* at that moment Mary Jane thought she had gone mad, grief-stricken by the one she had lost and loved dearly.

Mary Jane's gaze did not leave the figure of the man in the swirl as he walked away from her into the nearby barley field. Mary Jane felt compelled to follow the figure, she slowly walked towards the barley field, her feet felt cold as she realised, her shoes has fallen off. Mary Jane could feel the winter barley brush against her, she stretched out her hand as they glided over the top of the barley stocks.

The swirl dropped into the barley about ten feet in front of her, as the mysterious figure of the man disappeared the night fell silent, and the strange winds had calmed. Mary Jane continued to walk towards the place where the figure once stood, she looked down onto the ground to see a small linen blanket, suddenly there was a twitch.

Mary Jane was startled, her thoughts were going crazy, *'It's an animal.'* Mary Jane took a deep breath and composed her thoughts. She leaned over with caution, she reached out and nipped the edge of the small blanket with her finger and thumb, she slowly peeled the blanket back, Mary Jane, *"gasped"* stepped back, stumbled and fell hard onto her bum. Mary Jane crawled forward on all fours and started to peel the blanket back again. This time she paused; her eyes had not deceived her. Under that small corner of the blanket was a foot, the foot of a small baby. Mary Jane continued to pull the blanket back further, two small feet and legs. Suddenly a small kick, Mary Jane gasped, her heart was pounding in her chest, as her thoughts went wild *'It's alive,'* Mary Jane continued to draw the blanket completely back from covering the baby.

On the ground, in her barley field was a tiny baby boy, his eye's sparkled blue as he stared directly at Mary Jane, he did not cry he just lay there silent in the cold of the night. Mary

Jane noticed that there were small blood smears on his chest, arms, and head she frantically picked the baby up looking for any injuries the child may have, she wiped the blood smear from his body, but no wound was to be found.

Mary Jane wrapped the baby back in the blanket, she stood up clutching him tightly in her arms and close to her chest.

"Your mother, where is the mother, she must be nearby," said Mary Jane as she started to walk around in close proximity of where the child was found, calling out.

"Hello, Hello can you hear me? if you can hear me call out!"

Mary Jane began to feel a sense of panic, *'There is a mother in this field who has given birth she has lost her baby and she may be hurt."* Mary Jane began to run up and down the barley field shouting *"Can you hear me?"* Mary Jane shouted for a considerable amount of time.

After what seemed like hours, Mary Jane fell to her knees weeping. She held the child in her arms and close to her chest she looked down at his little face, he was fast asleep, she softly spoke to the child.

"I'm sorry, I'm so sorry, I cannot find her," she said.

In the far distance Mary Jane could see the glimmer of light from the rising of the autumn sun, she stood up, tired and exhausted she walked to the house. As she walked, she felt the warm breeze come from behind her, the same breeze she had felt that night standing in the farmyard, strangely she thought *'Can I hear the flapping of bird wings,'* Mary Jane turned sharply and the noise stopped suddenly, and the wind died instantaneously.

Mary Jane hurried up the farmyard, she got to the small white front door of the farm cottage, she placed her hand on the thumb latch, she glanced over her shoulder, she had this eerie feeling that she was being watched.

*

Inside the cottage was dull and dark, the sun had not broken the horizon, the fire had small cinders glowing and the candle that Mary Jane had lit last night had just gone out. Mary Jane looked around, *"Where can I lay you?"* Mary Jane said as she looked down at the baby. In front of her on the wall unit was John's wash basing a large blue and white pattern basin, she grabbed the basin placed it on the kitchen table and laid the baby into the basin.

"Fire let's get this fire going its cold and I need a cup of tea," said Mary Janes as she looked down on the baby. Mary Jane picked up some fire sticks she had gathered the day before; she had placed them in front of the fire to dry out. Mary Jane laid the sticks on the fire; she took the poker and stirred the cinders up. It was not long before they took light. Mary Jane picked up some logs that lay beside the slated hearth and placed the logs on the fire, it was not long before the logs caught fire giving light and warmth to the farm kitchen. Mary Jane then turned to the large kettle and with a towel in her hand took the kettle to the sink, where she pumped some water into it. She turned towards the fire and placed the kettle on the steel hook which hung over the fire.

Slowly the morning sun started to rise and shine through the two small front windows of the kitchen of Hog Hill Farm. The room lit up, Mary Jane had poured herself a cup of tea added a little milk. She walked towards the big wooden farmhouse table and looked down at the baby, he was wide awake, staring directly at Mary Jane.

"What I'm I to do with you?" Mary Jane said, as the baby kept looking at her with his big blue eyes, he made a gargling noise. Mary Jane smiled as she picked the baby up and held him in her arms, Mary Janes had an overwhelming feeling, something she could not explain. Mary Jane looked up at the photo of John Roberts that was sitting on the farmhouse wall unit. It was a black and white photo; he was a handsome young man. Suddenly the image came to life and the face of John Roberts came out of the photo and spoke to Mary Jane. *"Keep him!"* he said.

Mary Jane let out a small cry of fright, she thought she had gone mad.

"*Lack of sleep,*" she said out loud as she rubbed her tired eyes. Mary Jane looked at the photo of John Roberts good and hard. It did not move; it did not speak again.

"*I need some rest, I need to sleep,*" said Mary Jane as she laid the child back into the large blue and white, washbasin. '*Clunk,*' something hard hit the kitchen table which appeared to have come from underneath the child. Mary Jane continued to place the baby into the basin, once the baby was safe, she glanced towards what looked like a small wooden box.

"*Where did this come from?*" Mary Jane said as she picked up the box, it felt heavy, much heavier than it looked. The box was made of oak wood, smooth and glazed. There was gold beading around the center edges of the box on all four sides with a small gold latch hook, that kept the box closed. Mary Jane turned the box upside down to see if she could find a name or a mark, she thought it may lead her to the child's mother, the bottom of the box was plain, no name, no marks, no clue to finding the baby's mother or family.

The top of the box had four strange symbols engraved into the wood with a cross 'X' the symbols sat inside each segment of the cross. The top segment had a fish, the fish was engraved into the wood with gold embroidery, the fish appeared to have small blue stone as the eye that glistened in the sunlight from the kitchen window. The second segment had a tree that was embroidered in gold with small leaves made of tiny green stones.

The third and bottom segment had a symbol of a man with wings spread wide as if in flight. The gold embroidery lit up as Mary Jane tried to get more sunlight on the box, at the same time the winged image wings flapped in the sunlight.

The fourth image was peculiar, there was no gold embroidery, there was no shining stone. Instead, there was a skull engraved into the wood. Which made Mary Jane feel cold, she looked hard at the hollow dark eyes of the skull, they looked deep, cold, and empty. Mary Jane placed the box on the table. Her eyes were heavy with tiredness she crossed her arms on the kitchen table, resting her head on her arms she quietly fell into a deep sleep.

*

"Bang, Bang, Bang" Mary Jane was startled, what was going on, the noise *"Bang, Bang, Bang"* It was the kitchen door, someone was knocking on the door. Mary Jane stood up rather sharply. *"Baby,"* she said, what to do with the baby. Mary Jane looked around, the towel she had lifted the kettle with was on the kitchen table. Mary Jane picked the towel up as she looked down, she whispered *"Sorry,"* and covered the large basin with the towel.

Mary Jane looked towards the door *'Bang, Bang, Bang'*

"In a minute," Mary Jane shouted.

As she moved from the table, she looked down to see the box glowing, the gold embroidery was glowing. Mary Jane was startled; however, she had the most compelling feeling to open the box. Mary Jane picked up the box, it felt heavier, and it was warm. She placed her thumb on the hook latch that kept the box closed and pushed it up. Mary Jane had unlocked the box, once the latch was lifted and the box stopped glowing. Mary Jane's desire to open the box had not gone. Mary Jane had to look, she lifted the lid, she looked inside and to her surprise was a small piece of paper, as she lifted the small piece of paper she could see some symbols, strange symbols, then the symbols started to move, coming together to form words. Mary Jane read the mysterious note and all it said was *"Hire the work hand!"*

Mary Jane looked back into the box, there was a silver coin, a sparkling new silver crown with King Edwards VII's head on it.

Mary Jane quickly picked up the silver crown and placed it in her pocket. She walked towards the door and opened it. At first, she could not see anything.

"Good morning mam," said a strange quirky voice.

Mary Jane looked down to see a small boy or was it a small man, she was unsure. He was not very tall at all, standing at her kitchen door.

"*Good morning,*" replied Mary Jane.

The small person gave Mary Jane a big smile. It was at this point Mary Jane realised his even stranger appearance, he had ridiculously small teeth, evenly sized and very white. He had a lot more teeth than any person she knew. On his head was a peaked tweed hat, strangely his ears were small and very close to his head with small points at the end of each ear. Mary Jane thought, '*what a very strange, odd-looking man, boy, person he was.*'

The strange little man removed his peak tweed hat, to reveal silver-white hair, swept back over his head, it was not long, and it was well-groomed. The strange little man bowed as he removed his hat and stated his name.

"*My name is Murrigan-Sham, mam,*" and again he gave Mary Jane a big smile.

"*Good morning, sir,*" replied Mary Jane.

"*My name is Mary Jane Roberts; how can I help you this fine morning?*"

Mary Jane felt nervous, the strange happenings had completely startled her and this strange little man at her kitchen door even more so.

"*Mam, I believe you were advertising for a work hand for your farm at a crown a month, well I'm your man, mam.*"

For some reason, he looked and nodded towards the crown in Mary Jane's pocket. Mary Jane remembered the note '*Hire the work hand,*' Mary Jane was confused, '*I'm I in some sort of dream,*' she thought, has the past two days been a nightmare.

From behind her, the baby let out a cry, as she turned around, Murrigan was standing over the baby.

"*Isn't he such a beautiful baby?*" Mary Jane ran towards the baby and quickly picked him up from the big blue and white washbasin.

"*Yes, he is,*" Mary Jane replied. Mary Jane paused, "*How did you get past me at the kitchen door, how did you know he was a boy, how do you know of the farm hand job at a crown a month?*" Mary Jane asked in a frantic voice.

"*About that job are you hiring or not mam? I can start straight away,*" said Murrigan-Sham, he had distracted Mary Jane from her questions, she sat down at the table, Murrigan sat at the other end.

"I suppose I am, I could really do with the help on the farm."

"It's agreed then," Murrigan got out of his chair and reached out his hand, Mary Jane placed her hand into Murrigan's hand, as their hands met to shake. Mary Jane could feel the warmth of his hand, a reassuring warmth, making her feel calm and relaxed. She looked at Murrigan and thought *'what a kind face,'* Murrigan looked up at Mary Jane and gave her a big smile, *'We are going to have to work on that smile,'* Mary Jane thought.

"Cup of tea Murrigan?" Mary Jane got up to place the baby gently back in the basin. She then placed the kettle onto the hook over the fire.

"What's his name?" Murrigan asked.

"His name!" Mary Jane was taken by surprise; she did not know the baby's name. She was about to splutter out, *'He is not mine,'*

"Yes, what do you call him?" replied Murrigan.

"He is called Thomas Roberts, yes, we named him Thomas Roberts," said Mary Jane as she turned towards Murrigan.

"Yes, that's a good name for him, Thomas Roberts, I like that name," replied Murrigan.

"How old is he?" asked Murrigan, Mary Jane choked on her tea, all these questions she only met Thomas Roberts last night and Murrigan thirty minutes ago.

"Well," she paused *"He was born yesterday,"*

"That's amazing," said Murrigan.

"What is?" replied Mary Jane.

Murrigan replied *"You had him one day ago and here you are up and about like you'd never given birth,"*

"I'm a very strong woman," scowled Mary Jane.

The farm kitchen fell silent after Mary Jane's, little outburst.

"Bang, Bang, Bang" Mary looked at Murrigan, Murrigan looked at Mary Jane. Out of the corner of her eye, Mary Jane could see the emblems on the box glowing bright. She picked up the

box, the box felt warm, she quickly fumbled the box in her hands, the latch flipped back, and the box opened. There was a note and a silver crown, Mary Jane forced these into her pocket and open the kitchen door.

"Good morning mam, I am Moria-Sham, and I have been informed that you are seeking to employ a handmaid at a crown a month."

Mary Jane looked at the strange little woman, girl, she was unsure what she was looking at. Moria pushed past Mary Jane and walked directly to Murrigan.

"Good morning, sir," she said, as she started it introduce herself to Murrigan. There was this strange sense that these two had met before. Moria had all the same peculiar features as Murrigan, the silver-white hair, the pointy little ears, they were the same height and they even sounded like each other.

Moria looked at Mary Jane, *"This job, I take it, I, have it?"*

Moria placed her hand in front of her, to shake Mary Jane's hand. Their hand met and strangely enough, Mary Jane felt the strange warmth from Moria's hand, it made Mary Jane relax in her presence.

"Yes, the position is yours," Mary Jane answered. Moria looked up at Mary Jane and smiled she looked across to Murrigan and he was smiling. *'These two musts! be related,'* she thought, as they both grinned at each other.

Mary Jane showed Moria and Murrigan around the house. She showed them the three small bedrooms with the low laying roof and allocated a room to each of them.

"Hog Hill farm cottage is small but very cosy, where are your belongings?" Mary Jane asked.

"Belongings?" Moria and Murrigan looked at each other.

"Your clothing, suitcase?" replied Mary Jane.

"Oh yes, we have brought them, they are at the front door," Murrigan opened the small kitchen door, where two small wooden trunks sat outside the door both were identical, what Mary Jane failed to notice was the four emblems of the fish, tree, bird-like creature and the skull, on top of the trunks. Murrigan grabbed both handles of each of the trunks and dragged them in.

Mary Jane spoke loudly *"Let me give you a hand with those."*

"No, no Murrigan can handle them," said Moria, just as Mary Jane reached down towards one of the small trunks, she grasped the handles at each end, she bent her knees slightly and tugged up. To her surprise the box did not move, she tugged again, and still, the box did not budge, *'Strange'* Mary Jane thought.

Moria moved beside Mary Jane, she looked at her with an odd gaze.

"I have this, you shouldn't be lifting a heavy trunk in your condition," said Moria.

"What condition?" replied Mary Jane.

As Mary Jane stood up from behind the trunk, Moria reached her hand out and laid it across Moria's stomach,

"You know!" said Moria. Mary Jane felt a strange warm sensation across her stomach as if something had kicked her. Mary Jane placed her hand on her stomach and felt that her stomach had become swollen.

Mary Jane walked towards the table, where the baby was still wrapped in the blanket and sleeping quietly in the big blue and white washbasin. She leaned forward and touched the baby's hand. Just as she touched him another kick occurred, this time there was pain. Mary Jane leaned forward and clutched her stomach with both hands.

'What's happening to me?' she thought, her stomach had swollen again and again. What a strange sensation, Mary Jane had never felt anything like it. She looked across to Moria and Murrigan who had lifted the small trunks and started to walk up the set of stairs to the bedrooms. Mary Jane felt dizzy and a little confused, tiredness she thought, *'I'm just so tired,'* Mary Jane's world just started to fade as her heavy eyes closed, she had gone into a deep sleep at the kitchen table with her head in her arms as a pillow.

"Bang, bang, bang," came the sound from the small kitchen door. Mary Jane woke up suddenly in a daze. She stood up quickly, her head went light and dizzy.

"Heavy," Mary Jane said, *"I feel so heavy,"* Mary Jane looked down, still dazed and body swaying. She saw a glow coming from her apron pocket. The box was glowing again, Mary Jane

picked the box out of pocket and opened it, yet again a silver crown and a note. *"Pay your debt,"* it said. *'Bang, bang, bang,'* went the kitchen door. Mary Jane waddled towards the kitchen door. She opened the door to find farmer Giles, standing in front of her.

"Good afternoon, Mrs. Roberts, I hope I find you well and our condolences on your loss, Mr. Roberts was a fine gentleman."

"Thank you, kindly sir," replied Mary Jane.

"Mrs. Roberts, we need to talk, important talk, about the farm and your keeping of the farm, the mortgage is overdue, the farm is going to struggle with no man to run it and you in your condition and all," Farmer Giles was looking towards Mary Jane's stomach.

"What condition that might be, Mr. Giles?" Mary Jane scolded. Mary Jane placed both her hands on her stomach. Her big stomach, massive stomach, Mary Janes head had gone wild, what is going on, *'have I woken up from my sleep or am I still dreaming she thought,'*

"With child, Mrs. Roberts, with child," replied farmer Giles.

Mary Jane collected her thoughts *"We will manage just fine,"* replied Mary Jane. Mary Jane reached into her pocket and pulled out the silver crown from her apron pocket.

"Your payment, sir, and I bid you a good day," Mary Jane closed the door and closed it tight, she leaned against the door. Sat at the table was Moria and Murrigan, both smiling at her with big grins.

"Right!" Mary Jane shouted, *"Since that baby has turned up in my barley field, things have been very strange, and what are you two sitting there smiling for, what do I pay you for, to sit around all day and drink tea?"*

Suddenly Thomas Roberts started to cry. Mary Jane walked towards him and could see he was distressed, she picked him up and held him close.

"I'm sorry, I didn't mean to scare you, Oh, I think he's hungry, we must feed him."

'How to feed a baby,' she thought. Mary Jane stood in the middle of the kitchen looking around her, looking for something to feed the baby with.

"Lamb's" shouted Mary Jane.

"The baby can't eat a lamb," said Moria.

"No, he can't," replied Mary Jane.

Mary Jane was thinking about lambing season and on occasions, younger lambs would need to be bottle-fed. Mr. Roberts had lambing bottles in the house, she handed the baby over to Moria, and started to look for the lambing bottles. In a few minutes, she had three bottles in her hands.

"Moria, we need to get the fire going," stated Mary Jane, for some reason it had gone out. Moria started to run about the kitchen.

"Fire, I need to get a fire going," Moria kept repeating out loud.

"Moria, calm down, put Thomas back in the basin," Mary Jane said in a stern voice. Moria took a deep breath and placed Thomas Roberts back in the basin.

"Moria, go to the log shed at the side of the house and bring in some logs for a fire," Mary Jane gave Moria the instructions in a very quiet controlled voice. Moria opened the kitchen door and went outside.

"Murrigan," Murrigan stood up very quickly as if he were a soldier standing to attention when Mary Jane called his name.

"Yes, mam," he replied.

"Murrigan, fetch a pale of milk, Maisy is in the milking shed," Murrigan stood still as if he had frozen to the spot.

"Murrigan, did you not hear what I said?" asked Mary Jane.

"Yes mam, fetch a pale of milk, Maisy is in the milking shed."

"That's correct, what are you waiting for? we got a hungry baby that needs feeding, chop, chop," said Mary Jane.

Murrigan hurried towards the kitchen door, chattering to himself, *"Hungry baby that needs feeding, chop, chop,"* Murrigan opened the kitchen door and ran out, closing the door behind him.

Mary Jane, turns towards Thomas Roberts, she picks him up, holding him in her arms she looks down into his little eyes *"Don't you worry my little one we will have you fed in no time."*

Murrigan was standing just outside the kitchen door, he was breathing very heavily he was also extremely nervous, Mary Jane had sent Moria and himself on their first task. *'Crash bang,'* the noise was coming from the log shed. As Murrigan approached the log shed a load of logs landed at his feet.

"Do you think that's enough logs for the fire?" asked Moria.

"Yes, I'm sure that is enough," replied Murrigan.

There were a lot of logs laid outside and inside the log shed.

"Well then, you going to help me or not?" scolded Moria.

"I will help you if you help me first," Moira could sense that Murrigan was nervous.

"Yes, yes, I will help you; we must work together we cannot give her and doubt or suspicion, what's your task?" asked Moria.

Murrigan started to repeat his task, *"Fetch a pale of milk, Maisy is in the milking shed."*

"Oh!" replied Moria.

"Oh what?" replied Murrigan.

"It's a riddle, we must work out Mary Jane's riddle, let's start at the milking shed," said Moria.

Murrigan and Moria look around to see what they could see, the chicken shed, the pigsty and a large shed detached from the others. *"There,"* as Murrigan points to the large shed, *"This got to be the milking shed."* Moria and Murrigan made their way to the milking shed. They get to the door, there was some rope holding the door shut, wrapped around a rusted nail. Murrigan unwraps the rope from around the rusty nail *'Mooooooo'* Murrigan jumps back in fright and takes Moria with him, both are laid on the ground with Murrigan on top of Moria.

"What in bells was that?" asked Moria. The wind had caught the milking shed door and blown it open.

"What is that foul evil smell?" asked Murrigan.

"Draw a blade," Moria commanded. Murrigan reached up his sleeve and drew out from the sleeve of his jacket a large silver dagger. Murrigan and Moria got up, Moria nudges Murrigan to

take the lead. Murrigan positions his body and blade in a position ready to attack.

As the light started to shine in from the open doorway, Murrigan catches sight of the smelly beast, that dwells there.

"Are you Maisy?" Murrigan asked.

"Yes, I am, and you better have some nice grass for me."

"What are you, friend or foe," asked Moria.

I'm no foe and I'm no friend unless you got some nice green, juicy grass for me."

Maisy was a large black and white cow, she was extremely big and fat, all she wanted to do was eat grass all day. Murrigan slowly approached Maisy, *"We need your help, Mrs. Roberts has sent me on a task,"* Murrigan started to tell Maisy that he needed to fetch a pale of milk from Maisy and that he didn't know-how. Maisy started to 'Moooooo' so loud with laughter that she could be heard at farmer Giles farm a mile up the road. The 'Mooooo' was that loud that Mary Jane thought they were killing, poor Maisy.

"What do you need the milk for?" Maisy asked.

"For baby *Thomas Roberts,"* replied Murrigan.

"Baby who?"

Just then the milk shed door opened and Mary Jane was standing there with Thomas in her arms.

"What's all the racket about, what are you doing to my cow?" demanded Mary Jane.

"It's fine, mam, Maisy is just being stubborn, we will be right with you in a moment, you get young Thomas Roberts back inside, it's getting a bit chilly out here."

Moria started to lead Mary Jane back to the kitchen door, once inside, Moria attended to the wood for the fire.

"Stubborn, who you calling stubborn?" scolded Maisy.

"Sorry, this is my first day on the job as a farmhand, I will make you a deal, you help Moria and me and I will cut you fresh grass each day." stated Murrigan.

"Deal," replied Maisy.

"Good then, give us a pale of milk," asked Murrigan.

"*Give you, you're going to have to take it yourself and you can put that thing away before you start,*" said Maisy, Maisy was referring to the large silver dagger Murrigan was still holding in his hand. "*Grab the pale, also known as the bucket, hanging up on the hook beside me,*" Maisy said, as she rolled her big brown eyes as she instructed Murrigan to get the bucket from the hook. "*Place it below me, under my udders, take the udders, one in each hand and pull and squeeze, you will need the small stool to sit on,*" Maisy instructs Murrigan.

Murrigan was in position sitting on the small stool, "*Take an udder and pull and squeeze,*" Maisy said, "*That's it, you got it just pull and squeeze, pull and squeeze,*" repeated Maisy. The first squeeze of milk landed center of the bucket.

"*I think I have the hang of this now,*" shouted Murrigan, all excited about milking a cow, the second squeeze land directly in the center of his face. This was a continuous trend, one in the bucket one in the face.

"*You have lovely warm hands, you can milk me anytime you want,*" Maisy said, and she gave a long relaxing "Mooooooo" of delight. "*You should have enough now, to feed ten babies,*" Maisy informed Murrigan.

"*Yes, thank you, you have helped me quite generously, I will honour our deal,*" said Murrigan as he picked up the pale of milk, dripping from head to toe in milk.

Murrigan opened the small kitchen door, to see Mary Janes looking at him.

"*What have you been doing? it looks like you have had a bath in it,*" Mary Jane started to laugh, just then, Moria comes barging in with a large stack of logs, she trips over the small mat under her feet, the logs are in the air and come down with a thud, Moria joins them, and her body hits the floor with a bang. Mary Jane is stunned by Murrigan dripping wet with milk and Moria laid out on her kitchen floor. Mary Jane breaks into laughter once more. Murrigan gives his hand to Moria to help her up from the floor, they both look at each other and burst into fits of laughter.

Thomas Roberts gives out a short cry as to say, *"I'm still here and I'm still hungry,"* Mary Jane takes down a small pan hanging above the stove and pours some milk from the pale into it. *"Moria, can you please get the fire started, so we can warm up some milk for Thomas Roberts,"*

"Yes mam," replies Moria. Moria picks up a few logs and some sticks and places them on the fire. Moria was thinking to herself I need some flame. Moria places her hand into the logs, she looks to see if Mary Jane is watching her. Mary Jane has her head turned and is distracted by Thomas Roberts. Moria mutter the words *"Ignato,"* suddenly Moria's hand started to let off a small, magical spark, the sparks are generated into flames, the sticks catch fire and the logs were lit.

"Your hand," screams Mary Jane. Mary Jane pounced on Moria, pulling her away from the blazing fire, *"Pump water,"* Mary Jane screamed at Murrigan *"Her hands-on fire,"* Murrigan ran to the large white sink and started to pump hard on the metal handle of the water pump. The pump began to splutter and suddenly the water came gushing out. Mary Jane swung Moria around and pushed her towards the sink. Mary Jane lifted Moria's arm and forced her hand under the pump gushing out water. *"Keep pumping,"* Mary Jane instructs Murrigan. Murrigan keep pumping after a few minutes the sink was full.

"Keep your hand in the water until the stinging soothes," Mary Jane instructs Moria.

"Get the aid kit in the top drawer of the kitchen unit," Mary Jane command Murrigan. *"We must get a dressing on this wound quickly before you get an infection,"* said Mary Janes, as she starts to feel uneasy, her vision is blurred, her speech is slurred, and her hearing is dull and muffled, as she falls to the ground Moria catches her, Moria's face is the last things she sees.

Mary Jane opened her eyes and starts to see the sunlight from her small bedroom window, she knows it was morning as she can hear Errol the farm cockerel giving his morning wakeup call.

She lay on her bed, thinking *The nightmare is over, I'm awake now,'* Mary Jane placed her hand on her stomach, she was not pregnant, there was no swelling, a feeling of relief overwhelmed Mary Jane. She rolled over with a smile cuddling up to her nice warm blanket. When a cradle catches her eye, *'Why is there a cradle in my room?'* she thought. Mary Jane started to edge her way slowly towards the cradle, she started to lift her head to peer into the cradle, Mary Jane noticed the cradle was woven from willow tree branches it was perfectly woven. On the side was a small carved wooden plaque with the emblem of a tree, fish, bird-like creature, and the skull, there were also the letters TR engraved below the emblem. Mary Jane was familiar with the markings; she was a little curious as to why the marking had been made on the small wooden plaque and placed on the cradle. Mary Jane peeked over the top of the willow cradle; she was filled with excitement. Mary Janes paused she was holding her breath, inside the cradle was a small baby, looking directly at her, she breathed out slowly, her heartbeat which she could feel pounding in her chest had stopped pounding, *"Thomas Roberts,"* she whispered.

"Morning Mam," as the door opened, Mary Jane looks up as Moria barges in through the door, with a tray in her hand.

"Morning," Mary Jane replies.

"Some breakfast for you and your son,"

"Thank you very much," Mary Janes replied, as Moria laid the tray on the bedside table, Mary Jane looked at Moria's hand.

"How is your hand?" Mary Jane asked, looking at her hand Mary Jane noted, no dressing, no burnt skin, *"which hand got burnt?"* Mary Jane asked.

"My hands are fine both of them," Moria raised both hands to show Mary Jane. Moria turned to leave Mary Janes bedroom,

"Enjoy your breakfast, and don't forget to feed Thomas Roberts,"

Mary Jane thought *'There was no way possible that Moria had not burnt her hand, there is something peculiar going on.'* Mary Jane looked at her tray two boiled eggs and toast that was black and burnt.

"They can't burn a boiled egg!" Mary Jane said out loud. Mary Jane took the egg in her white ceramic egg cup, picked up her small silver teaspoon, and chopped the top of her boiled egg. To her surprise, the yoke started to flow, looking closely Mary Jane realised that the egg was raw.

Mary Jane looked at Thomas Roberts, lay in the cradle, she felt overwhelmed that this little baby was in her room. She picked him up and held him in her arms. She reached across and picked up the bottle of warm milk and started to feed Thomas Roberts his breakfast, he was very small she thought, *"We will soon make you big and strong,"* Mary Janes said softly.

From downstairs Mary Jane could hear, banging noise, pots and pans clashing and Moria scolding Murrigan. Downstairs was a mess, cup, pans, dishcloths, broken eggs, flour, Moria was scolding Murrigan however, it was her that had made the mess. Moria was not a real housemaid, after all, she never had been. Moria could hear Mary Jane coming down the stairs. Moria closed her eyes and muttered the word *"Perfecto,"* the small kitchen started to come alive, the broom started to sweep, the cups and saucers started to dance through the air back in the cupboards, the flour that lay over the kitchen table and floor gathered its self together and formed a dancing woman in a white swirling dress, she danced her way to the large flour jar that sat on the kitchen floor she hovered over the jar and spun herself into the jar. The fire that was out, lit up, just then the door opened, and Mary Janes walked into her tidy little kitchen.

"I see you have been busy Moria," said Mary Jane.

"Yes Mam, it's busy work being a house-made" Moria replied.

"You have done a grand job, thank you," both Mary Jane and Moria looked across the kitchen table, *"Slurp, Slurp,"* Murrigan was slurping on a big mug of tea the mug seemed massive in his hand and when he realised, he was being watched he lowered the mug from his face, only to reveal bright red strawberry jam running down the side of his mouth.

"Oh, no! the sheep have got out again," shouted Mary Jane as she glanced out the window.

Moria started to shout at Murrigan.

"You're the farmhand, get out there and sort those sheep out," Murrigan grabbed his peak hat and coat and ran out the door. Mary Jane and Moria started to giggle at the reaction of Murrigan.

*

Murrigan stood outside from the farmyard he could see about thirty sheep, wandering down the dirt track towards William Gile's Farm. Murrigan started to run across the yard and up to the dirt track, when he got to the sheep, he shouted at them *"You lot stop right there, turn around and get back into your field,"*

"Ma," The sheep replied.

'Ma, is this some strange language these animals speak?' Murrigan thought.

"Do you not know that sheep are dumb animals?" the voice was coming from behind Murrigan. Murrigan turns swiftly his hand up his sleeve ready to draw his hidden dagger. Laid on the grass was a young border collie dog.

"Are you speaking to me?" asked Murrigan.

"Who else would I be speaking to, there's just you, me, and the dumb sheep and they don't speak or listen or obey," stated the young collie dog.

"What's your name?" asked Murrigan.

"They call me lassie, but you can call me Bimbo, I like being called Bimbo," replied the dog. Bimbo was a year-old tan brown and white border collie he was lean and had one bright blue and a dark green eye. He was a handsome dog and full of mischief.

"I will make a deal with you, if you help me round these sheep up and get them back in the field, I will return the favour," said Murrigan.

"What type of favour?"

"Anything you desire," replied Murrigan.

"Deal," Bimbo jumped up and started to dart back and forth, up and down, herding the sheep together and moving them back into the field. Murrigan stood there in amazement, within a few minutes all the sheep were back in the field that belonged

to Hog Hill Farm., *"Amazing!"* shouted Murrigan *"You think you were born for this job,"* said Murrigan.

Bimbo just stood staring at Murrigan.

"My favour now," requested Bimbo.

Bimbo laid on his back all four legs in the air. *"Rub my belly,"* said Bimbo.

"What! rub your belly?" Murrigan replied.

"Yes, rub my belly, you said anything I desire, I want you to rub my belly," said Bimbo.

"How long for?" asked Murrigan.

"For as long as I say,"

Murrigan got down and started to rub Bimbo's belly,

"Faster," Bimbo shouted. The faster Murrigan rubbed Bimbo's belly the more he giggled.

"Ok stop," Bimbo commanded.

Bimbo jumps up on all four legs and starts to walk back to Hog Hill Farm.

"Where you going?" asked Murrigan.

"Dogs work is down its dinner and nap time," replied Bimbo.

"Who will guard the sheep and stop them from escaping?" asked Murrigan.

"I'm no guard dog," Bimbo said, as he waddled down the track tail swishing left and right.

"Murrigan," shouted Mary Jane.

Murrigan was perched like a bird on the stone wall. He was fast asleep until Mary Jane had startled him. In the shock of hearing Mary Jane's voice Murrigan, still half asleep, dropped off the back of the wall. 'Thud,' he hit the ground, as quick as he hit the ground he jumped back up onto the wall, this time covered in mud.

"Murrigan, what are you doing?" demanded Mary Jane.

"Well mam, Bimbo, helped me gather the sheep up and herd them back into the field, he then refused to guard the sheep and that's why I'm here to stand guard, so the sheep don't escape," said Murrigan, very fast and flustered.

"What are you waffling on about man and who is this Bimbo?" asked Mary Jane.

"He is your farm dog," replied Murrigan.

"Our dog is called Lassie," stated Mary Jane.

"Well, mam, he told me he would like to be called Bimbo, as he doesn't like being called Lassie,"

"And the dog told you this?" asked Mary Jane. Murrigan went quiet, he paused and realised that Mary Jane was asking too many questions.

"It was just a bit of fun mam," replied Murrigan.

Mary Jane looked around the farm, her mind wandered, she wished John was here, it had only been a few days since she buried him in the village cemetery. Her heart was broken and there was nothing that would bring her John back. Murrigan was standing beside her, he saw the sadness in her eyes.

"What would you have me do, mam?" asked Murrigan. She looked down at Murrigan, she could see his compassion upon his face.

"Catch me, for I feel that I am falling into the dark place, and I am scared that if I ever hit the bottom, I will never get up, if only John were here, he would tell me what I must do," said Mary Jane as her tears rolled down her cheeks.

Murrigan stepped up beside Mary Jane he took her hand, she felt the warmth of his hand. As they both looked over the ragged fields with walls that had fallen.

Do not fear this darkness it will keep you safe, only in the darkest place can you see the clearest light, do not fear my lady for you are blessed."

Mary Jane wiped her tears with her hands, *"Thank you for your comfort and companionship, I must tend to my baby, and you must tend to these walls,"* said Mary Jane.

"Yes mam, tend to your baby and I will tend to the walls," Murrigan said with his big smile. Mary Jane started to walk down the track with a smile on her face, as mad as Murrigan was, she had a soft spot for him and Moria, but most importantly for her new baby boy Thomas Roberts. Mary Janes, thoughts took her to plan the next few weeks. She would tell others that she was pregnant, to John and that he sadly died just before Thomas was born. Thomas Roberts was John's and her son, and no one

would be any the wiser. Her thoughts were with Thomas Roberts real mother, who was she, where was she, one day would she come knocking on Hog Hill Farm door seeking her son. Mary Jane looked up towards the barley field, where she had found Thomas Roberts, was his mother still in the field, *"Tomorrow we will find out!"* she said aloud.

Before Mary Jane walked through the kitchen door, she turned to look up towards the sheep fields she could hear Murrigan singing at the top of his voice and piling stones. She smiled and walked into the little farmhouse.

Murrigan was standing in the hole in the wall he was looking at this one big sheep, who was staring at him, as if to say, *"Get out of my way,"* Murrigan *"Growled,"* very loud, and the big sheep turned and ran. *"A fortress is what I will build and you pestering sheep will never escape,"* said Murrigan. Murrigan had a good look round, dusk was settling in, and the sun was just about down.

"Excelar," he muttered, and clicked his finger and thumb together, the ground started to rumble and the boulders that were piled up started to fly through the air. Some had stopped in mid-air and when the time appeared to be right these rocks slotted themselves into the wall, this occurrence was not just one wall it had spread, the wall was rebuilding itself. The wall was getting thicker taller and stronger. Wooden gates were hanging off, damaged and rotten, they flipped into the air, the old rotten wood dropped off and was replaced, magically by perfect new wood, these new wooden gates then slotted nicely into the gaps where the old gate once where. The wall continued to build and soon as they were complete, the new gates swung shut and a steel bolt shot into the wooden gate post to secure the gates. The walls were five feet high, two feet wide, and straight with smooth edges. Murrigan's work was almost complete, Murrigan hopped onto the wall. The sheep were all huddled together, above the sheep were thousands of rocks, spinning around and around. Murrigan, looked at the sheep, *"I don't like you sheep much,"* said Murrigan as clicked his fingers one more time and the rock s fell, not onto the sheep but around them. Murrigan had built the sheep a wind pen, a

shelter the sheep could cuddle up in on the cold winter nights ahead.

*

Mary Jane woke the next morning the sun was up and Errol the farmyard cockerel was doing his thing. Mary Jane opened her window curtains to let some light in, she looked out of the small bedroom window and had to look twice. Mary Jane was breathless, *"The walls!"* she said, *"How did he manage that?"* Mary Jane said to Thomas Roberts, as she turned to pick him up. *"Look what your uncle Murrigan has done, he is such a clever man,"* Mary Jane said to Thomas Roberts as she turned him towards the window to show him the perfectly built stone walls.

Moria and Murrigan were both in the kitchen, Moria had a concern, a concern that Mary Jane would find out about Murrigan and her identity, who they really were, and why they were here on Hog Hill Farm.

"Murrigan," said Moria. Murrigan had his spoon and head in a large bowl of fresh porridge. *"Murrigan listen to me we need to talk,"* said Moria, just as Murrigan lifted his head from his bowl, Moria's wooden spoon that she was using to mix some cake mix bounced off his head.

"Talk then," replied Murrigan.

"We need to be careful, and we need to stop using magic, Mary Jane is starting to get suspicious," said Moria. Murrigan looked at Moria

"Suspicious, of course, she suspicious, she has a baby, she never had, she has a box that gives her gifts and tells her what to do, who wouldn't be suspicious. (Murrigan paused) she is just curious about her surroundings and her new life, Mary Jane will be fine, she needs us, and she needs Thomas Roberts, let her be happy," said Murrigan.

"I suppose when you look at it that way, your right let her be happy, we will make her happy, but what if she starts to ask questions?" asked Moria.

"When the time is right, we will tell Mary Jane the truth about Thomas Roberts," said Murrigan, just as Mary Jane had come down the stairs and opened the door leading to the kitchen with Thomas in her arms.

"Thomas Roberts, what about Thomas Roberts?" asked Mary Jane.
"I was just saying, the little fella must be hungry," Moria replied.
"Yes, so am I, make sure we all eat a hearty breakfast, we all have a busy day ahead of us," said Mary Jane.
"I'll eat to that," said Murrigan as he reached out his bowl to Moria for more porridge.

"Moria, if you gather and twine, Murrigan and I will get on with the cutting. Mary Jane instructed. The winter was drawing nearer, and the leaves were starting to change, it wouldn't be long before the first winter frost sets in. Mary Jane knew that the autumn harvest needed to be gathered and the winter barley need to be cut. The harvest wasn't the only thing on her mind, Mary Jane wondered if the body of Thomas Robert's birth mother lay in the field. *"Murrigan, you start at the top and I will start at this end,"* explained Mary Jane. Murrigan walked to the far end of the barley field, with his scythe in his hand wondering what it was for. Mary Jane had Thomas Roberts harnessed to her back, in blankets, for some reason Mary Jane felt the need to have him close, also to be there in the event they find his mother. Mary Jane dropped the scythe, onto the ground, the sharp end away from her, she took a firm grip of the top and bottom handle raising the blade a few inches off the ground, she swung it right, then to the left, the cut barley fell to the ground. Murrigan was looking at Mary Jane's actions, his eyes had changed shape and he was focused on Mary Jane, his eyesight allowed him to see exactly what Mary Jane was doing. Off Murrigan went, left then right and the barley fell. Moria followed behind picking up bundles of cut barley and tying them together with twine. They stopped only for a short lunch and a few water breaks. As the day started to draw to an end and the sun started to dip behind the glens. *"I think it's time we stopped and had our tea,"* Mary Jane shouted, Mary Jane, Moria and Murrigan, stood over the half-cut barley field and took joy in the day's hard work.

"We can finish that off by tomorrow evening," said Murrigan. All three of them walked down the track, along the perfect stone wall, into the yard, and up to the front door.

The following morning the sun was up, and Errol was up also crowing his morning wake-up call. Mary Jane, Murrigan and Moria, were on the edge of the barley field, *"Are we ready to go again?"* asked Mary Jane.

"Yes mam," replied Murrigan, and with his big wide smile scythe in his hand, he marched back to the top of the field. Mary Jane and Murrigan started cutting and Moria started to gather and tie the barley clumps together. After what seemed like an hour,

"Mam, Mam," shouted Murrigan.

"What is it?" shouted Mary Jane, Murrigan was looking down at the ground.

"It's something dead," he shouted back, Mary Jane's heart sank, her face turned pale, she felt as if she was going to throw up, she dropped her scythe and ran up the field towards Murrigan. As she drew closer, she stopped.

"What is it Murrigan?" she asked.

"I'm not sure mam," He replied. Mary Jane slowly eased herself towards, the object laid on the ground in front of her. The first thing that caught her by surprise was the smell of death. Mary Jane plucked up her courage and stepped closer brushing the top of the barley away with her hands. Her heart was racing she could feel it pounding in her chest. She looked down,

"Deer!"

"What is it?" asked Murrigan.

"It's a deer," replied Mary Jane. Mary Jane started to calm down, *"Let's drag it to the side, we can burn it later,"* That day was long and hard for all three of them, Mary Janes burden was lifted, Thomas Robert's mothers' body was not in the barley field after all. Mary Jane, Moria, and Murrigan retired to the farmhouse for a good wash, some supper, and a good night's sleep.

The winter had started to close in, and it was the eve before Christmas. Snow had started to fall and laid over Hog Hill Farm like a perfect white blanket on a bed. Thomas Roberts was growing and becoming aware of his surroundings, Mary Jane, Moria and Murrigan had grown very fond of the little man.

"Thomas Robert's must be two months old now," said Moria.

"We must start to be thinking of his future, his schooling, his profession," Murrigan said.

"I agree, but tonight is the eve before Christmas and there is plenty of time to think about his future," Mary Jane said, as she held Thomas Roberts in her arms, she opened the first page of Dickens, Christmas Carol.

Thomas Roberts had lived eight years very happily at Hog Hill Farm, he had grown to love Mary Jane as his mother and Moria and Murrigan as his aunt and uncle. The summer of 1910 was hot, humid with plenty of thunderstorms. Thomas Roberts ran bursting through the back door of the farmhouse, that led onto the garden at the rear of Hog Hill Farmhouse.

"Woo, slow down young man," scolded Moria, stood in front of her was Thomas Roberts at eight years old and four feet tall with jet black hair, shining blue eyes, and tanned skin from the summer sun.

"Auntie Moria, Mother said we can have a picnic for afternoon tea, we have picked some fresh strawberries, raspberries, and gooseberries, can you whip up some cream?" asked Thomas Roberts.

"Sound nice, get the picnic basket, I have some fresh scones, go find Murrigan and we will meet you by the pond," said Moria.

"Aunt Moria, can I ask you a question?" said Thomas Roberts.

"Of course, you can, you can ask me anything you want," replied Moria.

"Why does Murrigan, talk to the animals?" asked Thomas Roberts.

"Well, that is a very good question, your uncle Murrigan has a gift, he hears what they say, and he speaks their language, you could speak to them also, take some time to listen to the animal, you, maybe surprised in what you hear, do you have any more questions?" asked Moria, Thomas Roberts shook his head to say no. *"Run along now and find Murrigan."*

The sun was out and bouncing off the pond that lay to the north of Hog Hill Farm about three hundred meters from the house. Mary Jane had laid a large red and blue tartan blanket on the grass, about twenty meters from the pond bank. Moria placed the large basket packed with scones, sandwiches, and fresh cream for the strawberries. Murrigan and Thomas Roberts were skimming stones along the surface of the pond.

"I got four," shouted Thomas Roberts, with a big smile on his face.

"Well done young man, that's going to be hard to beat," said Murrigan, as he bent over to find a smooth stone to skim across the pond. Murrigan looked over the water as he fondled for his stone. Thomas Robert bounced a stone, however, something strange was occurring, Murrigan noted that the bounces were coming towards them, Thomas Roberts looked at Murrigan with a strange look upon his face, suddenly a weed from the pond wrapped around Thomas Roberts ankles and pulled him into the pond, Mary Jane *"Screamed!"* out loud, Murrigan, ran to the pond edge, Moria, ran up behind Murrigan, she placed her boot on Murrigan bum and forced him into the pond screaming *"Save him."*

Moria held Mary Jane tightly as she tried to fight Moria off.

"Where is he? I cannot see him," Mary Jane shouted.

Mary Jane fell to her knees, Moria was reassuring her that Murrigan would save Thomas Roberts. Thomas Roberts and Murrigan were nowhere to be seen, they had vanished into the depth of the pond. A large splash came up from the center of the pond, there was a large, winged creature with a serpent creature wrapping itself around the winged creature, they were fighting violently with each other. Both creatures rose about ten meters into the air, the winged creature was flapping its wings that caused strong winds and a sense of chaos was all around. Both creatures slammed back into the center of the pond and a long silence began. Mary Jane and Moria sat on their knees at the edge of the pond holding on to each other tightly.

Thomas Roberts felt himself sinking, his legs were bound by the weeds, he could not kick to get to the surface for air, as he looked up, he could see Mary Jane and Moria at the edge of the pond, as he sank deeper and deeper, the sun that shone upon the lake had started to fade. Thomas Roberts could feel himself falling into the darkness. *'Thud,'* Thomas Roberts had hit solid ground. He was dazed and his eyes could not focus. Thomas Roberts noticed two figures in front of him, they were the same height and shape. His sight was slowly coming back, Thomas noted a smell, a strange musky smell. Thomas got to his feet and started to follow the two figures in front of him. He could see they were two women in front of him as he got closer, he called out *"Mam, can you help me?"* the two ladies stopped and turned around. At this stage, Thomas Roberts noticed they looked the same, identical, but there was something different one was of flesh, human the other looked like a ghost almost transparent. The identical ladies were holding hands. *"To the gates, you must go through the gates,"* said the flesh lady, she seemed quite normal as she pointed to the big black gates that were in front of them. The two identical ladies continued their journey towards the gates. Thomas Roberts followed with caution.

Once at the gate a deathly-looking creature was stood by a table, on the table was a book the book was large and looked very old, there was a quill pen and an inkpot. The identical ladies were standing by the book when the deathly-looking creature pointed to the book with his bony fleshless finger.

"Make your mark," the creature said as he pointed to the book. The ghost-like image of the identical ladies picked up the quill and made her mark on the book. *"Walk on,"* said the creature. Thomas Roberts approached the table and the deathly creature, yet again, pointed to the large old book on the table, Thomas could see his bony finger, he could also feel the cold that surrounded the deathly creature, the air was cold, and it made Thomas Roberts shiver. Thomas picked up the quill, the table was too high for him to reach, *"Make your mark,"* said the deathly creature. Suddenly the table and book got smaller, Thomas Roberts was able to see the book, hundreds of names and marks, where people could not write their names. Thomas Robert's thoughts wondered, *'Where is this strange place and what is this book, he is about to write on?'* Thomas Roberts showed no fear, he picked up the quill dipped it in ink, and wrote *'Thomas Roberts,'*

"Walk on," sated the deathly creature.

Thomas turned to walk on, he could see the identical ladies walking slowly towards the gates. Thomas caught up with the identical ladies and slowly walked behind them.

"Welcome to Creeve my lady," The voice was ragged and hoarse and had a wicked tone. For the first time, Thomas Roberts had a sense of fear and that he should not be here in Creeve.

"You've signed the line now pay the way," the voice said.

The identical ladies looked at each other *"Goodbye,"* they said together, letting go of each other's hand the ghostly lady stepped towards the large figure, Thomas could not make the figure out completely as the ghostly identical lady was obstructing his vision. The ghostly lady kept walking into the large figure and was consumed, she was gone. Thomas looked to see a large beast with a black face, its eyes were white and lifeless, on his head was swept back long jet-black hair and two large white horns, and a long platted black beard, dress in a black robe, that sparkled with shards of sharp glass, on his arm was a large black raven, in his hand was a long black staff with a black shiny stone embed into the top of the staff. Thomas stepped back and fell to the ground, he had never seen anything like this before, fear had now swept over Thomas Roberts and his thoughts were of Hog Hill Farm, his mother, Moria, and Murrigan.

"Thomas Roberts you are dreaming wake up now," he said aloud to himself,

but he was not dreaming, this occurrence was real. Thomas Roberts lifted his head, and a kind hand was in front of him a woman's hand well-tended and clean, Thomas Roberts looked up to see the identical lady in front of him offering her hand to help him up. Thomas took the hand and the woman pulled him up to his feet. Out of the corner of his eye, Thomas Roberts could see the other identical woman, the one of flesh and bone, she looked ill, not the same woman he met on the path to the gates. The identical lady looked as if she had her soul ripped out of her, and that is exactly what this beast had done, however, it was no longer a beast it had changed into one of the identical ladies.

"Well come to Creeve young man, we don't get many young people coming through these gates these days. My name is Arawn, keeper of the gates, guardian of Creeve, who might you be?" asked Arawn in the voice of the identical lady.

"My name is Thomas Roberts from Hog Hill Farm of the town of Trim."

"Well then Thomas Roberts from Hog Hill Farm of the town of Trim, do you have something for me?" requested Arawn.

"Something for you mam! no, I don't have anything at all," Thomas Roberts replied with a confused look on his face.

"Do you know where you are boy, do you know how you got here?" asked Arawn.

"No mam, I don't," replied Thomas.

"What's the last thing you remember?" asked Arawn.

Thomas had a flashback he remembered falling into the pond and sinking to the bottom of the pond, not able to swim back to the surface. *"Yes, I recall now, I was drowning in the pond,"* replied Thomas Roberts.

"That's correct, you drowned, you died, my boy, where is your payment, where is your soul? you signed the line so pay the way," said Arawn.

"I don't know, I don't seem to have a soul," replied Thomas Roberts.

"You don't have a soul; everyone has a soul, and you must pay with your soul to dwell in Creeve," said Arawn.

"I'm sorry, I don't have a soul to give you, what happens now, can I go home?" asked Thomas Roberts.

"Well, if you got no soul to give then you're not coming in!" shouted Arawn.

Suddenly Arawn turned from being the identical lady, into the beast, he lifted his staff and struck Thomas Roberts on the head, Thomas Roberts felt himself falling once more, into the deep and dark.

Arawn was angry and confused, who was this boy without a soul, what was his purpose and why did he come to Creeve?

"Ram-say, come forth," commanded Arawn.

From the mist and shadows behind Arawn was a tall black creature, with two short black horns and white hair and the blackest of eyes, he had razor-sharp teeth and as he spoke in a soft voice

"*Yes, my lord?*" and bowed as he spoke to Arawn.

"*A boy was here, not long ago, his name, Thomas Roberts from Hog Hill Farm of the town of Trim. You are to watch him, report back to me, and speak to no one of this happening.*"

"*Yes, my lord,*" said Ram-says, Ram-says bowed and dissolved into thin air.

Thomas Roberts could feel himself, sinking to the bottom of the pond once more, he was now in the darkness when suddenly he felt himself being lifted from the bottom of the pond and into the air. Mary Jane and Moria looked over the water, the wind was blowing once more, the noise of powerful wings could be heard, flapping in the wind. Up from the pond and into the air Mary Jane and Moria could see Thomas Roberts floating about two meters above the water. Mary Jane looked on in amazement, she could see the outline of an invisible angel, the sun and water had created a transparent image of the creature that had risen Thomas Roberts from the depths of the pond. The wings kept flapping as Thomas Roberts was suspended in the air moving closer to the bank of the pond to where Mary Jane and Moria stood, Thomas Roberts was laid on the ground at the side of the pond. From, nowhere Murrigan appeared dripping wet,

"*He has fallen, he has fallen into darkness.*"

Murrigan cried out.

"*No, it cannot be, it can't be,*" Moria cried out.

Moria knelt beside the small lifeless body of Thomas Roberts, she placed her hand upon his chest and started to whisper and chant, words that Mary Jane had never heard before, Mary Jane fell to her knees and started to pray. Thomas Roberts took a deep breath and life returned to him, coughing and gasping for air, Mary Jane sat him up and held onto him tightly.

"*I thought, we had lost you, I cannot lose you,*" Mary Jane cried.

"Let's get back to the house," Murrigan said with an anxious voice, he was looking all around him as if cautious that danger was near. Mary Jane picked Thomas Roberts up and started to move back to the farmhouse, holding onto Thomas Roberts as tight as she could.

Murrigan grabbed Moria by the hand and pulled her away from Mary Jane. *"They know he is here,"* said Murrigan.

"What makes you think this?" replied Moria.

"Today was no accident, Thomas Roberts was attacked by a 'Serpent of Keel," said Murrigan.

"That's not possible, they are friend not foe and how did he get here, the portal was locked from this side," replied Moria.

"There must be a new portal, or they have found a way to open the old one. I know what I saw and what I destroyed," said Murrigan.

"Why would a Serpent of Keel, come to these lands and want to attack Thomas Roberts?" Asked Moria.

"Something is not right in Drumtara, was he paid or forced to attack Thomas Roberts," said Murrigan.

"I agree, the creatures of Keel are friendly they don't attack unless they are being attacked, something is very wrong here, we must ensure Thomas Roberts is protected," replied Moria.

"We must leave now and take Thomas Roberts away from this place," said Murrigan,

"Really, and what about his life here, his mother, would you take him away from Mary Jane?" asked Moria.

"We swore to protect him, it was his birth mother's last wish, we must leave to protect him," said Murrigan.

"Yes," Moria said as she took Murrigan's hand. *"We also swore that we would give him love, the love of a mother and we choose Mary Jane, we cannot, and we will not leave or take Thomas Roberts away from Mary Jane and the love he has here at Hog Hill Farm,"* said Moria, in a soft calm voice.

Murrigan bowed his head *"Yes we did,"* he replied. *"In that case, we must defend Hog Hill Farm, Mary Jane, and Thomas Roberts, we will do whatever it takes to defend them,"* said Murrigan in a defiant voice.

Mary Jane dried Thomas Roberts and placed him in his fresh, stripped red pyjamas, she kissed him on the head, *"Sleep tight my love,"* she said as she brushed his jet-black hair away from his forehead, and slowly Thomas Roberts fell into a deep sleep. Mary Jane made her way down the stairs and closed the door behind her. She walked up to the table where Moria and Murrigan where sat. *"Use two, pack your things and get out,"* said Mary Jane in a calm stern voice. *"Since you have arrived, I feel I have been going mad, strange happening, you* (Mary Jane was pointing to Murrigan), *talking to the animals as if they understand you, what that all about? and you* (Mary Jane was pointing at Moria) *all this work you have been doing it should take you hours and it appears to be done in minutes. This is not right, this is witchcraft, the devil himself sent you, to hunt me."* Mary Jane was in tears as she let it all out, she turned around and took a handkerchief from her apron and blow her nose, she looked up to see the box with the four emblems of, fish, tree, bird-like creature and the skull glow, *"And another thing this box, what is it for, why does it offer me gifts and tell me what to do?"* shouted Mary Jane. As she held the box in her hand, she opened it and a small note was inside the box, Mary Jane took the note out of the box, the muddled-up letters on the paper magically formed a sentence, for her to read. *"If you send them away, he will die,"* Mary Jane dropped the box and note on the floor, she felt faint after reading the content of the note. Murrigan stood up and took hold of Mary Jane who was unsteady on her feet and lead her to the kitchen table and sat her down on a chair. Moria picked up the box and the note, after reading the note she gave it to Murrigan to read.

"Now is the time to tell you the truth, mam, you may not believe what we say or fully understand why things have happened or why they are going to happen, please do not fear us or what I'm about to tell you, and what I say must never leave these four walls," Moria paused as Mary Jane acknowledged her.

"We are from a place called Drumtara," said Moria.

"Is that somewhere in Europe?" asked Mary Jane.

"No *Mam, Drumtara is not of this world,*" Mary Jane sat back on her chair and listened intensely as Moria started to tell her the truth. *"Drumtara is where the souls of all living creation go when their life is spent, their soul and spirit are reborn in Drumtara as a new creation, the fish, trees, and birds go there and so did humans until one human broke the laws of creation and violated a secret constitution. His name was Tirk, he was a powerful wizard and the ruler of Drumtara he was a good, kind wizard and kept the balance of creation in harmony. Until he violated the rule of creation. No Drumtarian should cross over worlds nor any other source of living creation cross into Drumtara. Tirk's magic and knowledge were so powerful, he started to work on portal creation to other worlds and was successful. He had created a portal to the human world and his curiosity got the better of him.*

Tirk crossed over many times to the human world, this is where he met Isbeth, Thomas Robert's birth mother. Tirk fell in love with Isbeth, and they conceived and Isbeth gave birth to Thomas Roberts in Drumtara. said, Moria.

Mary Jane looked puzzled, *"All these years and Thomas Roberts has a mother and father, why have they never come to get him, take him home, why is he here with me?"* asked Mary Jane.

"Children cannot be born of the flesh and bone in Drumtara, creation is *through the soul and spirit entering the creation of a Drumtarian, for example, the spirit can enter a tree and give the tree a new creation, give it new life, many creations in Drumtara have magical powers, fish can transform into amphibians and walk the land, even talk. It's a magical place full of life and wonder. When Isbeth gave birth to Thomas Roberts in Drumtara, the balance of creation was disrupted, and an entity of darkness spread over the lands. "Tirk had created black matter, the black matter grew to evil, and chaos and madness spread over Drumtara like an unseen virus.*

The creations of Drumtara turned on each other, dark powers and magic was used to violate each other, greed and hate were born for the first time in Drumtara. There was one who corrupted the souls and minds of Drumtarians, his name was Nicopulas, a dark warlock who thrived on evil and chaos, his powers grew strong in the darkest places of Drumtara.

He made deals with chieftains, he lied and deceived many of them. There was one deal that was important to him one deal he needed to seal, this deal was with the collector of dark souls, his name is Arawn lord of the underworld. The deal was that the souls and spirits of humanity would go to the underworld a dark place ruled by Arawn, his responsibility was to collect evil, bad souls, now he is collecting the souls of all humanity, good souls, this has halted new creation in Drumtara and corrupted the creation already created in Drumtara this gave power to Nicopulas the power to rule over Drumtara. Nicopulas demanded all wicked souls are to enter Drumtara as his servants."

"What's this got to do with Thomas Roberts, how did he get here, who are you?" asked Mary Jane as she starred at Murrigan and Moria. *"I know you have many questions, Mary Jane, let Moria explain,"* said Murrigan. *"Nicopulas had convinced, witches, wizards, giants, and many more Drumtarians that Tirk had brought black matter to their lands and that their very existence was in danger, a great army of Nicopulas was formed and they stormed the great city of Lantara the heart of Drumtara, many guardians of Drumtara perished, the battle lasted seven days and seven nights, many souls were lost. In the end, Lantara was defeated and overrun by Nicopulas army."*

"Thomas Roberts father, Tirk and Isbeth his mother loved him dearly, they vowed they would not let him be captured and spend eternity in the prison towers of Nicopulas. On the seventh night of the great battle, Isbeth gave birth to Thomas Roberts. Thomas Roberts was the first and only human to be born in Drumtara. As Nicopulas army stormed the castle, Tirk and Isbeth planned to save their son. This is where Murrigan and I come into the story, we had been by Tirk's side for over five thousand years, we were his closest and loyal guardians and we trusted each other with our souls. said Moria as Mary Jane looked at Moria and Murrigan in astonishment.

"You are both crazy, why are you telling me this stuff, none of it makes sense, are you telling me your five thousand years old?" asked Mary Jane, *"No, we came into creation about fifteen thousand years ago,"* replied Murrigan. Murrigan stood up *"Don't be scared mam, for what I'm about to show you is my true image,"* Murrigan stepped backed from the table and within a few seconds had

36

transformed. Mary Jane fell off her chair in fear and shock of what she just witnessed, *"Do not be afraid Mary Jane, for we are your friends,"* Mary Jane could hear Murrigan's voice, but it was not Murrigan in the room, Mary Jane lifted her head, she was at the end of the table, slowly she started to peer over the top of the kitchen table. Mary Jane *"gasped,"* standing in front of her was a magnificent creature, something she had never seen before, Murrigan true image was seven feet tall, his skin was pale almost white, His hair was silver and braided and shaven on both sides, his ears where small and pointed and lay close to his head. His eyes were blue, they caught Mary Jane's attention, dazzling blue eyes, he looked strong and brave like a centurion warrior of days of old. He wore silver-plated armour on a kilt, Mary Jane could see his powerful muscles on his legs. Upon his chest was a silver chest plate was the emblem on the magic box, with the fish, tree, the bird-like creature and the skull split into 4 segments. Murrigan wore a long silver-handled sword in a silver cladded scabbard which laid over his left hip, on his right hip was a sheaf, full of arrows, but no bow was to be seen. On Murrigan's right hand was some sort of silver laced tattoo embedded into Murrigan skin, Mary Jane could see the tattoo move under his skin, like a snake coiling around his arm. Murrigan walked towards Mary Jane bumping his head of the low ceiling rafter, Murrigan, most impressive feature was the large white wings he had tucked behind his back, the wings were too big to be opened in the small kitchen of Hog Hill Farm, Murrigan placed out his long hand to help Mary Jane up off the floor, *"We are your friends, we will never harm you,"* said Murrigan. He had that Murrigan smile on his face that reassured Mary Jane, that it was Murrigan. Mary Jane took hold of Murrigan's hand, Mary Jane could see his long muscular arms, suddenly she felt the warmth the calming warmth from Murrigan's hand. Mary Jane sat on the chair *"Please continue Moria, I want to know everything."* Murrigan transformed quickly back to Murrigan the farmhand and sat down at the table.

"The plan was to take Thomas Roberts out of the castle at Lantara and flee Drumtara. Isbeth only had a few moments with Thomas Roberts, before Tirk reached him to me. Tirk gave Murrigan two other items, the box of requirement, which you have used many times, this box is a gift to you as his human mother. I think you know how it works by now. The other gift was a key a magic key with the power to open the doors to the human world. Tirk told us exactly where the magic door was, on top of Mount Slem, one of four mountains that surround the city of Lantara, we followed his orders as requested. While the castle was being stormed by Nicopulas army we escaped through underground passages that took us to the valley of Slem at the foot of the mountain.

As we started to climb, we stopped to look down at the city of Lantara we could see the chaos that had taken place the city of Lantara was engulfed in white flames, this is the flame of the witch. We saw Lord Tirk perish at the stake, surrounded by witches who rained white fire upon him until his body and soul perished to ash. Before they destroyed Tirk, they made him watch as Isbeth was tied to a pole, and whipped by Nicopulas with a snake whip, each strand of the whip is a venomous snake. Each lash unleashes unbearable pain. The witches finished Isbeth with white fire.

Murrigan and I could not bear to watch anymore we made our way to the top of Mount Slem quietly, stealthy, unheard and unseen. We located the large round rock, Murrigan muttered the spell, and the rock produced a small wooden door, the key was inserted into the keyhole and turned. Murrigan, Thomas Roberts, and I crossed over into your world. We had little time to adapt; it was with the grace of Drumtara we found you. Standing in the yard of Hog Hill Farm, we could feel your loss and your goodness, your love, we knew you were the one to help us, we didn't need to decide you were chosen to look after Thomas Roberts and become his mother. The night in the barley field the first night you found Thomas Roberts laid on the ground, we were there, Murrigan and I and we have been here all this time. We are the guardians of Thomas Roberts, and we must protect him from the evil that haunts him, all three of us."

"Mary Jane," said Moria, as she looked at Mary Jane who was sitting in a daze at the kitchen table, *"Yes,"* replied Mary Jane as she lifted her gaze to look at Moria.

"Do you fully understand what I have said, do you believe what I have just told you?" asked Moria. *"Yes,"* replied Mary Jane. *"What do you mean to protect him?"* asked Mary Jane.

"Today's event at the pond, was no accident," replied Murrigan.

"What do you mean?" asked Mary Jane with concern in her voice.

"There was a creature in the pond that pulled Thomas Roberts under, this creature is a water serpent of Keel, we know of such creatures they are water folk good creatures not aggressive, friend not foe, however for some reason we had one in the pond, and I believe he tried to kill Thomas Roberts," said Murrigan.

"How did he get here and if he is friendly why did he try to kill Thomas Roberts?" asked Mary Jane. *"These are good questions Mary Jane, and we need to find the answers.* replied Murrigan.

"Where is the Serpent of keel now?" asked Mary Jane.

"He perished by my sword, and he will no longer harm Thomas Roberts," replied Murrigan.

"We need to understand what has happened we may need to ask Thomas Roberts if he fell," said Moria

"Yes, he fell into the pond," replied Mary Jane.

"No, Mary Jane that's not what I meant when humans fall, they must pass over, they go to a place called Creeve a place of the dead, this is where they meet Arawn lord of the underworld, the collector of souls. This was the deal between Nicopulas and Arawn, Nicopulas rules over all Drumtara and Arawn rules over the souls of man forever."

-Chapter 4-
The Running Boy

The decision was made to prompt Thomas Roberts to talk about what had happened to him at the pond. Murrigan and Moria had grave concerns, they knew that other Drumtarians could enter the realm of the human world. What they did not know was how or where they had entered, what they did know was that the Serpent of Keel was on a task to destroy Thomas Roberts. There were so many questions unanswered.

Mary Jane stood by the kitchen sink, Moria was baking some bread, that appeared to be burning.

"What is he doing?" asked Mary Jane. Mary Jane could see Murrigan gathered at the foot of the sheep field with all the farm animals around him. *"He is asking them for their help, asking will they be the eyes and ears of Hog Hill Farm and telling them the story of Thomas Roberts,"* replied Moria.

"The important thing my friends is that we raise the alarm once you see anything, hear anything that is not normal, Errol!" said Murrigan as he looked directly at Errol.

"Yes, my lord," replied Errol the farmyard cockerel, with his chest pointing out and head held high.

"You have my permission to give it all you got day or night," said Murrigan.

"Understood my lord," replied Errol.

"The time will come when we have to fight to defend Hog Hill Farm, your home and to ensure that no harm comes to Thomas Roberts, some of you may perish, but I make this promise, it is not the end, it's only the beginning and our souls will meet again in this world or the next, you all know your duties, to your posts," commanded Murrigan in a voice of triumph as if giving the kings speech before the great battle.

"When the time comes can I fight?" asked bimbo, who was dancing about, snarling and growling.

"Sure, you can, better than that, I have a special mission for you," replied Murrigan. Bimbo sat still, like a good obedient dog, looking up at his master.

"Yes, my lord," said Bimbo. Murrigan looked down at him and said, *"You must protect the sheep,"* Murrigan walked away laughing as Bimbo sat on the ground speechless.

"I used to think Murrigan was crazy talking to the animals," said Mary Jane.

"I think he has always been crazy," said Moria, Mary Jane and Moria were having a good laugh about Murrigan when Thomas Roberts walked into the kitchen, he had a smile on his face, he looked at Mary Jane. *"I'm ready for school mum."* Today was Thomas Robert's first day at school, his uniform was a grey, jumper, white shirt, black and grey tie, and grey shorts. On his feet were the shiniest new school shoes.

"Look at you, first day at school, I have made you your lunch your favourite, strawberry jam sandwich and a rock bun for afters," said Moria as she reached him his school bag containing his lunch. Mary Jane realised that the monthly school fees, needed to be paid, she felt nervous as she never demanded from the box of requirements. Mary Jane could see the box on the shelf, it had not started to glow. She walked to the shelf picked the box up and placed the box in her pocket.

"I will walk you to school this morning as it's your first day and I need to speak to your teacher," said Mary Jane as she ran her hand over Thomas Robert's head. The cost for each month was seven shillings, seven shillings that Mary Jane did not have. She always wanted Thomas Roberts to go to school and get a good education and here he was his first day, and she didn't have the school fee. Mary Jane and Thomas Roberts pulled on their coats, Moria approached Thomas Roberts fixed the collar on his coat, Moria had a small tear in her eye.

"You will be fine and you're going to make lots of new friends," said Moria. Mary Jane and Thomas Roberts started to walk along the lane towards the village school, Thomas Roberts, spotted Murrigan.

"I'm off to school now uncle Murrigan," shouted Thomas Roberts,

"Good lad, you have a good day," Murrigan shouted back. Mary Jane looked up across the field, Murrigan was gone, Mary Jane could feel a warm breeze pass over her and she know that he was with them, not seen, not heard just watching.

Mary Jane and Thomas Roberts got to the front gate of the school. Mary Jane could sense that Thomas Roberts was nervous, she knelt beside him and took his hand.

"You need to be a brave boy, go in there with your head held high and do your best, know not to fight with any of the other boys, if you get scared or don't know what to do run, run fast and hard, run home," Mary Jane said.

"I will mum," replied Thomas Roberts. Just as Mary said *"Goodbye,"* Mrs. Sorter the headteacher was standing at the door of the school, looking across the playground. She was a frightful woman very tall, thin, skinny-faced with dark eyes almost black, she wore a pair of half-rim glasses that sat on the end of her nose.

"Come along boy, your late on your first day," Mrs. Sorter scolded. Mary Jane felt a warmth beside her, she could sense Murrigan's presence, she placed her hand into her coat pocket and drew out the box, it was glowing, she opened it quickly, coins clattered on the ground and a small piece of paper floated softly to the ground. Mary Jane fell to her knees to pick up the coins and note, she forced the box back into her pocket. Mary Jane gathered the coins and the note. It read *"Don't forget to pay for his milk!"* Mary Jane was confused. Mary Jane could see the black pointy shoes of Mrs. Sorter under her nose.

"Good morning, Mrs. Roberts," said Mrs. Sorters.

"Good morning," replied Mary Jane.

"Your son's monthly subs are due at the sum of eight shillings," said Mrs. Sorter as Mary Jane was getting to her feet.

"Yes Mam," replied Mary Jane. Mary Jane looked down at her closed fist and began to open it slowly, in the center of her hand were eight coins to the total of eight shillings.

"Payment in full Mrs. Sorter," said Mary Jane as she reached the money to Mrs. Sorter

"I bid you a good day," replied Mrs. Sorter as she walked away with the monies held tightly in her hand.

Mary Jane sat on the kitchen table, it was nearing three fifteen in the afternoon, school finished at three, it should take Thomas Roberts thirty minutes to walk home, Mary Jane was thinking. *"Bang!"* the kitchen door swung open and there was a hot and flustered Thomas Roberts. *"Everything ok son?"* asked Mary Jane,

"Yes, mother I have had a good day," replied Thomas Roberts.

"Good, come sit beside me and tell me all about your day, did you make friends?" asked Mary Jane.

Murrigan had just opened the kitchen door, Mary Jane could see Murrigan was not smiling.

"Did you run home?" Mary Jane asked.

"Yes mum," replied Thomas Roberts as he pulled a book from his school bag.

"I got some reading to do, I'm off to the barn to find a quiet place to read," said Thomas Roberts. Thomas Roberts picked up the book and left the house. Mary Jane sensed something was not good.

The next morning Thomas Roberts was up early, breakfast eaten, and dressed for school.

"Do you want me to walk you to school this morning?" asked Mary Jane.

"No mother, I'm a big boy now and need to walk to school myself." Thomas Robert picked up his school bag, opened the kitchen door, and started to walk towards the lane leading to Trim. Murrigan picked up his peak cap, slurped the last of his tea.

"Must tend the sheep," as he opened the kitchen door to leave.

"Don't fret mam, Murrigan will watch over him, no harm will come to the boy," said Moria. Mary Jane know that Murrigan would protect Thomas Roberts with his soul.

That Afternoon at three fifteen, Thomas Roberts ran into the kitchen. He was hot and flustered. Mary Jane could see his knees were scuffed, and his school jumper was torn at the elbows.

"What happened to your knees and your jumper?" asked Marry Jane.

"I fell in the playground at break time," replied Thomas Roberts.

"Go get yourself cleaned up, your dinner will be nearly ready," said Mary Jane.

"There something not right here," Mary Jane said to Moria.

"*He's a boy, he is probably up to mischief, he will be fine,*" replied Moria.

Murrigan walked into the kitchen and sat on the armchair. Mary Jane sat at the kitchen table, staring at Murrigan.

"*Well then?*" said Mary Jane.

"*Well then what?*" replied Murrigan.

"*What's happening to Thomas Roberts at school?*" asked Mary Jane.

"*What happens at school stays at school, it's between Thomas Roberts and the other boys,*" replied Murrigan,

"*What you mean other boys, what's happening with these other boys, how many are there?*" cried Mary Jane.

"*The boys, tease, call him names, chase him, push him over, and beat him occasionally,*" said Murrigan.

"*What! and you think this is normal?*" Mary Jane shouted at Murrigan.

"*What were your words mam?*"

"*Don't fight with the other boys, just run, run hard, run fast, run home, this is what he does every day and why? the person he trusts and loves the most on this earth is you, Mary Jane, he is loyal he is obedient and if you say run, he will run,*" replied Murrigan in a stern angry manner.

Mary Jane sank to her knees, in despair, "*I don't know how to do this,*" Mary Jane cried. Moria walked over to Mary Jane and picked her up.

"*You are his mother, you are scared for him because you love him, let us help you, we can teach him how to look after himself,*" said Moria.

"*I can teach him to destroy the other boys at school' only if you want me to,*" said Murrigan.

"*Murrigan!*" Moria said in a serious tone and a glaring stare at Murrigan.

"*We are a family, we must work together to make Thomas Roberts, strong, wise and courageous,*" said Moria. Murrigan, Moria, and Mary Jane were standing in the middle of the small kitchen all three of them embraced in a family hug.

The next morning, Thomas Roberts went off to school as normal, at three o'clock Mrs. Sorter, rang the school handbell.

"Ding, ding, ding," over and over again. Murrigan was perched on top of the school roof, in his full guardian splendor, invisible to any seeing eye.

The school doors opened, and the children started to leave the school. Murrigan could see Thomas Roberts, as he left the school he was walking quickly towards the gate, followed by a group of ten boys. Thomas Roberts kept walking and the boys still followed. The boys started to pick up stones, Thomas Roberts, looked over his shoulder, he knew what was about to happen, 'thud,' Thomas Roberts had a sharp pain on his left shoulder as a big stone hit him. Thomas Roberts started to move faster and faster; he was running hard. Thomas Roberts came to a dead stop and went flying through the air, it was as if someone had stuck their foot out and tripped him up. 'Crash!' Thomas, hit the ground hard, he was shocked, winded, and dazed, he could make a figure out of a boy standing not too far from where he fell, did this boy trip him up? Thomas felt pain in his head a stone struck the back of his head hard. The boys were still there throwing stones at him. Thomas knew he needed to get up. Thomas Roberts stood upturned to face the boys throwing stones, just then the strangest thing was happening, the stones were coming toward Thomas, he could see them, however, none of them were hitting him. There was some sort of invisible shield and the stones hit the shield and dropped to the floor. "Run," a voice said to Thomas, 'I know that voice thought Thomas.'

"Run, Thomas Roberts, run," said the voice.

"Murrigan is that you?" said Thomas Roberts.

"Run," once again said the voice, this time it was loud and aggressive. Thomas Roberts turned and ran as hard and as fast as he could. The boys gave chase, but not for long.

One after another, each boy came to a sudden stop, they bounced back and fell onto the floor, others tripped over each other. Murrigan had created an invisible wall, with his wings that the boys had just ran into, Murrigan then showed his full glory and gave the boys a loud roar, snarling and growling bearing his teeth like a wild animal. The boys got back up still shocked, screaming, and trying to run away without tripping over each other. Once the boys were out of sight Murrigan changed into the farmhand, out of the corner of his eye, he could see a small red-haired boy, the boy was bout nine years old. The boy just stood there and stared at Murrigan. Murrigan gave the boy a growl out of the corner of his mouth, the boy did not move or say anything. *"Strange boy,"* Murrigan thought, as he hurried to catch up with Thomas Roberts.

Murrigan managed to catch up with Thomas Roberts, *"You ok lad?"* Murrigan asked.
"Yes, I'm fine," replied Thomas Roberts.
"We need to speak to your mother," said Murrigan.
"No, can we just tell her I fell over?" asked Thomas Roberts.
"We can, however, the bullying will not end, you have options lad, keep running and you will trip and fall, and they will beat you, or you stand tall face up to them, you may need to fight," said Murrigan.
"Mother said, I'm not to fight, I must run away from the fights," replied Thomas Roberts.
"I agree with your mother, there is a time to run, a time to hide, but there is a time when you cannot do either, you have no choice, get hurt or fight to survive, it's making the right choice in the heat of the moment. The most important thing is that you have more than one choice," said Murrigan.

Both Murrigan and Thomas Roberts walked through the small kitchen door at Hog Hill Farm. *"Oh, my goodness!"* shouted Mary Jane as she throw the trousers she was mending on the floor. *"What happened to you?"* Mary Jane cried. Mary Jane could see dry blood on Thomas Robert's face, there was a cut on top of his head where a stone had split his head open. Thomas Robert's trousers were torn at the knees and blood could be seen. *"Why is this happening to you?"* cried Mary Jane.
"Tell your mother what's been happening," said Murrigan.
Moria stood up, *"I will prepare a hot bath."* she said as she left the kitchen to allow Mary Jane and Thomas to talk.
Thomas Roberts told Mary Jane of the everyday bullying, name-calling, teasing about his father and that he ran away

when he was born. Thomas Roberts, told Mary Jane that they would hit him most days or be pushed, tripped, they would take his lunch and he would go without food. Mary Jane looked at Thomas Roberts, with pain and sadness in her eyes. *"Get yourself upstairs and ready for your bath,"* said Mary Jane. Thomas Roberts gave Mary Jane a hug *"Don't worry mum, I will be ok."* said Thomas Roberts as he left the kitchen to go upstairs, Mary Jane broke down, she was in pain, Murrigan could sense her distress and her breaking heart. *"What, I'm I to do Murrigan?"* asked Mary Jane.

"Sometimes mam, we have to fight, sometimes we have to go to fight our own battles, Thomas Roberts must fight, be strong or this will never end for him, sometimes fighting back is the only answer," said Murrigan.

"No, I don't want him fighting, there must be another way," cried Mary Jane.

Mary Jane left the kitchen and went up the stairs to see Thomas Roberts. He was standing in the master bedroom, with a large towel wrapped around his waist. Mary Jane could see, the bruising, all over his body, she was saddened, angry, and confused that Thomas Roberts had to endure suffering at the hands of other nasty boys. *"Our they sore?"* Mary Jane asked.

"Yes, they can be, especially when I touch them or in bed when I roll onto one," replied Thomas. Mary Jane gave Thomas a hug she held him tight, her thoughts had turned to anger, *'why should my son suffer at the hands of these thugs?'*

"I promise you; these boys will not hurt you again," said Mary Jane as she hugged Thomas Roberts even tighter.

"Mum, Mum!" said Thomas Roberts.

"What?" replied Mary Jane.

"To tight," said Thomas Roberts. Mary Jane released her tight hug, kissed Thomas Roberts on the forehead *"Go have your bath, tell Moria to go easy on the scrubbing brush,"* said Mary Jane.

"Murrigan, can we talk?" asked Mary Jane.

"Yes, mam, of course, we can, I just want to say, I'm sorry for being so pushy about teaching Thomas Roberts how to fight, I know he is not my

son, but it hurts me to see him get hurt, I will do what I can to protect him," said Murrigan.

"Thank you, I know you and Moria love him and will do anything to protect him, I don't know the future or how long we have left, but one thing I do know is that I want him to defend and fight for himself and for those who need protection from, those who would do wrong to others," said Mary Jane.

"What would you like me to teach him?" asked Murrigan.

"Everything you know," said Mary Jane.

"Yes mam," said Murrigan with his big grin across his face.

It was an early Saturday morning on Hog Hill Farm, Murrigan had made cleared a square in the barn and had found two sets of fifteen oz boxing gloves, the gloves were old, and the leather had toughened up. Thomas Roberts was standing in the barn with a pair of long blue shorts and a white vest, Thomas Roberts was shivering in the cold barn.

"Thomas, put the gloves on," said Murrigan.

"I don't know how," replied Thomas.

Murrigan picked up the gloves and attempted to put them onto Thomas Roberts's hands. Murrigan ended up putting the gloves on the wrong hands, Murrigan attempted to put two left gloves onto Thomas Robert's hand. Murrigan got a little frustrated, picked up the gloves, and throw them into the corner of the barn.

"We will go bare-knuckle," said Murrigan. Murrigan started to dance around in the clearing *"hands up,"* Murrigan was still dancing around with his hands clenched into a fist and rolling them in a circle in front of his face. *"Come on then, hands up just like me, jab, jab,"* said Murrigan, every time he said jab, he would punch the air. Thomas Roberts started to copy Murrigan actions. *"Jab high, Jab low,"* said Murrigan as he made a low jab followed by a high jab. *"Good lad, well done, let's take a breather, have you ever hit anyone?"* asked Murrigan.

"No!" replied Thomas Roberts.

"Well then, you're going to have a go now," said Murrigan.

"Who am I going to hit?" replied Thomas Roberts.

"There is no one else in this barn, you're not going to hit yourself, me boy, you're going to hit me as hard as you can on the chin don't hold back," said Murrigan. Thomas Roberts lined himself up to jab Murrigan, *"Ready?"* asked Murrigan,

"Ready," replied Thomas Robert. Thomas Roberts picked up both hands into a good boxing stance. *"Bang,"* Murrigan was knocked off his feet and fell lifeless to the floor he was completely unconscious.

"Murrigan, Murrigan are you ok?" asked Thomas Roberts who thought Murrigan was messing about and pretending to be unconscious. Thomas Roberts ran out of the barn and ran towards the small kitchen door of Hog Hill Farm. Thomas burst in through the door and shouted, *"I've killed Murrigan,"* Moria and Mary Jane turned to look at the wild face of Thomas Roberts and burst into fits of laughter. *"Come see, I cannot wake him,"* shouted Thomas Roberts.

Mary Jane grabbed her shaw, wrapped it over her shoulders.

"Let's go have a look then," Moria followed a few paces behind them. Sprawled on the barn floor was Murrigan. Moria called out,

"Murrigan, get up you fool, you're scaring the boy," Murrigan did not move.

"Is he snoring, I can hear him snore?" said Mary Jane. Moria picked up the bucket of water that was laid on the floor and throw it over Murrigan. Murrigan started to come round, he shook his head straightened his chin.

"What happened?" asked Murrigan.

"Apparently you were knocked out by an eight year old boy," scolded Moria.

"Yes, Yes the boy can pack a punch he knocked me clean of my feet, what a punch," said Murrigan with excitement.

"Don't tease him," said Mary Jane.

"I'm not, this boy has strength," replied Murrigan with a big smile and a glazed look in his eyes.

The following morning, Murrigan and Thomas Roberts were standing in the cut barley field, Murrigan had cloths laid on the ground, there was something under the cloths and Thomas

Roberts was keen to find out. Murrigan pulled two wooden swords from under the cloths, they were made of oak, the wooden swords were finely made, with the emblem of the fish, tree, bird-like creature, and the skull, carved into the wooden handles of the swords. Murrigan reached one of the swords to Thomas, *"Woo, is this mine?"* asked Thomas Roberts, *"Yes, but it's not a toy, it's a training aid, to teach you to fight and become skilled with the sword,"* replied Murrigan.

"Will I get to kill people with it?" asked Thomas Roberts *"No, it's not a toy, the sword is a weapon of defence and offense, killing is always the last option and showing mercy at the time needed is more powerful than taking the soul of another, what you are learning is not a game and one day you may need to make important decisions of sparing or taking another life,"* replied Murrigan.

Murrigan was patient with Thomas Roberts, he taught him wisdom as well as fighting hand to hand and the use of the sword, he taught Thomas Roberts to swim, climb, hunt, and build shelters. Murrigan had his own agenda, and that was to make Thomas Roberts a warrior fit to fight any deviant beast that may be sent from Drumtara to kill him. Thomas Roberts saw the events as fun and enjoyed his time with Murrigan, unaware of Murrigan's true motivation.

One fine Saturday morning, Murrigan woke early, he has special plans for Thomas Roberts. Murrigan didn't knock on Thomas Robert's door, *"Get up young man, we got plenty of work to do before we can play,"* shouted Murrigan as he passed Thomas's bedroom door. Thomas Roberts did not hesitate he jumped out of bed and quickly got dressed.

"I will meet you at the top field when you have finished your chores," said Murrigan. Thomas Roberts finished his chores and started to run to the top field, standing, waiting for him was Murrigan. Murrigan looked at Thomas Roberts, he had a very serious look on his face.

"Today, my boy we are going to fire some arrows," as Murrigan reached Thomas Roberts an arrow made from a long thin straight

willow tree branch, the arrow was about a foot long, it was split at one end and had bird feathers inserted to make four fins, the bark had been stripped of the willow tree branch which made the arrow smooth. The other end was simply a pointed end sharpen by a penknife.

"Great, is this arrow for me, where's the bow?" asked Thomas.

"Bow, we don't use a bow, what you think we are Cowboys and Indians, bootlace, please," demanded Murrigan. Thomas stood looking at Murrigan, thinking he had gone mad. *"Boot lace!"* Murrigan repeated. Thomas Roberts knelt down and untied his bootlace, which he reached to Murrigan. Murrigan had a similar arrow that he laid on the ground, he took the lace and tied a knot at one end. *"Look here, at the arrow, do you see the notch just below the feathers?"*

"Yes," replied Thomas.

"Good, take the lace at the knotted end and wrap it around the notch, the knot and notch will hold the lace in place, keeping the lace tight draw the lace down, just above the tip, warp the remaining of the loose lace around your hand, like so," instructed Murrigan.

Murrigan repeated the actions and instructions to Thomas. Thomas then followed the instructions, he practice the looping of the lace, his hand were fumbling the lace, but it didn't take long before Thomas could loop the lace and extend the lace near the tip of the arrow, it was holding the arrow and wrapping the lace around his hand, which caused the most problems for Thomas. After some time of practicing Thomas got the hang of what Murrigan was asking him to do.

"Good, I think you got the hang of this part, the next step is the throw," said Murrigan. Murrigan then picked his own arrow up from the ground, looped it with the lace from Thomas's boot. Murrigan raised his hand and arrow above his head, his left leg slightly forward, and stood at a stance ready to throw. Murrigan whipped his hand forward and the arrow shot high into the sky. Thomas could see the arrow fly through the air *"Woo,"* he said in amazement, the arrow hit the ground with a thud about three hundred meters down the field.

"That was amazing, and no bow," said Thomas Roberts.

"No bow required, now go fetch the arrow," laughed Murrigan. Thomas Roberts set off at speed to retrieve the arrow he got about ten paces, when his boot without the lace, came off his foot and stuck into the mud, Thomas Roberts landed face-first into a bog of muddy water, Thomas could hear the laughter of Murrigan from behind him, Thomas pulled his stuck boot out of the mud and placed it back on his foot, *"Yuck,"* said Thomas as the squelchy mud came over the top of the boot as he forced his foot into it.

Thomas retrieved the arrow and ran back up the hill towards Murrigan. *"This arrow is a long to medium range, this means that no aim is directly taken, a good arrow-man could land a long-range arrow on your head from four hundred meters, give it a go,"* said Murrigan.

Thomas took the arrow in his hand, stood the stance, steadied himself, arm up and to the rear over his right shoulder, he stepped forward and released the arrow, that fell at his feet, *"Keep trying it's important that you practice and practice,"* Murrigan said as he walked away. Thomas Roberts spent hours on the top field of Hog Hill Farm practising the use of the lace and arrow, he started to get better, faster, and more accurate. Murrigan was impressed at Thomas Roberts dedication and the achievement of becoming an arrow-man.

Late one evening, Murrigan could see Thomas at the top field practicing with his arrow, whoosh, it went through the air fast and with good distance. Murrigan picked up some buckets and walked to the bottom of the field, he picked up Thomas's arrow from where it had landed and laid the buckets down, about five meters apart.

"Well done my boy, you have worked hard and improved so much, I have a gift for you, where I come from the arrow is called the Arrows of Lantara, they are used by guardians, warriors that protect my homeland and the great city of Lantara." from behind him Murrigan produced a sheath, silver lining and embroidered with the emblem of the fish, tree, bird-like creature and the skull. Thomas Roberts thought that it looked splendid and had never seen anything like it. Inside the sheath were ten arrows the flights made of pure white feathers the stem was silver coated and the tip of

the arrows was of a silver metal, which looked extremely sharp. *"I think you are ready for the Arrows of Lantara, these are not toys, they are weapons, for hunting and in some cases the taking of souls. Keep them safe look after them, but first let's see you use them, do you see the buckets at the bottom of the field land your arrows as close as you can to the buckets."*

Murrigan took the sheath and placed the waist belt around Thomas's waist and buckled the belt, there was a lace at the bottom of the sheath that Murrigan tied around his leg, to hold the sheath firmly in place. Thomas was amazed at how light the sheath and arrows were. Thomas Roberts had a bootlace in his hand. Murrigan paused and looked Thomas Roberts in the eyes,

"Do you believe in magic?" asked Murrigan.

"I'm not sure, if I do, do you?" replied Thomas Roberts.

"Yes, where I come from, there is much magic, yes, I do believe," Murrigan replied.

"What is about to happen and what I'm going to give you is a secret you cannot tell anyone; you must make a life promise," said Murrigan.

"Life promise, what's a life promise?" replied Thomas Roberts.

"It means boy if you tell anyone I will have to kill you," said Murrigan.

"Woo! I don't want you to kill me, so I don't want to know," cried Thomas Roberts with a look of shock and fear on his face. Murrigan started to laugh.

"I'm only kidding you; I won't kill you, just cut out your tongue." Thomas realised that Murrigan was making fun of him, again.

"Give me your right hand, do not be afraid, trust me I would never hurt you," said Murrigan in a calm voice. Thomas Roberts trusted Murrigan more than anyone, he was like a father to him. Thomas placed out his right hand. Murrigan had a small black bag in his left hand he reached into the bag and pulled out a long thin silver snake, the snake glistened in the remaining sunlight of the day. The snake's eyes were white, Thomas could see his white tongue, every time the snake hissed. *"Don't be afraid, this snake will not hurt you, this is a silver snake from my homeland of Drumtara, they are secret and ancient creatures should this*

one accept you it will become your silver lace, it will read your thoughts and command your arrows to fly and hit the target you command it to," said Murrigan. Thomas held his hand out in front of him, his fears had gone as he trusted Murrigan, the silver snake slid from Murrigan's hand to Thomas's hand, sliding up the back of his hand coiling around his wrist and halfway up his arm, the snaked turned and started to move toward Thomas's hand, the snakes head stopped over the top of Thomas's thumb it lay there very still for a few seconds and then dissolved into his skin.

"There, you have been accepted, use this weapon wisely, control your thoughts, control your silver snake, and your arrows will land on your target, look at the two buckets concentrate," said Murrigan. Thomas took the stance and put his hand down to pull out an arrow.

"No, no, command the lace, tell it what you want it to do, concentrate," demanded Murrigan. Thomas could see the silver lining of the snake moving under his skin. Thomas paused, in his head, he thought take the arrow out of the sheath, lace it and place it in my hand. As quick a Thomas thought it, it happened, the snake slid out of his hand, picked the arrow, laced it, and flipped the arrow into the air, Thomas Roberts caught the arrow, swung his arm back then forward, *'whoosh,'* the arrow was in flight, thud the arrow landed directly on top of the bucket, splitting it in two.

"Again," screamed Murrigan. Thomas repeated the same thought, and the second arrow was in the air, *'thud,'* the arrow hit the bucket dead center. Murrigan looked at Thomas with a big smile *"Our secret."*

Arawn was sitting on his throne at the gates of the underworld. Not many souls had passed through the gates recently and Arawn's mind had drifted into deep thought of the boy called Thomas Roberts, the boy without a soul. Arawn had never met anything like this boy, and he was deeply troubled by his presents. As Arawn sat on his large throne, stoking his raven that was perched on the arm of the throne. He shouted out aloud *"Ram-Say come forth."*

Ram-Say was perched on top of the barn roof of Hog Hill Farm, he was cloaked in an invisible spell, even Murrigan and Moria could not see him and never did. Ram-Say heard his master's call, on hearing Arawn's call Ram-Say shot into the air and evaporated, within moments he had appeared in front of Arawn, walking towards Arawn from behind a mist. Ram-Say bowed at Arawn's feet. *"You commanded me, my lord?"* Ram-Say asked as his head bowed.

"Ram-Say, my faithful, what news do you have of this boy Thomas Roberts? the boy without a soul," commanded Arawn.

"He is weak and pathetic, my lord, however, he is in the presents of two guardians of Drumtara. I believe they were protectors of Lantara and close to Tirk, possibly his personal guard," said Ram-Say.

"What evidence have you of this?" asked Arawn.

"I have seen the one they call Murrigan in his guardian glory and he teaches the boy the arts of the guardians," replied Ram-Say.

"Strange, why are their two guardians in the human world with this boy? we need to find out who this boy is, does the boy have ability?" asked Arawn.

"Ability my lord!" Ram-Say asked with a curious look upon his face.

"Does the boy have magical ability?" Arawn asked in a stern voice.

"No, my lord he is weak, I could bring his soul to you if you so desire it," replied Ram-Say.

"No" screamed Arawn *"This boy has presented himself and he had no soul, he cannot enter the underworld until he has paid with his soul,"* Arawn screamed out loud, he calmed down and looked at Ram-say with a gentle mischievous glare.

Strange Occurrences

"No, my faithful you must go back and keep watch, you are my eyes and ears, they must never find you, I will go and consult with Nicopulas."

"Yes, my lord," Ram-Say replied, as he stood up turned around, and walked back into the mist until he had disappeared. Arawn walked towards his throne, he outstretched his arm, and the large raven flew to his outstretched arm. Arawn kept walking into a mist that mystery appeared, as he walked towards the mist he faded into the haze and disappeared.

Back on Hog Hill Farm, Thomas Roberts was standing by the barn, he looked all around him in a very suspicious manner. He got to the door and slowly creep into the barn, just having a sneaky peek back to ensure that he was not being watched. He walked across to the back end of the barn and passed by Maisy the farm cow. *"Good morning, Maisy, fine morning it is,"* Thomas said as he passed Maisy. *"Mooorning,"* replied Maisy. Thomas stopped and looked back at Maisy, he thought, did Maisy just say, *'Morning to me,'* Thomas shook his head and continued to walk to the back of the barn, Thomas bent down and lifted a bundle of straw, under the bundle of straw was his arrows and sheaf which held the silver arrows, as Thomas picked up his arrows the silver snake lace started to glow and slither around his fingers, hand and up to his elbow. Thomas could feel the strange sensation under his skin, the snake lace moved as Thomas touched the arrows, the snake lace protruded from his fingertips and slowly caressed the arrows.

As Thomas was leaving the barn, he looked at Maisy *"You did not see a thing, our little secret,"* Maisy looked directly at Thomas and winked, Thomas, looked at Maisy with a strange look and thought to himself, *'Did this cow just wink at me?'* Thomas closed the barn door behind him and walked across the yard and up the hill to the far-field. There was a large oak tree at the bottom of the field. Thomas's plan was to use the tree as target practice. Bimbo the farm dog had followed Thomas up onto the field and was dashing about Thomas's feet. Thomas took a throwing stance as he stood at the top of the field, he could feel the sensation of the silver snake lace under his skin, Thomas grabbed the arrow with his fingers and flicked the arrow from his sheaf into the air the snake lace shot out of his fingertips and took hold of the arrow just below the feathers and directly over the lace holding notch, as the arrow began to drop, Thomas caught the arrow between his forefinger and thumb of his right hand, just above the arrowhead, which was extremely sharp. Thomas whipped his hand back over his shoulder and then forward. The arrow whizzed forward with the silver snake lace giving a whipping sound as the arrow released from the lace. *"Thud,"* the arrow hit the large oak tree with such force that Thomas could hear the *"Thud,"* that was made when the arrow struck the tree.

Thomas had a total of ten arrows each one struck their mark every time. Thomas had learned to master the Arrows of Lantara with skill, he was getting faster and accurate with each arrow. Once all the arrows were fired into the large oak tree, Thomas started to walk down the field to the tree, he had a big smile upon his face and was feeling extremely proud of himself as Thomas approached the large oak tree. *"*YOU!*"* said a very loud voice Thomas stopped suddenly; he was looking around him *"Who's there?"* he shouted out.

"You, you little toe rag, sticking your pins in me," Thomas stumbled back and fell into a muddy puddle, Thomas realised that the tree was talking to him, he could see a face on the tree, not a very happy face, *"Do you know what it's like to have someone stick a pin into you? bend over boyo and I will show you,"* screamed the tree.

"I'm, I'm so sorry" stuttered Thomas in reply *"I didn't realise that I was hurting you, please forgive me. I can remove them,"* said Thomas.

"That would be nice, please be gentle," said the big old oak tree. Thomas slowly started to remove the arrows from the big oak tree, *"Sorry,"* Thomas said each time he pulled an arrow out. Once all the arrows were out the large oak tree looked relieved.

"Thank you, are you the one they call Thomas Roberts?" asked the large oak tree.

"Yes, I am Thomas Roberts, I will not fire any more arrows at you, I promise," replied Thomas.

Strange Occurrences

"Murrigan has asked me to keep an eye on you," said the large oak tree.

"What do you mean?" asked Thomas. The large oak tree paused, *"Well, Murrigan told me to keep an eye on you, to ensure you were not up to no good with those arrows,"* said the tree, with a strange unconvincing smile upon his face. The large oak tree knew the real reason why, there was a threat to Thomas Roberts life, and it was everyone's responsibility to watch over him.

Thomas Roberts picked up all his arrows and started to walk back up the field *'Talking trees, have I gone mad?'* he thought to himself.

"Nice meeting you Thomas Roberts," shouted the large oak tree as Thomas walked away. Thomas got to the top of the field; he could see an old wooden fence post at the bottom of the field not far from the big oak tree. Thomas threw his first arrow at the post and missed the post. *"No!"* Thomas said out loud.

"I could fetch that for you," said a voice from behind. Thomas turned around sharply, to see no one standing behind him. He looked down, to see Bimbo laying on the grass.

"Don't tell me you're a talking dog?"

"Actually, I will talk to anyone who hears me," said Bimbo.

"I'm going mad, talking trees and dogs," said Thomas.

"I will make a deal with you, if you give me extra food each evening especially, Moira's tasty bread, I will retrieve your arrows," said Bimbo. Thomas stood there amazed; the farmhouse dog wasn't just talking to him he was making deals with him.

"Ok then," Bimbo shot down the field located the arrow and brought the lost arrow back to Thomas, and dropped it at his feet. Thomas spent most of that morning firing arrows and Bimbo retrieving them. Thomas Roberts felt strange talking to Bimbo, after a while, it started to feel normal. On the way back to the farmhouse, Thomas peered over the sheep wall and started to talk to the sheep. *"Hello sheep, I hope you been having a fine day,"* he said. The sheep never replied,

all he got was *"MAAAA"* Thomas looked down at Bimbo who was rolling on his back laughing out loud.

"You really have gone mad, talking to sheep, sheep don't speak," said Bimbo, who was laughing the whole way back to the farmhouse.

Thomas got back to the yard, *"Keep an eye out, make sure no one is watching me,"* Thomas said to Bimbo. Thomas opened the barn door and walked in *"Good afternoon, Maisy,"* said Thomas as he passed Maisy.

"Good afternoon master Roberts," said Maisy.

"I knew you understood me," replied Thomas.

"Yes, I understand you, I was worried in case I startled you," said Maisy.

"I'm not afraid, I have had a tree shout at me and Bimbo speaking to me, so having our cow speaking to me is not a surprise," replied Thomas.

"You are a special young man, this is why you can talk to the animals and the tree's you are one with all creation, you are connected with every one of us, be careful mind, keep your gift secret, you must not tell anyone, you must stay safe. said Maisy.

"I will, keep my secret safe, can I tell my mother," asked Thomas.

"For the time being keep your gift safe, the time will come when you can tell Mary Jane, but for now keep it safe," replied Maisy.

"I will do." Thomas Roberts said as he ran out the barn door.

Thomas Roberts walked in through the kitchen door; "BOOTS" screamed Moria. Thomas took off his muddy boots at the kitchen door.

"Can you help me, young man, I need some onions chopping, grab that knife, watch your fingers," said Moria. Thomas started to chop and talk.

"Where is Murrigan? 'Ouch," shouted Thomas as he held his hand up with blood pouring down his hand,

"Put it in your mouth," shouted Moria as she ran to the sink and pumped water onto a tea towel.

"Let's have a look at that cut," Moria unwrapped the tea towel. Thomas took his cut finger out of his mouth and looked at the cut, Thomas kept staring at his finger, the pain had gone, and so had the cut. Moria took hold of his hand and stood staring

also at Thomas Roberts hand. *"Strange!"* said Thomas. Moria started to wipe the dry blood away from Thomas's hand. The wound on Thomas Roberts hand had self-healed. Thomas stood there looking at Moria.

"Don't be afraid, this is a gift, you must not tell anyone about," Moria said as she placed her hand on his cheek and gave him a compassionate look.

"I know," replied Thomas.

That evening after two large bowls of Moria's stew, Thomas sat on the large armchair close to the fire, the day had been long and full of strange events. Thomas sat on the comfy chair and found himself nodding off into a deep sleep. Thomas opened his eyes and realised that he was standing in a pond, up to his knees in water. The water was dirty and smelt foul. Thomas looked down and could see a pebble beside his feet, the pebble was small and black and laid on the bottom of the pond, strangely, the water around the black pebble was clean and very clear. Thomas bent down to pick the pebble up, each time Thomas tried to pick the pebble up the water became murky and dirty. Thomas tried to feel for the pebble at the bottom of the pond each time he could not feel or find the pebble with his hand. Thomas pulled his hand out of the murky water and the water turned clear he could see the black pebble on the floor of the pond, he just could not get hold of it.

Thomas was aware that he was being watched as he looked up, Thomas could see a small stone wall, sat upon the stone wall was a young boy, dressed in a white robe, the robe had the emblem of Drumtara, embroidered in silver thread, the emblem was large, covering the entire front of the

robe. Thomas looked at the child, he was about five years old, Thomas felt that he recognised the boy.

"Hello," said Thomas.

"Hello, my name is Thomas," said the young boy with a smile on his face. Thomas realised that the boy was harmless and sat beside him on the wall.

"My name is Thomas as well, what a strange coincidence," replied Thomas.

"It's not a coincidence at all, I knew your name, I know who you are," said the boy.

"Who are you?" asked Thomas as he looked at the boy.

"Look down," ordered the young boy, Thomas looked down and was sitting on the edge of a very high wall, a hundred feet from the round, *"Woo,"* shouted Thomas.

"Are you afraid?" asked the boy.

"Yes, how did we get so high?" asked Thomas as he tried to move back on the wall and away from the edge.

"I am you; I am a small particle of your soul; I am your courage," said the young boy.

"I don't understand," replied Thomas.

"Every emotion you have is a particle of your soul, you laugh when your happy that feeling is attached to your soul, your sad this emotion is all so a part of your soul, each emotion is a particle that creates the soul, these particles never die, they cannot be seen or heard. I am courage, your courage, you will need me soon, trust me, take a leap of faith, JUMP," the boy screamed at Thomas *"JUMP, I 'am courage JUMP"* The boy screamed at Thomas again and again, the young boy was screaming *"JUMP"* over and over again. Thomas took one look down and pushed himself off the edge. Suddenly Thomas woke up.

"You, having a dream son?" Thomas looked up to see Mary Jane's smiling face.

"Yes, mother a dream."

It was Monday morning at six am. Mary Jane, Murrigan and Moria, were up at crack of dawn and with Errol, giving his morning song. *"Thomas Roberts, get up young man or you will be late for school, and you got your chores to complete,"* said Mary Jane with a big smile on her face. Mary Jane opened Thomas bedroom curtains *"It's a beautiful day and Moria has a fresh pot a sweet porridge on the stove, you better hurry up or Murrigan will scoff the lot,"* Mary Jane turned round just as Thomas had left the bedroom, Mary Jane had a little giggle to herself, she was extremely happy, and her life was very content, as she looked out Thomas Roberts bedroom window, she could see a young lamb had got out and wandered into the newly seeded barley field.

"Thomas once you finish your breakfast can you go up to the barley field a lamb has escaped and place it back in the sheep field?" asked Mary Jane.

"Will do mum," replied Thomas Roberts. Thomas quickly ran upstairs and dressed into his uniform for school. He ran down the stairs, grabbed a bread bun from the table, and dashed out the door. Murrigan was sat on a large log smoking on a long clay pipe, while the long axe was magically chopping wood, with no hands holding it. Thomas paused to look at the axe as it smashed down and chopped another log. Murrigan sat on the log with a big grin on his face. He jumped up and the axe fell to the floor. *"Should you not be off to school young man?"* Murrigan shouted across the yard.

"Yes, I need to rescue a lamb that has escaped," replied Thomas.

"Well then, on your way, chop, chop," shouted Murrigan.

Thomas shouted *"Bimbo,"* on hearing his name his head poked up from behind the large log Murrigan was sitting on. *"Come on boy we have a lamb to rescue,"* Bimbo hopped over the large log and raced towards Thomas.

"Yes, you can have extra, at dinner time," said Thomas.

Bimbo shot off up towards the sheep field. Thomas ran after him. It did not take long to find the lamb Bimbo darted about chasing the lamb while Thomas kept the large wooden gate open.

"There you go, she's in," said Bimbo.

"Good job," replied Thomas. Thomas looked up at the newly sown barley field, the young seedlings were starting to sprout.

"She made a bit of a mess of the field, I will let Murrigan know, I'm sure he can fix it," said Thomas. Thomas noticed a new

scarecrow had been placed in the middle of the field. *"Is that a new scarecrow?"* asked Thomas.

I don't know, I don't recall seeing Murrigan put it up." said Bimbo.

"I must get off to school, I will grab my lunch, I might even save you some," said Thomas.

"Yes please," said Bimbo jumping about with joy. Suddenly Bimbo stopped, he started to growl loudly.

"Run Thomas get back to the house," commanded Bimbo.

"What's wrong?" Thomas asked just as he turned around to see the scarecrow running towards him. Bimbo ran toward the scarecrow, who had a pitchfork in his hand, as bimbo got close to the scarecrow he jumped up at the scarecrow. The scarecrow grabbed hold of Bimbo by the throat and throw him to one side. Thomas had started to run back towards the house. The scarecrow kept chasing him, Thomas slowed down to look round. *"Smash,"* Thomas found himself on the floor he had tripped up, the air had been knocked out of him when he fell. Thomas realised that the scarecrow was looking over him. Thomas could see the disfigured face of the scarecrow, he had sunken dark eyes and crooked, razor-sharp teeth. The scarecrow leaned over Thomas and placed his long stick fingers around Thomas's throat.

"Get your hand off him you filthy scarecrow," growled Bimbo, snarling and presenting his own sharp white teeth, as he pounced onto the scarecrow's back. The scarecrow did not let go of Thomas's throat, as the scarecrow leaned closer to Thomas.

"Your soul is mine," the scarecrow said in an evil voice. *"Whoosh, Whack,"* and the scarecrow's head went flying, it landed to the left-hand side of Thomas, the body of the scarecrow fell lifeless on top of him, while Bimbo was ripping clumps of straw from the body of the scarecrow.

Thomas pushed what was left of the scarecrow of him, to see Murrigan standing over him with the long axe in his hand.

"You ok, lad?" Murrigan asked.

"Yes, I'm fine," replied Thomas. Murrigan could see the red marks around Thomas's throat.

"Can you get up? we need to get back to the house," asked Murrigan.

"I think so," replied Thomas as he stood up and fell to his knees.

"It's my ankle, I must have twisted it when I fell," said Thomas.

"It's ok, take my hand, and I will help you back," as Murrigan helped Thomas to his feet, he placed his arm around Thomas and helped him as he limped back to the farmhouse.

"Sound the alarm!" Murrigan shouted at Errol as he passed him sitting on the gate post close to the house. Errol started to screech *"Cock-a-doddle dooooooo,"* as loud as he could, all the animals know exactly what the warning meant and were ready for an attack on Hog Hill Farm.

Mary Jane and Moria heard the alarm, Mary Jane grabbed the fire poker and ran into the yard followed by Moria.

"No, no, no what happened," cried Mary Jane as she ran towards Thomas.

"He is safe, get him inside and lock the door," commanded Murrigan. Mary Jane and Moria took hold of Thomas as he hopped towards the farm kitchen door, once inside, and Murrigan heard the door locked, he looked down at Bimbo, *"Stay alert, inform the others to be prepared, all buildings to be checked, I will have a look from above,"* said Murrigan as he shot into the air, Bimbo ran about the farm informing all creatures to be prepared, Errol was still sounding the alarm. After checking the area was secure Murrigan landed in the yard all the farm animals, ducks, hens, rats, mice, small birds even a hedgehog could see him as they had all gathered to find out what has happened. Murrigan transformed from the guardian back to the farmhand.

"Gather round everyone, gather round, this morning, Thomas was attacked by a scarecrow, however, I believe this creature was from my world Drumtara, this creature was sent to take Thomas away from us. We must never let this happen, you are all guardians of Hog Hill Farm and protector of Thomas Roberts, be prepared, stay alert

and be prepared to defend him with your lives," said Murrigan with passion in his voice. All the animals let out a loud cheer in support.

"Moria, can you go to the school this morning tell them that Thomas Roberts is unwell and will be staying at home for the next few days," said Mary Jane. Just then the kitchen door opened Mary Jane raised the old shotgun to her shoulder.

"Steady on with that thing," said Murrigan as he peered his head around the door.

"It's you," replied Mary Jane with a sigh of relief.

"What happened this morning?" demanded Mary Jane.

"Thomas was attacked by a scarecrow up on the barley field," said Murrigan.

"Was it someone dressed as a scarecrow? I don't understand," Mary Jane asked as she burst into tears *"Why can't they just leave him alone? he is just a boy."* she cried.

*

Arawn had just entered the kingdom of Drumtara at the foot of the great city of Lantara, as he walked to the gates they opened, and he entered unchallenged. The great hall was on the lower grounds of the city. There was a long walk, through the great courtyard. In the courtyard were charred, glass statues, these were statues of the residents who once lived in the great city of Lantara, many had been tied to posts, hanging upside down and burnt by the white fire until their souls had perished in the flames. This was Nicopulas, method of cleansing the city of would-be enemies. Arawn kept walking towards the great hall, the large doors opened, yet again unchallenged. The hall was alive with heat as Arawn walked down the center of the great hall white fires burned. In the flames of the white fires where the remains of the guardians who had been stripped of their wings and left to burn on the eternal flame, the pain would have been unbearable. Arawn could see witches, hanging from their feet from the roof of the great hall, these were witches loyal to Tirk they still lived, Arawn was in no doubt they would suffer at the hands of Nicopulas. As Arawn walked further he could see blue blood,

65

the blood of guardians splattered all over the floor, he could see red eyes in the shadows watching him. Suddenly a winged beast leap from the shadows and landed in front of him. The beast was a servant of Nicopulas, a demon from a dark place loyal only to Nicopulas, the creature stared at Arawn, he never flinched a muscle, Arawn feared no demons, after all, he was the ruler of the underworld. The demon picked up an arm that was laid on the floor. Arawn realised that Nicopulas was giving the demons a victory feast and the menu was the souls and flesh of Lantarians. Arawn smiled and kept walking to the end of the great hall of Lantara.

-Chapter 6-
Offspring Off Nicopulas

Sat in front of Arawn, upon three thrones were three figures. The middle throne sat higher than the other two thrones. The middle throne was made of bones and sat upon it was an old man wrapped in a fur coat and a silver thorned crown upon his head. To the left of the old man was a large creature who sat upon a throne that appeared angry and gruesome. This creature was grey in colour and had massive hands with a ball and chain in one hand and a large axe in the other. Its face was scared, and he had an ear missing, his eyes were sunk into his head, they were dull, dark and lifeless. His mouth hung open, however, half of his razor-sharp teeth appeared missing. Arawn could smell the aroma of rotten flesh coming from the thrones a decaying smell of death. On the other side was a long thin grey creature it sat upright and was starring directly at Arawn, it was growling quietly under its breath at him, he could see all its razor-sharp teeth, they had blue blood on them which told Arawn it was a flesh eater. Both creatures nerved Arawn, he knew that Lantara was safe for no one and that he had to remain cautious.

Arawn, bowed before the three thrones, *"My lord's, I have come to seek consultation with Nicopulas lord and master of Drumtara, I come to seek his wisdom on a matter of grave concern."*

The old man sat upright upon his chair.

"Arawn come closer my sight is not what it used to be," said the old man in a croaked voice.

"My Lord, forgive me, for I did not recognise you," replied Arawn.

"Let me introduce you to my children, on my left is Gear-ra, my daughter," Gear-ra bowed her head, to acknowledge Arawn, as she sat on the throne. Arawn bowed back.

"To my right is my son Zoda," Zoda just stared at Arawn.

"Your children my lord?" Asked Arawn.

"How dare you question my father! do you think he would defy the secret laws of Drumtara, we are not born of this world, we are our father's creation, made of his flesh, blood and soul. He gave us life so that we may rule by his side." growled Gear-ra.

Zoda stood up from his throne and walked towards Arawn as Zoda walked around Arawn

"I smell you; I smell your vile, the smell of evil. I do like you," said Zoda, with an evil grin on his face. *"Chair, get our friend a chair, he has got news, he wishes to share,"* shouted Zoda, from the shadows came a creature dragging a wooden chair along the floor. The chair was dropped in front of Zoda. Arawn walked forward, uprighted the chair and sat upon it. The chair was small, and he realised that he was looking up and they were looking down. Nicopulas leaned across to Gear-ra and whispered in her ear *"Father is hungry, fresh souls, NOW,"* Gear-ra shouted, her voice was piercing and echoed through the great hall, her voice was unnerving and startled the creatures that lurked in the shadows of the great hall.

From the shadows, came two demons, they were holding a young girl, Arawn knew she was a young witch, he could tell by her bright green eyes. The girl was brought before Nicopulas, he took her by the hand, her body started to dissolve in small bright particles, these particles hovered in the air for a moment. Suddenly they shot into Nicopulas body and were gone. Arawn realised that Nicopulas was consuming the souls of witches and that strange dark magic was being conjured.

"My children! Come forth," commanded Nicopulas.

Zoda and Gear-ra knelt at Nicopulas feet, the soul he consumed started to regurgitate and came out of Nicopulas mouth and into the mouth of Zoda and Gear-ra. Arawn realised that Nicopulas was taking the souls to feed his children.

"They are getting stronger," said Nicopulas who fell back onto his throne.

Arawn thought *'As you get weaker,'* Zoda and Gear-ra stood up they looked stronger, they were transforming with each soul that was feed to them. They were feeding off Nicopulas strength.

"Speak of your grave importance and we will consult," Gera-ra said.

68

Arawn started to tell, Nicopulas, Zoda and Gear-ra about Thomas Roberts the boy without a soul and how this boy had come to him in Creeve with no soul to offer. He told them of his spy Ram-Say and what he had found out about the boy and of Murrigan and Moria, the two guardians of Drumtara who are protecting the boy. He also told them that he believed that this boy was the lost son of Tirk, who had escaped while the battle for the city of Lantara was raging. He told them also of Mary Jane and that she had taken the boy as her own.

Nicopulas, Zoda and Gear-ra sat quietly and listen to Arawn story, when he had finished telling the story they all started to laugh out loud.

"The story is very true," shouted Arawn with a deep roar.

They all stopped laughing, and the great hall fell into a deadly silence.

"I do not, doubt your story, Arawn, lord of the underworld, I doubt your ability to think that I do not know of this boy without, a soul, I have requested his soul on two occasions and on each my servants have failed," said Nicopulas in an old frail voice.

"How is that possible? there is no access to the human world from Drumtara it is forbidden" said Arawn.

"Forbidden!" screamed the old man.

Nicopulas stood up from his throne, he grabbed Zoda by the throat and started to drain the soul out of Zoda. Nicopulas body started to grow, his arms grow long and muscular. He had transformed into the might of Nicopulas. A tall white demon with jet black hair and two long black horns, protruding through his jet black hair, just above his pointed ears down the centre of his head was a row of smaller horns. His eyes were pitch black, and Arawn could see his own reflection in them.

Arawn bowed at the magnificent sight of Lord Nicopulas ruler of Drumtara. This was the Nicopulas that Arawn knew, powerful, feared.

"Who are you to tell me what is forbidden, I am the creator of life, taker of soul's master of the keys to the human world, I say what is forbidden and nothing is forbidden to me,"

'Look at me!' said the roaring voice of Nicopulas.

Arawn looked up and looked Nicopulas in the eyes, cold black eyes.

"If this boy is the son of Tirk and his wench human witch, I want him to endure an infinity of suffering and all that love him will perish, I want his soul as a pet so I can tease it and beat it for my pleasure," growled Nicopulas.

"Look what they made me do my son, my precious son," cried Nicopulas.

Nicopulas fell beside the stiff corpse of Zoda.

"What soul I have, I give to you,"

Nicopulas breathed into Zoda's mouth particles of Nicopulas soul left his body and transferred back into Zoda and he was restored back to life as he took a gasp of breath. Nicopulas reverted back to the old man, falling back into his throne looking weak and tired.

"Sit down and listen to what I have to say, this boy you claim has no soul, if he is the son of Tirk then he may be a threat to us, you say he has a mother, a human mother, I want her soul," demanded Nicopulas

"We will need to send a small legion to take her, the guardians are powerful and skilled warriors," said Nicopulas in a calm voice.

"And how are we going to get them there?" asked Arawn.

"The same way Tirk did, Tirk had learned that there were four hidden portals to the human world, one in the north, east south and west. The problem was they moved with the rotation of the stars; they would never be in the same place at any one time. Tirk had located one of the portals on the west and placed a marker on it, when the full moon shone, he would fly high on a warlock staff and look upon Drumtara the portal would shine a beam up to the sky that only he could see through a looking glass, I have that looking glass and I know where the portal is. To open it the Lepz forged a key, (Lepz where forest dweller green goblins, intelligent, greedy and vicious creatures that would provide the required service at the right price) *I also have that key, so to answer your question of the forbidden, Arawn lord of the underworld, who will stop me?"* said Nicopulas with a grin on his face.

"What do you command of me, my lord? my sword is yours," replied Arawn.

"Send me your spy, Ram-Say, he will consult with my children, and we will take the mother of the boy with no soul," said Nicopulas.

Thomas Roberts had gone to bed early and had drifted into a deep sleep, he found himself in a familiar dream, he was standing in a pond the dirty pond, he looked down and could see a clear part in the dirty water. Thomas thought *'This is the pebble dream, I have been here before,'* only this time when Thomas looked into the clear water, he could see the face of a girl. Thomas was taken back at how pretty she looked, the girl had long black hair, emerald, green eyes and a beautiful smile. She appeared to be smiling at Thomas, as he reached down to touch the water, it turned murky and the girl disappeared, Thomas stood back up, hoping the water would clear so that he could look at the girl again. The water remained murky, and the girl did not reappear.

Thomas looked up and saw the small wall that was in his previous dream. As Thomas walked toward the wall, he could see a figure on sitting the wall, it was the young boy.

"Is that you Thomas?" said Thomas Roberts to the young boy sitting on the wall.

"Yes, it is me," replied the boy.

Thomas Roberts noticed the young Thomas sitting on the wall was shaking he appeared nervous almost scared.

"Are you ok? you are shaking," said Thomas Roberts.

"No, I'm never ok, I'm afraid, always afraid,' replied young Thomas.

"Why? what has happened?" asked Thomas Roberts.

"You happened, you have created fear, you continue to create fear, I have been so afraid since you were born. Look down tell me what you see," said young Thomas.

Thomas knew it was time to jump, he has had the dream before. Only this time when Thomas Roberts looked down, he could see Hog Hill Farm, it was on fire, he could see the thatched roof of the farm in flames, the barn and the surrounding building were burning. All the animals were running wild, the fields were in flames, burning a strange white flame, he could see three bodies laid on the ground charred and burnt.

"Do you feel it, do you feel it now, fear, I feel your fear, I 'am your fear, I am you. Jump Thomas Roberts, Jump, you can save them."
Thomas Roberts jumped off the wall, he started to fall, he was falling into the inferno below of white fire, the flames got closer, and he could feel pain as he started to burn as Thomas fell into the flames, he shouted out loud *"NO."* Suddenly he awoke in his bed, to see Moria beside him.
"It's ok, you're having a dream, no one can harm you," said Moria in a calm voice, she leaned toward Thomas while sitting on the edge of his bed, she brushed his hair away from his forehead with her fingers. *"It's ok now, go back to sleep."* Thomas pulled the blankets up to his neck as Moria sat back in her chair and turned down the oil lamp to a dull glow. Thomas felt safe with Moria in his room watching over him. He turned over in his bed and looked towards the window, he could see a ray of moonlight and a transparent image of Murrigan standing by his window in his full guardian glory, with his hand perched on top of a long sword and a helmet sat upon his head like a Roman centurion ready to go to war. Thomas felt safe and soon drifted off into a peaceful sleep for the rest of the night.
The morning had broken, and Errol was in full chorus, Mary Jane, Moria and Murrigan were all sitting at the table sipping on milky tea.
"The time has come to tell Thomas," said Moria.
"Tell him what exactly? that he comes from a strange land in another world, you two are guardians of Drumtara and that I am not his real mother, he is only eight years old." scolded Mary Jane.
"Almost nine years old, doesn't matter how old he is, he should know the truth," said Murrigan.
"No, the time is not right, I think we should wait until he is older," replied Mary Jane.
Just then Thomas Roberts came through the door leading from upstairs.
"Tell me what?" asked Thomas.
"That it was your turn to clean out the chicken coop," said Mary Jane.

Arawn walked through the mist and was back in his own kingdom of the underworld, he was not happy with the experience he had at Lantara with Nicopulas. He had concerns about the new offspring of Nicopulas, Arawn did not want to lose favour with Nicopulas or be sacked to let Gear-ra or Zoda take his place as lord of the underworld. Arawn sat on his throne at the gates of Creeve, and roared *"Ram-Say come forth."* Ram-Say appeared through the mist and walked towards Arawn, Ram-Say knelt at Arawn feet.

"You summoned me my lord?" asked Ram-Say.

"Yes, my faithful, we have a problem."

Arawn, told Ram-Say about his concerns about, Gear-Ra and Zoda and the unpredictability of Nicopulas. Ram-Say sat at Arawn's feet and listen to every word that was spoken and the plan to take Mary Jane and present her to Nicopulas.

"My lord, may I speak?" asked Ram-Say.

"Freely, I command it," replied Arawn.

"Lord Nicopulas wants the mother of the boy, this Mary Jane for his own desires, he plans to send a legion through a gateway to the human world. Why don't you send one through who could bring her to you, you could use her to bargain with and make your favour with Nicopulas stronger," said Ram-Say.

'Em,' said Arawn in deep thought as he stroked his pet raven perched on the arm of his throne.

"I like your thoughts, Ram-Say, I could not send you, my loyal servant, the guardian's that protect the boy are too powerful, who would you send Ram-Say?" asked Arawn.

"There is one my lord, he dwells in the deep of Creeve and you have him at your command,' said Ram-Say.

"Pooka! I am really liken your thoughts, Ram-Say, Pooka is the one, he is cunning and destructive, POOKA COME FORTH," shouted Arawn. In the distance the hoofs of a galloping horse could be heard, the mist in front of Arawn parted and a velvet back stallion horse was standing in front of Arawn, Pooka stood up on his back legs and kicked his front legs into the air, with strength and power.

"Pooka, my loyal servant, I have a quest for you, you will cross over to the human world and bring me back the one they call Mary Jane, you will bring her directly to me. Ram-Say will show you where she is. You must act as a wild horse that has wandered onto their land, gain the trust of the one, they call Mary Jane and when the time is right destroy her and bring her wretched body and soul to me," commanded Arawn.

Pooka bowed his head and turned to walk through the mist and disappeared.

"Should this go wrong, we were never there, and this did not happen. I want you to watch over this quest I have given to Pooka, but you are not to intervene," said Arawn.

Ram-Say bowed his head *"Understood my lord,"* replied Ram-Say. Ram-Say stood up and walked into the mist. Arawn sat back on his throne, he stroked his black raven who was perched on the arm of his throne, Arawn sat with a grin upon his face.

"Look up there, is that a big horse on the top field?" shouted Thomas Roberts as he started to run towards the top field. *'Thump,'* as Thomas ran into Murrigan and stumbled back on his feet.

"No, you don't, get back down to the house and stay there," demanded Murrigan.

Thomas realised that Murrigan was serious, there was something in his tone of voice. Thomas turned and ran to the house. Mary Jane came out of the kitchen door,

"What's going on?" she asked.

"There is a big black horse in the top field mother, Murrigan asked me to go back to the house," replied Thomas Roberts.

"Get inside quickly," shouted Mary Jane as she pushed Thomas towards the kitchen door, once inside, Mary Jane locked the door, she reached up and took the shotgun down that hung above the door, she broke open the gun to reassure herself it was loaded, *'Snap, click,'* as Mary Jane snapped the shotgun closed and clicked back both hammers that sat at the top of the shotgun.

"Everything ok Mary Jane?" asked Moria as she removed the pinafore, she wore when she was cooking.

"There is a black horse at the top field, Murrigan is checking it now," Mary Jane said very nervously and with her eyes never leaving the door and forcing Thomas Roberts behind her, she was holding the shotgun with a firm grip pointing it towards the door. Her entire body was shaking with fear. Moria walked towards Mary Jane, *"Look at me,"* Moria said to Mary Jane as she took hold of the shotgun and eased it out of Mary Janes grip. *"It's ok, should there be any problems Murrigan can deal with it,"* said Moria.

"How do you know, it's safe? we need to protect, Thomas Roberts."

"It's ok, come outside," Mary Jane, Moria and Thomas could hear shouting coming from outside. Moria edged towards the small kitchen window, she could see Murrigan with the large black horse.

"It's ok, it's just Murrigan," Moria looked down at Thomas Roberts to reassure him that all was well. *"And he has the horse with him,"* said Moria.

Mary Jane unbolted the locked door, and they all went outside to see the horse.

"He's a bit wild, but he is a fine-looking horse," said Murrigan.

Thomas went forward to stroke the horse, the horse kicked out with his back legs and appeared nervous. Mary Jane steps closer to the horse.

"Calm, boy, it's fine, no one is going to hurt you," as Mary Jane put out her hand the horse stepped closer to her, he bowed his head and Mary Jane stroked his face and long black mane.

"He likes you," said Moria.

"I used to ride a lot when I was a child, I always had a way with horses, he must belong to someone, he is such a fine horse, I'm sure someone is missing him," said Mary Jane.

"I will keep an ear out for anyone who may have lost a horse, but I would say finders keepers," replied Murrigan.

"And I agree," said Thomas Roberts.

"That's it, then we will keep him unless someone has a legal claim over him," said Mary Jane.

Two weeks had passed, and no one had come to claim the horse, Mary Jane had spoken to the local policeman who had no reports of a lost or stolen horse. The decision was made they would keep the horse who was to be named Blackie.

Murrigan had found a saddle and reins for the horse, however, no matter how hard he tried he could not get Blackie to calm down. He attempted to bribe the horse with carrots, this did not work, he tried a nosebag with fresh oat, Blackie was having none of it and bolted across the field with the nose bag attached to his face. Thomas Roberts and Bimbo lay on the grass laughing at the day's entertainment. Murrigan throw the saddle to the floor and walked down to the house. This only made Thomas and Bimbo laugh even more.

"That horse is only good for horse meat, he will not stand still, and he won't take a saddle," said Murrigan with a big frown upon his face.

"I will have a go, after lunch," said Mary Jane.

"Good luck with that," replied Murrigan.

Moria and Mary Jane burst into laughter at the expression on Murrigan face.

That afternoon, Mary Jane, took her shaw that hung on the back of the kitchen door, placed it over her shoulders, she looked at Moria, Murrigan and Thomas Roberts, who were sitting at the table jam tasting. *"I'm off for a walk and a bit of fresh air,"* said Mary Jane.

Mary Jane stepped outside, she could feel the cold breeze of a light wind, summer was coming to an end and the days were cooler. Mary Jane looked up towards the top field where she could see Blackie, in her pocket was some sugar lumps. Mary Jane made her way up to the top field and Blackie came strolling up to her, he bowed his head, and she patted his face. *"I got something you will like,"* as she pulled some of the sugar lumps out of her pocket and gave them to Blackie, Mary Jane could hear the sugar lumps crunch inside Blackies mouth.

"I told you, I had something you would enjoy."

Mary Jane walked over to where Murrigan had thrown the horse saddle and reins.

"Stay calm, I won't harm you," said Mary Jane as she reached into her pocket and gave Blackie more sugar lumps. While Blackie was munching on the sugar, Mary Jane bent down to pick the saddle up, she had to use a bit of muscle to lift the saddle off the grass, she had forgotten how heavy saddles were and she know she had to find some more strength to heave the saddle onto Blackie's back. Mary Jane counted in her head *'123,'* lifting the saddle onto Blackie's back. He did not move as the heavy saddle landed on his back. Mary Jane continued to fasten the buckles and still Blackie did not move. *"Your such a good boy,"* said Mary Jane as she placed the bit into his mouth and pulled the reins over his ears and fasten the straps. Mary Jane was laughing to herself.

"I guess you don't like our Murrigan, and I don't blame you, he can be a real grump sometimes, let see what you can do," said Mary Jane as she placed her foot into the stirrup and pulled herself up onto Blackie's back, Blackie started to get nervous and took a few steps back. Mary Jane took hold of the reins and leaned forward. *"Calm boy,"* she whispered into his ear. Mary Jane pulled the reins to the right, away from the gate, she squeezed her legs into blackie's ribs, and he started to walk across the field, Mary Jane turned left then right.

"Let's see what you really got," as she gave Blackie a jab with her heels, off they went, galloping across the field, they got faster and faster and closer to the wall, Woosh, Blackie and Mary Jane jumped and cleared the wall. For the first time in a long time, Mary Jane felt a sense of enjoyment, the riding of Blackie across the fields had taken her back to her youth when she was young and carefree.

"Woo, come see this," shouted Thomas Roberts as he quickly opened the kitchen door and ran into the yard, quickly followed by Moria and Murrigan.

"Well stone me crows," said Murrigan.

"Stone me what?' asked Thomas with a strange look upon his face.

"It doesn't matter," replied Murrigan.

Moria, Murrigan and Thomas Roberts stood in amazement as they watched Mary Jane galloping along the top field on the back of a beautiful black stallion. Mary Janes hair was blowing in the wind, all three were even more amazed when she jumped the stone wall.

"Isn't she amazing," said Thomas Robert with a look of pride and a big smile.

"Yes, my boy your mother is a truly amazing lady," said Moria as she put her arms around Thomas and continue to watch the wonderful image of Mary Jane on horseback.

-Chapter 7-
Pooka

Today was a very special day, Hog Hill Farm was full of life, Moria was working her newfound magic of baking cakes and reading the morning paper and sipping on hot tea, all at the same time. The rolling pin was rolling puff pastry and the wooden spoon was mixing a cake mix the door from the landing opened and they all stopped dead, just as Mary Jane walked in.

"There is no point in halting your work Moria each time I walk in," said Mary Jane with a smile on her face, Mary Jane and Moria started to laugh. Moria clicked her fingers, and the kitchen became alive once more.

"Smell's amazing," said Mary Jane.

"Lemon drizzle with lemon buttercream cake, apple turnovers in puff pastry with fresh cream," said Moria.

"Sounds amazing," replied Mary Jane as she dipped her finger into the lemon buttercream.

Murrigan had just walked into the kitchen, morning everyone, *"Em, that smell's good,"* said Murrigan.

Murrigan leaned forward and looked into the bowl of lemon buttercream as he placed his finger into the bowl, Moria whacked his knuckles good and hard, with a wooden spoon.

"Hands off," she scolded.

"Where is the birthday boy," asked Murrigan.

"He is still in bed, I thought I'd give him the morning off from his chores and let him sleep a little longer, did you get it Murrigan?" asked Mary Jane, in a quite secretive manner.

"She is in the barn and she's a cracker," replied Murrigan.

Moria and Mary Jane were sorting out the kitchen for Thomas Roberts 12th birthday, the table was covered with all kinds of foods from sweet cakes to sausage rolls. Thomas and Murrigan were in the yard chasing Bimbo who had sunk his teeth into an old football they had been kicking about. Bimbo just thought it was such fun being chased about.

"Right use two let's go," shouted Mary Jane from the kitchen door.

As Thomas got to the door, Mary Jane placed a blindfold over Thomas Roberts eyes and walked him into the kitchen, Mary Jane, Murrigan and Moria all burst into song as Mary Jane removed the blindfold.

"Happy Birthday to you, Happy Birthday dear Thomas, Happy Birthday to you' 'Hip, Hip Hooray," they all shouted at the end of the song. Mary Jane placed the large lemon drizzle cake, covered in yellow lemon buttercream, iced on top of the cake *"Happy Birthday, Thomas Roberts, 12 Today"* with twelve candles around the edge. Thomas Roberts stood looking over the table in amazement, he had never seen so much food in all his life.

"Wahoo," he said.

"A feast fit for a king," Moria replied.

"Let's go then, blow those candles out before they melt the cake, don't forget the wish," said Murrigan.

Thomas Roberts closed his eyes, he made his silent wish, on opening his eyes, he blew all the candles out, followed by a big round of applause from Murrigan, Moria and Mary Jane.

They all sat down and tucked into the amazing food.

"I'm completely stuffed," said Thomas Roberts as he sat back on his chair rubbing his belly which was all bloated.

"How many sausages rolls did you have?" asked Moria as Murrigan was munching on another one.

"Nen," Murrigan replied.

"How many!" she scolded.

"Nen," as Murrigan held up his hands and showed all his fingers and thumbs.

"Ten, that's disgraceful," shouted Moria as Murrigan sat back on his chair rubbing his very swollen belly, with his large grin upon his face.

"Present time," shouted Mary Jane, as she placed the blindfold back over Thomas Roberts eye's, she stood Thomas up and Moria grabbed his other arm.

"Lead the way Murrigan," Mary Jane commanded.

Thomas could hear the kitchen door open and feel the cool breeze of the autumn air on his face. He could hear the opening of the barn door; he knew this as the wooden door scrapped along the yard floor. He knew he was inside the barn; he could smell the animals and feel their warmth in the air. Mary Jane slowly removed the blindfold and said softly. *"Happy Birthday Thomas Roberts."* Thomas was unsure what he was looking at as his eyes looked in front of him, his vision was blurred and once they had come back into vision, he could see a horse standing in front of him.

"It's a horse, you got me a horse?" asked Thomas Roberts.

"Yes, my boy it's your horse," replied Mary Jane

"He is beautiful," said Thomas with a look of surprise on his face.

"He is, she," said Murrigan.

"let's take her outside so you can have a good look at her," said Murrigan as he started to lead the horse towards the barn door. Once outside, Thomas could see the horse in daylight, she was about twelve hands high, she was white with brown patches, her mane was long and white, she looked young.

"How old is she?" asked Thomas.

"She is just over a year old, and she, really needs a name," replied Murrigan.

"Yes, I should give her a name, em," Thomas was in deep thought.

"I will call her Bella,"

"Bella it is then," said Mary Jane.

"Tomorrow, we will introduce Bella to Blackie, I'm sure they will be good together and they can keep each other company. We can both saddle up and go for a morning ride," said Mary Jane with a big smile on her face.

"That sounds good to me," replied Thomas Roberts. He took Bella by the rope that was tied around her neck and lead her into the barn. Thomas placed some oats into a bucket and gave them to Bella, who got her head stuck in the bucket.

"Get me out of this thing," said a muffled voice.

Thomas pulled the bucket from Bella's face.

"You need to get a bigger bucket," said Bella.

"Sorry, I didn't realise you would get your head stuck in the bucket," replied Thomas.

"Well next time bigger bucket and more oats and you and me will just get on fine," said Bella.

"I will remember that the next time, do you like your name, I have given you," asked Thomas.

"Yes, it's a nice name thank you, where I'm I actually and how come you talk to me?" asked Bella.

"You're on Hog Hill Farm on the outskirts of the town of Trim, it is a beautiful place and everyone is really friendly, and I don't know how I can speak to you!" replied Thomas.

"And it's to be kept a secret, can you keep a secret?" asked Maisy as she poked her head over the gate in the barn.

"Yes," replied Bella

"You'll do fine here," said Maisy.

"Good evening to both of you and I will see you in the morning," said Thomas Roberts as he closed and secured the barn door behind him.

Thomas Roberts walked into the kitchen with a big smile on his face, Murrigan was still eating sausage rolls. He sat down on the big armchair and thought *'What an amazing day.'* Slowly Thomas could feel himself drift off, the heat of the kitchen fire and the dancing of the flames soon had him falling into a deep sleep.

There he was again, standing in this murky pond, *"Why am I here again?"* Thomas said aloud. He looked down and could see, Mary Janes Face, she was smiling, and looking so happy. Thomas did not reach down this time, he was enjoying the moment of seeing his mother happy.

Thomas heard a *"Cough!"* he looked up to see himself on the wall, an identical, same age same clothes.

"Hello," Thomas said to the identical Thomas on the wall.

"What an amazing day, don't you think?" said Thomas on the wall.

"Yes, it was," Thomas Roberts said as he sat on the wall.

"Our lives should have been so much different, look down Thomas Roberts," Thomas looked down to see a small boy in a cage, he was holding onto the bars, his clothes were torn and he was filthy. Thomas Roberts looked closer and realised, that the small child in the cage was him, a younger him, cold, hungry

and alone. Thomas Roberts looked back at the identical of himself.

"Do you know why your life is different today? it's because of me," said the boy sitting on the wall.

"Who are you?" asked Thomas Roberts as he looked at his identical.

"I am you; I am what set you free from your cage, your world of rage and pain. I am love,"

Thomas awoke rapidly from the dreamy sleep.

"Go get yourself to bed," said the voice of Mary Jane.

Thomas got up from the large armchair and made his way to his bedroom. His thoughts were with the strange dreams he was having and what they meant.

The next morning Thomas Roberts was up bright and early, even Errol was caught off guard to see Thomas come out of the barn, with Bella, with saddle and reins already positioned on Bella.

"You having a late morning?" asked Thomas as he passed Errol.

"Goodness me, no young sir, I'm just fine-tuning my vocal cords," replied Errol.

Thomas Roberts kept walking with a big grin across his face as Errol burst into his morning chorus. Mary Jane had just come out of the kitchen door.

"Mount up and I will walk you up to Blackie," shouted Mary Jane.

Thomas took hold of the reins he realised that he was going to have problems mounting Bella as his legs were too short, Thomas decided to climb the gate with Bella beside him, he took a leap at Bella who decided to step forward at the same time. Thomas rolled over Bella's back end, completely missing the saddle and landing in her poo, which was very fresh.

"Op's sorry, but if you don't tell me what you want me to do then, I cannot help you," said Bella.

'Ok then, just to remind you I have a nice new bucket full of rolled oats ready for you to munch on, if you don't get a grip, it will be grass for you, my lady," scolded Thomas with his face covered in horse muck.

"Fine, keep your spurs on," replied Bella.

Thomas had his second attempt at mounting Bella, he got back on the fence, drew Bella closer, throw his leg over the saddle and he was on. Mary Jane took hold of the reins and all three took a long slow walk up to the top field where Blackie was watching every move they made. As they approached the gate Blackie leaned his head over the gate and both Bella and Blackie rubbed their heads together.

"That a good start they both like each other," said Mary Jane as she reached into her pocket to give Blackie some sugar lumps and stroke his face. Mary Jane opened the gate pulled the cover of her saddle that lay on the ground, she picked up the saddle and lifted the saddle onto Blackies back. Thomas had noted, how strong his mother was, he knew her saddle was a heavy one, but Mary Jane made it look easy.

The weeks had passed, and most days Mary Jane and Thomas Roberts would go for their morning ride, both Mary Jane and Thomas were extremely happy and life was very pleasant at Hog Hill Farm. The winter nights were closing in. It was one late afternoon, when Thomas Roberts noted that the sky had darkened very fast, there was a rumble of thunder in the distance.

"Looks like a storm is on its way," said Murrigan as he looked up to the sky.

"Let's get the animals indoors for the night," said Mary Jane, just as the rain came down slowly at the start and then got very heavy, the wind had picked up, the sky got darker, and a crack of lightning shot across the sky.

Mary Jane grabbed a rope.

"I will get Blackie, he won't respond to you," shouted Mary Jane as the thunder had just erupted above their heads followed by another crack of lightning. Mary Jane made her way up to the top field; she could see Blackie running around the field.

'Blackie' Mary Jane shouted.

Blackie came trotting towards, Mary Jane, she put her hand in her pocket and pulled out some sugar lumps, *"Calm down fella, it's fine,"* said Mary Jane as she gave him the sugar lumps and stroked his head.

Mary Jane turned to walk out of the field and towards the gate, the flashes of lightning kept lighting up the sky to make visibility, a little better in the dark field. Suddenly, Blackie stopped.

"Come on boy," said Mary Jane as she pulled on the rope.

Mary Jane turned around, standing behind her with the rope around its neck, was not a horse, it was a beast, a large horned beast about eight feet tall, his eyes were on fire. Mary Jane screamed and began to run, the lightning cracked, and Mary Jane could see the gate she had opened. Her feet were slipping and sticking as she ran towards the gate, the mud was thick and difficult to run in. Mary Jane could hear the roar of the beast, behind her, she could hear his breath as he breathed louder as he got closer.

"Cock-a-doodle-doo, Cock-a-doodle-doo," Thomas heard the alarm call of Errol, *"Mary Jane is in danger, Mary Jane is in danger,"* Thomas took to his feet he ran hard and fast up the path toward the top field, the lightning cracked, and he could see his mother trying to run and the beast chasing after her. Thomas Looked down to see Bimbo beside him.

"Arrows, Bimbo," Bimbo turned and set back towards the farm, he knew exactly what he needed to do, he had seen Thomas Roberts hide the arrows on many occasions. Bimbo ran past Murrigan, nearly knocking him off his feet, Bimbo dived into the loose straw and jumped back out. With the arrows in his mouth, he rush past Murrigan, Bimbo did not say a word to Murrigan, Murrigan knew that something was wrong. Woosh Murrigan transformed into the guardian and rose into the air, he could see that a beast was in the field chasing Mary Jane, Murrigan could see Thomas Roberts running towards the top field and Bimbo catching up on Thomas. Bang a lightning bolt hit Murrigan, and a gale of wind caught him at the same time. Murrigan had lost control and fell, crashing into the roof of the Barn.

Bimbo had caught up on Thomas Roberts.

"Stay close," commanded Thomas Roberts as he put his hand out and the silver snake lace, took hold of a silver

arrow, *'crack!'* went the lightning, Thomas could see the beast had Mary Jane and had her held to the ground, *"whip, lash,"* as the arrow left Thomas Roberts hand, the silver snake lace released the arrow.

The arrow landed directly into the back of the beast's shoulder, he roared in pain and dropped to one knee releasing Mary Jane, who had fallen backwards into the mud. The beast was about to grab Mary Jane again.

"Leave my mother alone," came the voice, standing in front of the beast was Thomas Roberts, soaking wet with an arrow ready to unleash. *"Whip, lash,"* as Thomas released the arrow this time the beast was ready and caught the arrow. The beast dived forward at speed and grabbed Thomas Roberts, he had him by the throat and was crushing his windpipe, Thomas Roberts could not breathe, Bimbo had jumped up sinking his teeth deep into the beasts arm, Bimbo was hanging off the arm that was choking Thomas Roberts.

Slowly Mary Jane appeared in front of the beast, she spoke to the beast very softly.

"It's ok, no one will harm you," said Mary Jane.

The beast looked at her, it grunted and stared at her. Mary Jane placed her hand on the beast face, He had a long horse face with a large steel ring in his nose. Mary Jane could see flames rage in his eyes.

"It's ok Blackie, calm down boy, you will be fine," said Mary Jane as she ran, her hand across the beasts face. Mary Jane looked into the eyes of the beast, the red flamed eyes turned slowly, bright blue, a beautiful blue and a tear ran down the beast face that turned into a diamond as it fell off his cheek. The beast let go of Thomas Roberts throat and dropped him to the ground. Bimbo was growling with his teeth still sunk into the beast arm. The beast fell back on his bum, he had a large sword in his hand which he dropped to the floor and started to sob.

"I can't do this," sobbed the beast.

Just then, Murrigan landed directly behind the beast his sword drawn back and was in swing ready to slay the beast.

"No," screamed Mary Jane.

Pooka

Murrigan sword stopped inches from taking the beasts head off, Murrigan stepped back, with caution blade still raised ready to destroy the beast.

Mary Jane looked across to Thomas Roberts, who was crawling towards Mary Jane, she took him in her arms.

"My brave boy, are you hurt?" Mary Jane asked as she felt his arms and legs.

"No, mum I'm fine, are you hurt?" replied Thomas.

"No, I'm fine,"

Thomas and Mary Jane sat in the pouring rain, covered in mud, staring at the beast who had tried to kill both of them, who was now sitting in the mud sobbing his heart out like a child.

"It's ok Murrigan, relax, I think he means us no harm," said Mary Jane as she beckoned, Murrigan to put down his sword.

"You're not going to hurt us, are you?" Mary Jane asked the beast with caution and sought reassurance that the beast was not going to trick them and slay them when their backs were turned.

"No, my lady, please forgive me, I have wronged you and the boy, and I deserve to die, I have lived for a thousand decades in confinement, in darkness, alone. My mind and thoughts were corrupted and I planned to kill you, my lady," stated the beast.

"Kill me, why?" asked Mary Jane with shock in her voice and surprise upon her face.

"I don't really know! what I do know is that you did something to me," The beast but his hand on his chest, *"I have the sensation in here, every time you spoke to me, every time you touched me, every time you gave me sugar lumps,"* said the beast with a smile upon his face.

"I was kind to you, it's called kindness," said Mary Jane.

"Kindness, your magic is powerful my lady for you have tamed the beast in me, with the touch of your hand and the words you speak, my soul and sword are yours, I will be your guardian and protector from this day forth if you will forgive me and spare my soul," said the beast as he looked directly at Mary Jane.

Mary Jane looked at the beast, she could see he was genuine, and she trusted him. Mary Jane placed her hand on the beast face, he closed his eyes in comfort from the touch of her hand.

87

"Beast, you are forgiven," said Mary Jane. The beast started to sob again.

"Mary Jane let's get back to the house, we are exposed here," said Murrigan as he watched all around his sword in hand ready to spring into action if needed. Thomas, Mary Jane and the beast got up from the muddy field. Bimbo just kept growling at the beast.

"Yes, you were brave also boy, a little extra for supper tonight for you," said Thomas Roberts. On hearing the word supper, Bimbo stopped growling and dashed away towards the farmhouse.

Murrigan transformed into the farmhand as Mary Jane, Thomas Roberts started to walk out of the field and down the path towards the house.

Mary Jane got to the door first, she opened the door and walked into to kitchen followed by the Beast. Moria looked at Mary Jane.

"What's Hap......," Moria didn't finish her words, whoosh, Moria transformed into a splendid guardian as the sight of the beast who had just walked into the kitchen directly behind Mary Jane. Mary Jane jumped back as Moria lifted the saucepan above her head, Thomas Roberts, followed by Murrigan.

"You take, one step closer and I will take your head off," screamed Moria as she stood there in her guardian glory with a saucepan in her hands,

"A fat lot of good that will do," said Murrigan, as everyone burst into laughter.

"It's ok Moria you can put the pan down, he is friendly," said Mary Jane as she tried to control her laughter.

"Who is he? what is he?" asked Moria.

"I'm not sure, who exactly are you?" asked Thomas Roberts.

"Why don't we all sit down, we have a lot to talk about and I have a funny feeling it's going to be a long night," said Mary Jane as she pulled out a chair for the beast to sit on. The beast sat down on the chair which he was too big for, He looked down at the

table and could see a bowl of sugar lumps. The beast looked at Mary Jane.

"Go on then, help yourself," the beast picked up a lump of sugar looked at it.

"Sugar Lump," he said with a big smile upon his face.

When everyone had sat down, and the beast had stopped crunching on sugar lumps he began to tell his story. *"My name is Pooka, I was once the prince of the Harras, many spirit horses, we ran wild and free in Drumtara,"* said Pooka.

"Yes, I remember the spirit horse, but they disappeared long ago," said Moria.

We were tricked, the Harras was protected by Tirk for many decades, his only wish was that he could ride on horseback occasionally, he was a good wizard and true to his word.

Tirk came to me in the wild and told me that a great war was coming between witches and Drumtarian, he knew we were peaceful and not warriors. He promised us that he would take us to secret lands where we would be protected. Tirk lead us to the lands himself we walked far and long, many spirit horses and younglings. When we arrived, the lands looked rich from a distance. Tirk took us through the Damson path, that crossed deep bog lands, a one-way path only he knew the return path. I realised that something was not right. Arawn mistakenly dropped his disguise and was revealed to me. I swore revenge and that I would destroy him. Arawn set his loyal servants on me, I fought long and hard, in the end, there were too many, I became weak and his minions, beat me hard until my spirit had almost left me. I was taken away in secret, the Harras, never knew what had happened to me. I was informed they had exiled me for my portrayal. The Harra believed that Tirk had betrayed them also. The place they were taken to was a barren wasteland, little grew, little rain fell. The swamp was uncrossable and many died trying, the water was undrinkable, and the swamp gave off toxic gases when it dried up in the heat. The spirit of the horse was betrayed by Arawn. I swore I would have my revenge, to this day justice was never served."

"What happened to you?" asked Thomas Roberts.

'Me,' replied Pooka, with a lost look upon his face.

"You don't have to talk about it now if you don't want to," said Mary Jane

"I need to tell you, my lady, you will learn how the beast in me was created," replied Pooka.

I was bound and dragged into the deepest dept of Creeve, the kingdom of the underworld, ruled by Arawn himself. I sat in the darkness, left lonely and in despair. Arawn would visit me, torment me with the death of the Harras and my kin. He would tell me the witches would hunt them for their souls, occasionally he would beat me hard. His minions would always beat me. Over time I lost myself, my spirit broke and my thoughts and memories left me."

"How long?" asked Murrigan.

"I'm not sure, when did the Harras disappear from the free lands of Drumtara?" replied Pooka.

"About three thousand years ago," said Murrigan with sadness on his face.

The room fell silent, Pooka had been in captivity for three millenniums, tortured and humiliated for so long, this would disturb the mind of any creature.

Murrigan stepped up behind Pooka and place his hand on his shoulder,

"Your safe now," said Murrigan as he yanked the arrow that Thomas Robert had hit Pooka with.

"Thank you," replied Pooka as Murrigan placed a tea towel on the wound.

"You stated you had come for me and not Thomas Roberts?" asked Mary Jane.

"Yes, my lady, my order was simple, bring Arawn the soul of the one they call Mary Jane," replied Pooka.

"Why does he want me?" asked Mary Jane with a confused look upon her face.

"Why not want you, you are a powerful witch, that can tame the beast at the touch of your hand, my lady you have powers that warlocks and witches could only dream off."

Mary Jane started to laugh I have been called a few things in my time but never a witch.

The whole kitchen burst into laughter. Pookas face did not change as he was too busy staring at the sugar lumps.

90

"I think it's bedtime for everyone, Pooka you can sleep in the barn tonight with the other animal's plenty of straw and hay," said Moria.

"I can show him," said Thomas Roberts.

"Yes, but be quick busy day tomorrow,"

"Yes mum," replied Thomas.

Thomas took Pooka's hand they were massive compared to Thomas's hand; Thomas lead Pooka out through the kitchen door.

"Do you really think my mother is a witch," asked Thomas.

"Yes, young sir, I do, her magic is like nothing I have seen or felt before, I have no doubt, she is a witch and a good one too," replied Pooka.

"I think it be a good idea, if you could get back to being Blackie, I don't want Maisy thinking you are going to eat her," said Thomas.

"Yes, young sir, good idea," replied Pooka.

Whoosh the wind swirled around, Pooka transformed back into Blackie.

"Can we trust him?" said Moria.

"Yes, I think we can, he is a gentle creature who has had a hard time, Murrigan what do you think," asked Mary Jane.

"I agree with Mary Jane, he has pledged to protect you and as a true Drumtarian, he will honour the pledge," said Murrigan.

"That's it settled, we keep him," said Mary Jane.

"We will be needed more sugar lumps then," replied Moria as she looked down at the empty sugar bowl.

-Chapter 8-
Whispering Winds

Ram-Say had just returned from Hog Hill Farm. He was standing in front of Arawn, who was sat upon his throne, he was fast asleep and snoring very loud. Arawn, open's one eye and quickly sits up on his throne.

"My lord, I have news's," said Ram-Say as he knelt before Arawn.

"Go on then," Arawn commanded in a loud voice.

"Pooka has failed you my lord,"

"Failed, what did the guardians slay, him?" asked Arawn, with a grin on his face.

"No, my lord, we have misjudged the one they call Mary Jane, Pooka was about to take her soul when she cast a spell on him with the touch of her hand, Pooka fell to his knees begged for forgiveness and offer her his sword," replied Ram-Say.

Arawn stood up from his throne and screamed a deafening scream.

"How have we been tricked? I want this witches soul, I don't care how you take it, just take it and bring her before me," screamed Arawn.

"My Lord, I will do your bidding, I have a question. Why does Nicopulas want her soul?"

"Good question, my loyal servant, is she that powerful that Nicopulas needs her soul, he must have plans for her, he must need her desperately, even more of a reason why we should take her soul, she is a bargaining tool and worth quite a lot. Ram-Say bid my command, you must not fail me," said Arawn.

Ram-Say bowed his head *"My lord,"*

Ram-Say stood up turned around and walked into the mist.

*

Thomas had a good night sleep, he was drifting in and out of his sleep, when he heard Errol, giving his morning wake up call. Thomas felt slightly strange, he couldn't feel the stiffness of the straw mattress he slept on, instead he felt he was floating in the air. To his surprise he was floating about three feet in the air, just hoovering, Thomas though he was in a dream and was about to start falling. He didn't know how to stop the floating and he was starting to get a little anxious.

Thomas could hear the door being opened, he looked across as the door handle was turning. *"Thud"* just as the door opened, Thomas landed on the bed.

"Get up sleepy head, where going into town for some shopping, and then visiting, your father's grave at the cemetery," said Mary Jane as she opened the curtains in Thomas bedroom.

"Will do mum," replied Thomas as he quickly jumped out of his bed. Thomas quickly got dressed and ran down the stairs.

"Morning all," said Thomas.

"Morning, Thomas Roberts," said Moria and Murrigan as they were having there morning debate about what was happening today.

"I hope nothing bad happens," said Moria.

"Why would something bad happen?" asked Thomas.

"What you mean?" replied Moria.

"You just said to Murrigan, 'I hope nothing bad happens," said Thomas.

"No, she didn't," said Murrigan as he tried to divert the subject.

Just them Mary Jane entered the kitchen, she was dressed in black, she always put on her black clothing to visit John Roberts grave. Mary Jane sat down. Thomas could hear Mary Jane cry, when he looked at her, she was just sipping on her tea, Thomas noticed that there were no tears, Thomas was feeling a little odd.

Thomas could hear Murrigan talking, without moving his lips. Thomas could also hear Moria voice, while she was humming a tune to herself. Thomas thought he was going mad, he got up from the kitchen table and ran out, he ran to the side of the farmhouse, placed his hands over his ears.

"Leave me alone, please leave me alone," He shouted aloud, he could hear lots of voices and they were driving him to despair.

"You ok Thomas?" Thomas looked up to see Moria.

"No, there is something wrong with me, I can hear voices, I can hear mother crying when she is not and this morning I was floating in my bed, have I gone mad Moria?" asked Thomas.

*"No, my boy there is nothing wrong with you, you have a wonderful gift'
you're a soul reader,"* replied Moria.

"What you mean, soul reader?" asked Thomas.

*"There are many gifts, being a soul reader in one of the rarest, some
people can read minds, but people don't always do or say what they think.
You my boy go deeper, the soul hearer knows the truth about peoples
thoughts, their true intentions, you can tell who is good or evil, a wonderful
gift,"*

"What about the floating?" asked Thomas.

*"I don't know anything about floating, but we need to tame, you soul
hearing,"* replied Moria.

"How do we do that?" asked Thomas.

"Pretend you have four ears, you place earmuffs onto the front,"

"I, I don't have four ears and I don't have earmuffs," replied Thomas,
looking all confused.

"Click," Moria clicked her finger and thumb together.

"You have now," said Moria as Thomas felt his head.

At the click of Moria's fingers Thomas had grown two extra
ears with a set of earmuffs on them. Thomas took the ear
muffs off and felt his ears, he was shocked to feel four ears two
on each side with one behind the other.

"Calm down, is only temporary," said Moria.

"Put the muffs on you front ears, and listen to my feelings," said Moria.

Thomas took the earmuffs and put them onto his front set of
ears.

*"I'm so excited, the boy has got, magical talents, he's going to be a great
wizard,"* said Moria without speaking a word.

"What, did you hear?" asked Moria.

*"I'm not sure, you are all exited, going on about someone with magical
talents and is going to be a great wizard,"* replied Thomas.

Moria seemed a bit uneasy about what Thomas Roberts had
heard from her, Moria was thinking *'I need to control my emotions.'*

"Yes, you do," replied Thomas.

"Good, very well, swap your earmuffs over," said Moria.

Thomas took the ear muffs off and swapped them over.

"Now all you should hear is each other's voices, what I want you to do is pretend you got four ears, and a set of earmuffs when you want to hear anothers soul take the earmuff off's when you don't place them back on,"

"I can't have fours ears and a set of earmuffs on all the time," replied Thomas.

Moria clicked her fingers, and the earmuffs and ears fell off the sides of Thomas head, the ear wriggled on the floor for a moment, "Puff," they disappeared in a puff of smoke along with the earmuffs.

"I want you to use your imagination, you will learn to control this gift, for the time being, keep this quiet," said Moria.

"I will," replied Thomas.

Moria and Thomas walked into the kitchen, Mary Jane was putting on her coat.

"Come on then, young man, let's go we can treat ourselves to some apple turnovers in town,"

"Sounds good to me," replied Thomas.

Mary Jane and Thomas started to walk into the town of Trim. The cemetery was their first stop, it was a good twenty minutes walked to the cemetery. Mary Jane and Thomas had got to the front gate, Mary Jane had gathered a small bunch of wildflowers on her walk to the cemetery. Thomas opened the old metal gate that creaked very loudly as he opened it. There where to large gargoyles on top of the gates posts, perched with their wings closed and long tongues sticking out.

The cemetery was old, with an old church which was only used for funerals and the rare wedding. There were two further gargoyles positioned at the entrance to the church door.

As Thomas walked in through the gate, he heard whispering.
"Did you say something' mum?" asked Thomas.

"No son," replied Mary Jane as she sorted out the flowers in her hand.

John Roberts grave was at the far end of the cemetery, past the old church, it was a dark area with large pine trees that blocked out the sun, on a cloudy day, it could be difficult to read the engravements on the head stone.

Whispering Winds

As Thomas and Mary Jane got closer to the church, Thomas could hear the whispering, this time it was like a chant.

'Cosantoiri an ardu marbh ordaim duit.' Thomas could hear the words being repeated over and over again, there was a breeze in the air, he could hear the whispers in the breeze as they passed through the tree's, Thomas thought about his invisible earmuffs and his four ears, the trick Moria had taught him, it was not working.

Thomas and Mary Jane got to John Roberts grave, Mary Jane bowed her head and stood quietly at the grave side. Thomas was looking around he kept hearing the words *'Cosantoiri an ardu marbh ordaim duit.'* Over and over again, he thought these words were in his head as he couldn't see anyone in the cemetery.

Ram-Say was sat on top of the old church roof, looking down at Mary Jane and Thomas Roberts, He was invisible to their eye's, however he was chanting *'Cosantoiri an ardu marbh ordaim duit.'* Over and over again.

The gargoyles at the gate of the church started to crumble, turning to dust which blew away in the breeze, their hard crust tomb was dissolving to the chant of Ram-Say. The two gargoyles at the church entrance also started the same process, in a short time the gargoyles had come to life, black and scaley and lashing their tongues like whips, they had long fingered claws, and red blood shot eyes, they growled and snarled at each other, suddenly they spread their wings and took flight.

Mary Jane had just laid the wildflowers, on John Roberts grave.

"Mum?" said Thomas Roberts in a quiet voice.

"Yes?" replied Mary Jane.

"RUN" screamed Thomas Roberts.

Thomas grabbed Mary Jane by the hand, she had not seen the gargoyles standing behind them at the grave side, but she heard their screams as they started their attack. Mary Jane and Thomas needed to get out of the graveyard and quick. The gargoyles where taking turns at lashing them with their tongues and clawing as they attacked. What Thomas and Mary Jane did not know was that the gargoyles tongue were venomous. Thomas picked up stones and started to throw them at the gargoyles, Mary Jane also started to pick up stones and throw them. Thomas spotted a concrete tomb stone that had a concrete table. He grabbed Mary Janes hand and ran to the table, Thomas forced Mary Jane down and under the table.

"Stay here," said Thomas just as a gargoyle had grabbed him and tossed him into the air, Thomas got back to his feet quicky, he could see all four gargoyles attacking Mary Jane, she had curled up under the table as they whipped her with their venomous tongues and clawed at her. Thomas picked up a large stick and started to beat of the gargoyles whacking them as hard as he could. It was working the gargoyle flow up and turned towards Thomas ready to attack, Thomas stood his ground stick in his hand and was ready to defend his mother to the end.

Suddenly the gargoyles fell to the ground and smashed into thousands of little pieces and turned to dust blowing away in the breeze. Thomas could feel blowing behind him, he could hear the beating of wings, he looked behind him, Thomas knew it was Murrigan, he could sense his presents. Thomas Roberts turned around to see Murrigan standing in front of him in his guardian glory. In one hand was a long silver sword dripping with green slime in the other was the head of a hideous beast, Murrigan held up the head,

"This filth has been watching us for a long time, it will watch no longer," said Murrigan, as dropped Ram-Say head to the ground.

"Mother," shouted Thomas.

Mary Jane laid under the stone table lifeless.

"She can't be dead, please don't let her be dead," cried Thomas Roberts.

'Listen to her soul, what is she saying,' said Murrigan.

Thomas knew exactly what Murrigan meant, he paused, and he listened.

"When, I get up I'm going to kill these foul creatures, leave my boy alone," Thomas could hear Mary Jane, scolding.

"She still got fight in her, we need to get back to Hog Hill Farm immediately," demanded Murrigan, as he pulled Mary Jane from under the concrete table, holding her tight in one arm and Thomas Roberts in the other, whoosh they were gone.

Murrigan crashed open the kitchen door at Hog Hill Farm.

"Clear the table," he shouted.

Moria ripped the tablecloth of the table, cutlery went flying across the kitchen floor. Murrigan laid Mary Jane on the table.

"She has been snake lashed by enchanted gargoyles," said Murrigan as he looked a Moria.

"Right, we need docking leaf and lots off it," said Moria in a calm voice.

"Docking leaf?" replied Thomas Roberts with a surprise look on his face.

"Yes, docking leaf's, you know the big green leafed plant you put on stinging nettles," said Moria with a stern look upon her face.

"Yes, I know what they are," replied Thomas.

"Well then go get them," said Moria as she stared intensely at Thomas.

Mary Jane, started to come round, she was in a lot of pain, her skin was red and burning, she has scratches all over her hand face and neck.

"Is she going to be, ok?" asked Murrigan.

"Yes, she will be fine, she will be sore for a few days, she is in good hand,' replied Moria.

Thomas returned with the docking leaf's, Moria placed then into a bowl and started to crush the leaves until it turned to mulch. Once mulched Moria gently laid it onto Mary Janes wounds.

A few days had pasted, Mary Jane was sitting up in bed sipping on a cup of tea, when Thomas walked, in, Mary Jane smiled at seeing him.

"You ok mum?" asked Thomas.

"Yes, are you?" replied Mary Jane.

"*Yes, I'm good,*" said Thomas.

"*I'm so proud of you, what you did at the graveyard was very brave, most young men would have run and hide, but you stood your ground to protect your mother,*" said Mary Jane.

"*Mum, I know, I am different, I know that Murrigan and Moria are different, what I don't understand is why,*" said Thomas.

"*My boy, my beautiful boy, yes, you are not different, you are just very special, when I fully recover, we will sit down and discuss this as a family, you need to know the truth and the truth will be told.*" replied Mary Jane.

*

Arawn sat on his thrown, in Creeve, he was growing anxious as he had not heard from Ram-Say for some time. "*Ram-Say come forth, I command you, Ram-Say come forth I command you,*" screamed Arawn,

Ram-Say did not come forth and never would, Arawn had assumed that something had gone wrong, that the witch called Mary Jane had destroyed Ram-Say.

Arawn sat on his throne, very quietly, he could see a figure come through the mist.

"*Ram-Say is that you?*" Arawn called out.

"*No, my lord, I'm a Torm a messenger from lord Nicopulas,*" Torm was very tall and slim she had, no hair and very small pointy ears, her nose was flat and her eyes where silver, her teeth where razor sharp, she was quietly spoken, Torm was dressed in a long white robe that came down over her feet. She walked towards Arawn very gracefully as if almost floating. As Torm approached the

throne she bowed. "*My lord Arawn, lord Nicopulas commands your presents at the great hall of Lantara,*" said Torm

"*Any reason, in particular, why our lord commands my presents?*" asked Arawn.

"*It's not for me to say my lord, I'm sure you will be informed,*" replied Torm.

Arawn was feeling nervous, had Nicopulas found out about his plan to take, Mary Jane, he did not trust Nicopulas and Nicopulas trusted nothing.

"Very well, I will follow soon," said Arawn.

"One more request, lord Nicopulas said, dress for the occasion," said Torm.

"What occasion?" asked Arawn.

"The feast, in honour of his children," replied Torm as she stood up and disappeared into the mist.

Arawn sat back on his throne, he had realised that his plan had gone wrong, he also realised that the feast Nicopulas was hosting in the honour of Gear-ra and Zoda was a trap and that he was possibly on the menu. Arawn stroked his black raven deep in thought.

Mary Jane, Moria, Murrigan and Pooka where all sat at the kitchen table. Mary Jane had called a family meeting. She wanted to discuss with everyone, that the time was right to tell Thomas Roberts the truth of his life and where he was from. Everyone was in agreement that the time was right. Thomas was now thirteen years old and was growing into a fine young man. He was now asking many questions on the events that occurred in his life.

"I have something that will help Thomas understand who he is and the truth about his life. We call it a memory stone, the memories are mine, but they will give Thomas a lot of information," said Moria.

Thomas entered the kitchen to find everyone sitting round the table and staring at him.

"Good morning," said Thomas.

"Good morning," everyone said at once.

"Thomas, we need you to sit down," said Mary Jane.

Thomas pulled a chair out and sat at the table.

"You know that a lot of strange occurrences have happened over the past few years, and we have told you to keep a lot of things secret. We have all agreed that the time is now right to tell you the truth, Moria is going to use something called a memory stone to help you understand the truth," said Mary Jane.

Thomas sat on the chair very quietly, Moria put her hand in her pocket and brought out a small wooden box and placed the box in the middle of the table. Moria looked at the small wooden box and then looked at Thomas Robert, Moria gave Thomas a smile and looked back at the box. Moria got closer to the box and spoke the word.

"REMORA"

The small wooden box began to open, inside was a small white stone that has small speckles of crystal embedded into the stone, the stone was perfectly round almost like a marble, the stone lay on a small black felt blanket inserted into the bottom of the box. Slowly the small round stone started to rise about one foot above the box. Everyone was watching the small stone, they all appeared hypnotised by the stones presents. The small stone started to spin, first of all very slowly and continue to speed up spinning very fast, suddenly beams of light started to shoot out of the stone. Thomas felt that he was being transported to another world, that's exactly what was happening, Mary Jane, Moria, Murrigan and Pooka where with him standing beside him. Thomas looked down, he could see beautiful lands, small houses, tree, rivers animals running free across the land.

"Thomas these, are my memories, I'm sharing them with you, don't be afraid as these are memories, some are good some are bad, what you need to know is that they happened and not happening, they are the past, some memories were a very long time ago," said Moria.

Thomas kept looking down, he did not speak.

"We are flying over the kingdom of Drumtara, this is our world, it is far from hear and cannot be travelled to unless you have a portal and portal key," said Murrigan.

"It's beautiful," said Thomas.

"Yes, it was," replied Moria.

The journey took them across a large lake which was so big you could not see where it started or ended, then came the forest which were just as big as the lake if not bigger. They flew over the forest until they came to a wide opening at the foot of a mountain range in the background. there were open plain fields with many horses running free.

"The Harras, my kin,' said Pooka with a smile on his face as he watched the horses running free. Suddenly they stopped in mid-flight, in front of them was a large city built into the mountain range, that rose halfway up the mountain, there were two bridges one on the left running up to the top of the mountains and one on the right, the bridges where high and large with three large arch ways under each bridge. The city had a large moat of crystal blue water, Thomas could see many creatures swimming and bathing, he could hear laughter and joy from the city. Running down the centre was a large road; the road was split in two with creatures of all types moving from the left towards the city and the right to come out. The city was surrounded, by a wall, a very high wall with towers spread along the wall, each tower had a guardian on top of each

tower. In the centre of the wall was a gate way with two large gates. The gates where open, both gates had the Drumtara crest embedded into the wooden gates, the four symbols in a divided X.

"Do you see the gates, Thomas?" asked Moria.

"Yes, they are big gates," replied Thomas.

"The markings on the gate is the crest of Drumtara, the fish on the top represents the creatures of the water. The lake we past was Keel, they are protected by the ancient goddess called Merrow. The tree is the souls of the forest, there are many woodland realms, some good some evil. The bird like creature at the bottom of the symbol is the guardians, we will introduce you to the guardians soon. The skull at the left represent all that is evil and bad," said Moria.

The next memory shown was, in the great hall of Lantara, there was two thrones, the hall was lit up with beams of light coming from sky lights in the roof of the great hall on each side where statues of guardian, in full armour, some with arrows of Lantara in their hand in the throwing stance other with swords and shields, as Thomas looked up, he good see more statues of guardians suspended in the air as if they were flying, Thomas was amazed a such sight, he had never seen anything like it. As they moved close to the Thrones Thomas could see two figures on the thrones to the left was a man, he looked hansom with his white and silver laced robe, he had white hair almost silver swept back he had bright blue eyes which smiled every time he did. The man was looking at the woman on the throne beside him, she was beautiful with long black hair, dark coloured skin with green eyes, she had a wonderful smile.

"They look beautiful and so happy," Thomas said, as the man and women on the thrones laughed and talked to each other.

"Yes, they were very beautiful and the happiest souls in all of Drumtara on this day," said Moria.

"Why this day?" asked Thomas.

"On this day they found out they were going to have a child," replied Moria.

Moria paused, she placed her hand on Thomas shoulder.

"Thomas, I'm going to tell you something that's, (Moria paused) *that's very important and may change the way you feel, the man on the left is called Tirk, he is the high guardian and protector of all Drumtara, and he is your father,"* said Moria.

"My father, I thought John Roberts was my father, I don't understand any of this," said Thomas Roberts in a voice of despair.

"Thomas, its important you listen and understand," said Mary Jane as she stood beside Thomas, she slipped her hand into his, they both held each other's hand very tightly.

"The lady beside your father is your mother, she is happy on this day because she found out she was having a child and that child was you," said Moria.

"No this is not true, this is a lie," shouted Thomas Roberts as he fell to his knee's crying.

Mary Jane fell beside him holding him tight.

"That's enough Moria stop this now, please," cried Mary Jane.

Suddenly they were back in the kitchen of Hog Hill Farm Thomas and Mary Jane where on the kitchen floor, still holding each other tight. Moria was standing over the kitchen table with her hand out in front of her, fist clinched tight, she opened her hand with the memory stone in the palm of her hand.

Murrigan sat at the table with his head bowed, he was full of sadness, he knew the whole story and the sadness that was to follow. Murrigan knew that Thomas Roberts world had just come crashing down. Pooka sat at the table, large droplet of tears were running from his eyes and hitting the kitchen table, each tear that fell turned into a diamond and tapped on the table each time the tear drop fell.

Thomas got up and ran out of the house, Mary Jane stood up to run after him. Murrigan stood up and grabbed Mary Jane hand. He looked her in the eye he could see her pain.

"Leave him, I will go and speak to him," said Murrigan.

Murrigan stepped out into the farmyard, he could see the small figure of Thomas Roberts sitting on a wall, facing up the fields. Murrigan walked up beside Thomas and sat beside him.

"Today is a difficult day, its day like today that define us, they make you or break you. There is two important, thing that should not be forgotten, those we have lost and those we still have. Mary Jane is not your birth mother, but she is your mother, she has given us all a great gift and something that is more valuable than any possession, she gave us her love, we are a strange family from different worlds, but we are a family. I never had a family, I have never loved anyone and now I have this feeling inside me, that I cannot explain, I know they call it love, it scares me very much, because loving someone means to suffer, at any hurt they may feel. I am not your father and Moria is not your mother, but we love you boy as if you were our son. Mary Jane loves you like her own son, and she always will." said Murrigan as he took Thomas Roberts by the hand.

"I know you love me; I know you all love me; I could never want for another family, like I already have. The memory stone feels so real as If it is happening, I guess I'm shocked, but I knew that I was different, I just didn't know how different," said Thomas.

Thomas and Murrigan sat quietly for a while.

"Your father was my friend, he was a great wizard, albeit he use to dwindle in some dark magic, he was never a seeker of power only the knowledge of magic. I would say he was a scientist or engineer of magic, yes, an engineer of magic. I think this scared many, but he was good, kind and he loved you although for a short time. He ordered Moria and me to protect you, look after you. Moria and I could not do this on our own, we needed help and we needed it fast. It was fate, that Mary Jane is your mother, she was presented to us, and we knew she was the one," said Murrigan.

"I have something of your fathers he, gave it to me to, he said 'use this to protect my son' I think it's fitting that you should have it," said Murrigan.

Murrigan put his hand into his pocket and brought out an old tissue, he started to peel the tissue back to reveal a gold ring, Murrigan picked the ring up and gave it to Thomas Roberts. Thomas took the ring and examined it, set in the gold ring was a blue stone, when Thomas looked into the blue stone, he could see the emblem of Drumtara embed deep in the stone.

"It's a nice ring, but it's too big for me," said Thomas Roberts.

"*Try it on, it goes on the smallest finger of the left hand,*" replied Murrigan.

Thomas placed the ring on the smallest finger of his left hand, the ring was too big, magically the ring shrank to fit Thomas little finger, Thomas looked at Murrigan with surprise upon his face.

"*Woo, that was amazing, it fits perfectly, why the little finger of the left hand?*" asked Thomas.

"*Your left hand is you shield hand, your right hand is to grip a sword or unleash the arrow,*" replied Murrigan.

"*I don't understand, it's only a ring,*" said Thomas.

"*Only a ring, there is no other ring like this one, this is a shield ring very rare very powerful. Hold it out in front of you,*" commanded Murrigan.

Thomas punched his left hand out in front of him nothing happened.

"*You have to do it like you mean it, you need to protect yourself,*" scolded Murrigan.

Murrigan stood up.

"*Prepare to protect yourself,*" as Murrigan pulled a large silver sword from his side, Thomas did not see the sword until it was drawn, Murrigan raised the sword above his head ready to strike Thomas Roberts. The sword came down hard and fast, Thomas punched out with his left hand, just as the sword was about to strike him, suddenly the ring opened up, Thomas could see a water shaped circle in front of his hand connecting to the ring, Thomas could see Murrigan through the water, he could see Murrigan sword strike the water ring, the sword bounce of the ring shield.

"*That it, my boy that's how you use a shield ring, nothing can get through it not even white fire, there is something else about the shield ring, it hides you from your enemy, give it to me, I will show you,*" said Murrigan with excitement in his voice.

"*Here, you take my sword,*" said Murrigan as Thomas reached Murrigan the ring and Murrigan reached Thomas the sword, the sword was long, Thomas took the sword in his hands, it was very light.

"Your sword is very light," said Thomas as he picked the sword up and started to swing it about.

"It might be light but its deadly sharp," replied Murrigan, just a Thomas hit the wall and cut through the stone as if it was made of butter.

"Woo, what is this sword made of?" asked Thomas.

"The sword was forged in Lantara by the Orcans, white fire breathing creatures, they are excellent sword makers. The sword itself is made of silver sands gathered of the coast of Rush, the sands are melted to make the silver ore, the melted silver is then placed into a sword cast and the Orcans shape the swords with diamond head hammers, The sword you are holding was presented to me by your father," said Murrigan with a distanced look upon his face as if he was reminiscing the day, he received the sword.

"Enough of that, let me show you what the shield ring can do," said Murrigan as he placed the ring on his little finger, the ring appeared to be getting larger to accommodate for Murrigan's stubby fat fingers.

"Attack me," shouted Murrigan.

Thomas swung the sword above his head and brought it down as hard as he could, Murrigan forced out his left hand which had the shield ring on. The sword came down hard, as Thomas appeared to be losing control as the shield opened, the sword that Thomas was wielding hits the shield, *"Bong"* as Thomas arms bounce back, and the force of the sword forces him to fall back on to the ground.

"Murrigan?" Thomas said.

"Yes" replied Murrigan.

"Where are you?"

Murrigan had disappeared, Thomas could not see him, he could only hear him.

Murrigan was behind the ring shield that had created an invisible wall as well as a protective shield, better still, Murrigan was looking through the shield, he could see Thomas.

"I'm here," said Murrigan as he popped his head over the shield, Thomas could only see Murrigan head as the invisible shied covered the rest of his body. Murrigan pulled his hand

back and the shield disappeared, standing in front of Thomas was a full bodied Murrigan.

"Woo, now, that was amazing, I have never seen anything like it," said Thomas with excitement.

"The ring is yours, young man, use it wisely, only to protect and for good, and the occasional trick," said Murrigan with a big smile on his face.

"I will, thanks you," replied Thomas Roberts.

"I think it's time, we went indoors, we have something we need to do." said Murrigan.

Thomas nodded his head; he knew that he had to know the truth and that the time was now. Murrigan picked up the sword as Thomas watched Murrigan place it by his side, as if sliding the sword into an invisible sheath. Murrigan stretched out his hand, Thomas placed his hand inside Murrigan hand, and he lifted Thomas back to his feet.

Thomas and Murrigan walked back to the farmhouse and entered the kitchen, Mary Jane, Moria and Pooka who was crunching on sugar lumps smiled.

"I think it's time I knew, everything," said Thomas as he sat down on a chair beside Mary Jane. Thomas took her hand and smiled at Mary Jane, Mary Jane smiled back, the small jester from Thomas, removed the thought that she may lose him if he knew the truth.

"We can do this some other time," said Mary Jane.

"No, the time is right," replied Thomas Roberts.

Moria opened the box, that contained the small white memory stone, it started to rise above the box and started to spin, within a few moments, Thomas, Mary Jane, Murrigan, Moria and Pooka where all back in the memory.

"What was she called?" asked Thomas as he put his hand out to touch her, his hand just passed through the image of his mother, it was only a projection of a memory of something that did happen.

"Isbeth, her name was Isbeth," replied Moria.

"Isbeth," repeated Thomas.

"She was such a kind person, Tirk had so much admiration for her," said Moria.

Murrigan looked at Thomas.
"This doesn't end well, your father Tirk, was, powerful, as I have explained, and he did things that broke the covenants of Drumtarians. Tirk had found a way to cross worlds, by exploring ancient magic. He found a way to cross into the human world, using key ports, they say there are four, to this world, however they never stay in the same place. When Tirk located one he marked it with a beacon that only he could see, he had keys crafted to fit the doors to the magic portals. When Tirk crossed over, he met Isbeth and fell in love. What he did next was to change everything, he offered Isbeth eternal life in Drumtara, she accepted his offer and Isbeth entered Drumtara as flesh and bone. The covenant states, 'Only the souls of the good from a past life can enter the Kingdom of Drumtara where it will be reborn into eternal life.' By bringing Isbeth to Drumtara without judgement on her soul, Tirk created an unbalance, a corruption amongst the creations of Drumtara. Nicopulas a dark warlock, sized the opportunity to grow his lies and hate he deceived many, including Pooka and his kin. He deceived the Witches, Warlocks and Wolfbeings who fought and destroyed each other, he tricked the giants and Lepz the keepers of the woodlands, he poisoned and polluted the water of Keel and the water folk suffered terribly.

Nicopulas tricked them all filled their souls with his vile hate and despair, he made them deceitful promises if they would rise up, and fight with him. The Drumtarians rallied to Nicopulas call and the great war began, for days and nights we the guardians fought against good souls who had been corrupted by Nicopulas on the seventh night of the battle of Lantara, you were born. On that seventh night your father and mother perished in the white fire casted by the Witches of Kincora."

As Murrigan told the story, Thomas could see, images of, the great war, witches flying, through the air with staffs in their hand, white fire shooting from the staffs, giants, banging on large drums, setting the drums alight and rolling them into the city walls and exploding when the smashed into the wall. Thomas could see the Lepz, thousands of them storming the city with arrows, swords, killing everything in their path. Thomas could see the mast destruction of the great city of Lantara.

The last image was hard to bare, two platforms in the middle of the great square, surrounded by many Drumtarians above the two platforms and suspended upside down in the air was Tirk and Isbeth, they were both bloody, Isbeth was in distress. Tirk was just staring at her. From the gathering of Drumtarians came a ring of about thirty witches standing side by side, dressed in black, muddy faced, bright green evil eyes staring at Tirk and Isbeth.

Then appeared Nicopulas, being carried on a throne, by four demon like creatures his image was that of an old frail man. The throne was placed at the edge of the ring, he raised his hand and dropped it. All the witches, tilted their staffs, long black thorn staffs with a black stone embedded into the top of each staff, the witches had a look of hate on their faces, suddenly white fire shot into the bodies of Tirk and Isbeth for a few seconds the white light from all the witches firing white fire, was blinding, after they had stopped the bodies still suspended above the platforms, where charred by the white fire slowly ash fell onto the platform, the entire bodies dropped onto the platform as ash, the ash blew away in the breeze, Tirk and Isbeth where no more.

The memory images disappeared; the small white memory stone hovered above the small box. It slowly dropped back into the box, the boxed closed by itself. Everyone sat quietly for a few moments.

"Who was the old man in the throne, who gave the order?" asked Thomas Roberts.

"He is Nicopulas, but don't be fooled by his frailty, he is powerful, cunning and very deceptive, he is a trickster, who is not to be trusted," said Pooka.

Moria picked up the, the small box that contained the memory stone.

"I want you to have my memories some are the best I ever had, the others you can discard," said Moria as she handed the small box with the memory stone inside.

"Thanks, you, Moria I will treasure these memories and thank you all, for being with me," said Thomas as he looked at Mary Jane, who had a tear in her eyes. Thomas got up of his chair and went to Mary Jane, he placed his arms around her.

"You will always be my mum," Thomas whispered into Mary Janes ear.

Arawn appeared through a cloud of mist, on the edge of a large dark forest, dark rain clouds hung over the forest with large bird like creatures flying high above. Arawn looked up to the sky as the creatures circled high above him. Arawn had a dark plan in mind, he needed to do something before he went to visit Nicopulas. Arawn needed a bargaining tool, and he knew exactly who she was, if only he could get his hands-on Mary Jane.

The wooded area was known as the Silent Forest, a place where evil and possessed spirits dwelled, the tale was that those souls that where tormented in their previous life's went to the silent forest to seek repentance. There was a spirit that dwelled in the silent forest that Arawn was seeking. She was known as Bana-Shea, she dwelled deep in the forest and had not been heard of in a thousand years. The story goes that Bana-Shea was once the queen of the witches, to become queen she committed a despicable act an act that would curse her for all eternity.

Bana-Shea was the witch who belonged to one of the most powerful Warlocks, in Drumtara, he was known to all as Slone, long ago witches where servants to warlocks and wizard, who would treat witches with cruelty, many witches were burnt at the stake, for talking back to a warlock. These where hard and cruel times for witches, they were made to walk in the shadows behind their warlocks somewhere known to be chained and forbidden to practice in witchcraft and magic. When younglings were created many young witches were sold off as slaves to warlocks.

Bana-Shea was a beautiful young witch, she was intelligent and curious about her magic. In secret Bana-Shea would practice old witchcraft and magic, conjuring up old ancient spells long forgotten by witches, she would study the old text of ancient witchcraft and magic. Over time she became confident and strong. Until one day Slone was cruel to her, Bana-Shea used the ancient magic against him, the spell she chanted in the ancient language was, *"is lisomsa agus is mianach do sou a Choinneail,"* translated it means, *"Your soul is mine and mine to keep,"* the spell was very powerful, which allowed Bana-Shea to suck the soul and life out of Slone, the soul would transfer through the mouth of Slone and enter Bana-Shea through her mouth. When Bana-Shea had completed the spell, Slone was drained of his soul and flesh. What stood before Bana-Shea was a weak-old creature, she did not destroy him as she wanted to punish him, Slone was to live for eternity as an old weak creature.

Bana-Shea, however, was gifted with extraordinary beauty, and powers beyond any warlock or wizards capability. All warlocks and wizards where gifted with a magical staff of hawthorn, these staffs where presented to warlocks and wizards, witches were forbidden to possess such a staff. The hawthorn staff had a black crystal embedded into the top of the staff this was the Stone of Braid. Braid was a very deep river which ran black as tar. Warlock and wizards would swim to the bottom of the river, a black crystal would present itself as a glowing light in the darkest place all the warlock or wizard had to do was reach out and grab the crystal that presented itself, once grabbed the warlock or wizard would be guided to the surface safely. Many warlocks and wizard where never seen again as not all of them where worthy of a black crystal.

Before Bana-Shea left the presents of Slone, she commanded his staff to honour and obey her. The staff came to Bana-Shea, without hesitation, giving her powers she had never wielded before. Bana-Shea had learned from the ancient text that the staff of power can be used to give flight, something warlocks or wizards could not do, she had learnt to cast white fire, a weapon that would burn through rock and steel. Bana- Shea had become a very powerful witch, however there would be a price to pay.

Sometime later Bana-Shea had come across a young witch, who was trying to drink from a river, the young witch had chains on her feet and hand, and a large steel neck brace that had the chains attached leading from her hands and feet. Standing not too far from the young witch was an old locking wizard, ugly with a scare that ran down his face, he had one eye and long tatty grey hair. The wizard yanked hard on the young witches chains, she was pulled back from the stream and fell onto the ground. Bana-Shea could see her pain as she laid on the ground.

The wizards shouted, *"Bring me some water witch,"* as he throw a large wooden jug at her. Bana-Shea walked through the trees, towards the wizard, the wizard caught a glance of Bana-Shea, and he was enchanted by her beauty.

"Good day," said Bana-Shea as she approached the wizard.

"Good day, my lady," replied the wizard.

Bana-Shea clicked her fingers, and the old ugly wizard froze, she picked up his staff which laid nearby. Bana-Shea looked at the young witch who was staring at her with fear in her eyes.

"Don't be afraid, I mean you no harm," said Bana-Shea as she sat down beside the young witch. *"Those look extremely painful,"* said Bana-Shea as she touched the chain wrapped around the young witches wrist. As Bana-Shea touched the chains they started to dissolved link by link until they had disappeared including the neck brace.

"You don't need to wear those chains anymore, you can be a free witch, but I need you to do as I say, I am going to give you a spell repeat after me, is mian liomsa anan a choinneail," said Bana-Shea. The young witch repeated the words that Bana-Shea spoke.

"Again, repeat it all again," demanded Bana-Shea.

"Stand up and follow me,"

Bana-Shea walked towards the frozen wizard she positioned the young witch in front of the old ugly wizard.

"Say the words," commanded Bana-Shea, as she clicked her finger the old wizard came back to life, he was shocked to see the young witch, standing in front of him. *"Is mian liomsa anan a choinneail,"* said the young witch, suddenly the old wizard braced up, his soul was being drawn out of him and into the young witch, as the soul of the old wizard left him and entered the young witch, he grew older and weaker the young witch started to change, her straggly black her, was starting to shine, her dark eyes shone bright and green, the wounds on her hand and neck disappeared, her teeth shone clean and white. The

old wizard stood on his two feet doubled over and struggling to stand, he was breathless and gasping for air. Bana-Shea picked up the old wizard's staff and gave it to the beautiful young witch.

"Take his staff and point it at him and repeat after me," said Bana-Shea as the young witch took the staff, she points the end that contained the black crystal at the old wizard.

"Sruthan," was the word that came from Bana-Shea's lips.

The young witch repeated *"Sruthan,"* suddenly white fire flowed from the end of the staff and the old wizard was disintegrated, where he stood and was converted into ash, A light breeze was blowing which blew away the light ash, all that remained of the cruel wizard.

"What is your name?" asked Bana-Shea.

"My name," the young witch paused, she had been enslaved for so long she had nearly forgotten who she was, *"My name is Ishka,"* replied the young witch.

"Ishka, I like your name, from today you are a free witch, never to be bounded by chains or feel the whip of a master, today is the beginning of the rise of the witch," said Bana-Shea, with a smile upon her face and triumph in her voice.

Over time Bana-Shea and Ishka, travelled across Drumtara, freeing witches from slavery, Bana-Shea had gathered a large covenant, she taught them the ancient magic, how to use the power of the staff they had taken from the wizards, she had taught them to consume the wizard's souls. Under Bana-Shea witches became powerful and strong.

Bana-Shea was powerful and wise, however she realised that there was a flaw, in her plan. To maintain the power, she and her coven had to continue to consume the souls of wizards and warlocks. The consumption of souls had become an addiction, a cruel craven had started to grow inside every witch, while warlock and wizards where plentiful at the start of Bana-Shea's crusade. They had now become scarce, many wizards and warlock had been consumed many had gone into hiding, from the fear of the witches and their newfound powers.

Bana-Shea had realised that something was not quite right in the early days of the gathering of the coven. On this day she had been feeling a strange sensation in her stomach a burning sensation that was getting worse, as she was walking through the forest with Ishka, she felt a sharp stabbing pain. Bana-Shea fell to the forest floor clutched her stomach a strange hunger was consuming her.

"My lady are you unwell?" asked Ishka as she tried to help Bana-Shea to her feet. Ishka could see that Bana-Shea was unwell, her face was pale, her red, rosy lips had turned blue, and the green sparkle had gone from her eyes, which had turned black. *"I feel weak, my strength is fading,"* replied Bana-Shea. Just then Ishka could see something through the tree's it was a young wizard, Bana-Shea sniffed the air like an animal on a hunt, suddenly, she lifted of the ground and flew directly through the tree's fast and like a ghost, passing through each tree. The young wizard was taken by surprise Bana-Shea grabbed him by the throat and pulled him close, within a few seconds she had started to consume the soul of the young wizard, he did not struggle. Bana-Shea had taken his soul all that was left was his skin and bone and the clothes he wore, once she had finished, she dropped him to the floor and looked at Ishka with a concerned look upon her face. The taking of the young wizards soul had restored Bana-Shea to her former beauty and her strength had returned. Bana-Shea was troubled by what had happened and soon learnt that with her newfound powers come with a price.

Bana-Shea decided that the witches needed to be ruled and that laws of the covenant where required these laws would be enshrined into the witches of the covenant, any breaches of the laws would be punished by death under white fire. Bana-shea gathered all the witches and read the new laws out aloud.

"Witches of the Covenant of Bana-Shea, my friends, my family, we must enforce the laws of the witch to ensure our existence prevails, to break our laws is punishment of death." Shouted Bana-Shea, an eery silence fell over the witches as Bana-Shea began to read the new laws from a scroll of paper. *"The first law is our most secret law; witches*

will not consume the souls of witches. Our second law, Witches would only consume the souls of warlock and wizards when craving. Third law, witches will declare their capture and share with those in need, this will prevent the hunger madness evolving in a witch which would drive a witch into hysterical madness. The fourth law, all-consuming of the soul of wizards and warlock would be a ritual held on the going down of the third sun. Commanded Bana-Shea." The ritual had two phases, the taking of the soul and the taking of the seed. The taking of the seed was ancient dark magic. Bana-Shea was the first to experiment with this magic.

*

On the day of the new ritual the first sun rose to break the dawn of the day, within a few hours the first sun lowers into the Drumtara horizon, and second sun begins to rise into the sky, the day stays bright as one sun lowers the other rises, as the second sun lowers the third and last sun of day rises when the third sun lowers, the cycle of the three moons occurs, initiating the beginning of the night. The cycle of the three moons is the same as the cycle of the three suns'. The first two moons shine white. The third and final moon of the night is known as the Blood Moon as it shines a blood red before the break of a new dawn.

In the coven the drums started to beat, and the dance of the witch began, many witches gather they danced and rejoice as the ritual begins. A young wizard who had been hunted down walks to the alter, he is smiling at the beauty of the witches dancing in the light of the fires and the last light of the day. The young wizard is unaware of what is about to happen, the witches that have captured him have cast a spell on the young wizard as he walks freely to the alter. The doorway to Bana-Shea house opens and she steps out followed by Ishka and four other beautiful witches. Bana-Shea is dressed in a long white silk dress, her long black hair shines in the last light of the third sun. Suddenly Ishka raises her hand into the air the drums stop beating and the dancing stops. Beacons of white fire start to light up around the coven of witches, shedding light as the last light of the third sun disappears into the horizon and the first moon of night begins to rise into the darkening sky.

Bana-Shea is glowing with beauty as she looks into the eyes of the young wizards who is looking back at her, her beauty has captured his gaze. Bana-Shea reaches her staff of power to Ishka, who takes the staff from her. Bana-Shea step close to the young wizard, with her bright red lips she kisses him softly on his lips, as she pulls away a bright glowing ball of light, no bigger than an apple appears from the young wizards abdomen and hovers for a few moments. The small ball of light then travels and disappears into Bana-Shea's abdomen. As Bana-Shea pulled her lips away, she started to consume the young wizards soul, slowly the young wizards and Bana-Shea started to rise of the ground, both stayed afloat until Bana-Shea had consumed the young wizards soul, once she had consumed the soul the young wizard falls to the ground, he is old, thin, and very weak, the four witches that had escorted Bana-Shea point their staffs of power and uttered the words

'Sruthan'

White fire shoots from their staffs in a steady flow until the wizard was turned to ash. Slowly Bana-Shea lowered to the ground, standing in front of the many witches who had gathered to watch the ritual.

"The ritual you have witnessed is the taking, we take their seed," said Bana as she placed her hand over her stomach. *"This seed is new life, the birth of the witch, the taking of the soul is the strength of the new life, new-born witches will live and grow strong in our coven, wizards will grow in the shadow of the witch and with the coming of age they will be taken,"* shouted Bana Shea. With this speech a loud cheer from the witches could be heard, the drums started to beat, and the witches danced the dance of the witches all night.

For a long time, the laws stood, and the rituals continued, Witches prospered under Bana-Shea's rule. Many witches and wizards where born, young witches would consume young wizards when they came of age, as the number of witches grew and the wizard depleted, the laws started to crumble. Older witches who had given birth to young wizards, started to crave for the taken, the addictions and cravings for souls was thriving and soon a new madness had started to grow within the coven. Witches had started to consume young wizards and even new-born, the chain of survival for the witches was cracking and crumbling. Witches had to be chained in caves to stop them from taking young wizards before their time. Bana-Shea was frustrated as she knew what the craving could do to a witch and she had no solution, she had sent hunting parties out to seek wizards and warlock and return them to the coven. Many hunting parties never returned with rumours that witches had taken the hunt for themselves.

One day, as the third sun has settled and the new moon had started to rise, Bana-Shea heard screaming across the coven, she could see witches running, screaming and flashes white fire, her first thoughts were an attack is occuring. *"Sound the alarm,"* she screamed at the guards, Ishka, came running towards her as the guard started to beat on the alarm drum.

"What is it, what's happened are we under attack?" Bana-Shea questioned Ishka.

"No, it's worse, the witches are possessed by the craving, many have gone hysterical, they are consuming each other and the young witches," replied Ishka, chaos had broken out in the coven, witches that had been possessed were seen consuming witches and witches burning witches to protect their younglings. Bana-Shea grabbed her staff and shot into the air, she landed hard in the middle of all the carnage, she could see with her own eyes the terror that the possessed witches had caused with the old weak witches laid on the floor begging for her help, she could see piles of ash where witches try to protect themselves having used white fire against their own kind.

"Stop," screamed Bana-Shea, her face had tuned white her lips black, and her eyes, rolled and turned silver. *"Stop, this madness, I command it,"* she screamed, with rage in her voice.

Suddenly all the madness stopped, the witches who had become possessed stopped their attacks. One witch was staring directly at Bana-Shea, her eyes and lips had turned black, she was pale, Bana-Shea looked at her with pity.

"What have I done?" Bana-Shea said softly.

Suddenly the possessed witch growled and ran directly towards Bana-Shea, Bana, Shea lifted her staff. *'Surthan,'* a flash of white fire shot from Bana-Shea staff, incinerated the attacking witch. From behind her came another witch then another, Bana-Shea was now destroying her own kind, the witches she had longed to save from slavery and here she was destroying them. In the mist of the attack, smoke and white fire was coming from Bana-Shea's home. Bana-Shea shot into the air and landed at the front of her house. Inside was her young daughter Nuska, the house was on fire, Bana-Shea ran into the house the flames engulfed her but did not harm her. After a few moments Bana-Shea came running out, there was no youngling in her arms. She looked around until she seen a figure on the ground not far from where she stood., as Bana-Shea approached she could see the witch had been consumed and was perishing, the old weak witch looked up at her, she realised it was Ishka, Bana-Shea fell to her knees and took Ishka in her arms Bana-Shea knew the end was near for Ishka. *"They took her,"* said Ishka in an old weak voice.

"I tried to save her, there where so many,"

"Who took her?" asked Bana-Shea as she held Ishka in her arms.

It was too late, Ishka had faded and had started to turn to dust in Bana-Shea hands. Bana-Shea had turned into a blind rage, she picked up her staff and a sword that lay nearby, her face had changed, eyes red, lips blacken as if she was possessed herself. In her blind rage she slayed witches with sword and white fire many ran some tried to fly, but she struck them down with white fire in mid-flight, turning them to ash, which fell to the ground like white snow.

When Bana-Shea had finished, many witches young and old had perished by her hands, that day was the end of the covenant of Bana-Shea, witches dispersed forming smaller covens many became isolated and hid in the darkness of the forests. Bana-Shea was last seen screaming as she flew through the forest where she was to remain in isolation for eternity.

Arawn walked through the silent forest until he came to an opening with a cave, he stepped into the cave that was lit by candlelight. He could hear voices speaking in a strange language.

"Who dares walk into my domain?" said an evil cold voice.

"I do, Arawn, lord of the underworld, I seek the company of Bana-Shea queen of the witch," said Arawn.

"Bana-Shea," said the voice from the shadows, Arawn could not see who the voice was coming from, but he was feeling a little edgy.

"Bana-Shea perished a long, long time ago," said the voice.

"I believe you to be her, come forth show yourself," commanded Arawn.

A figure in the shadows started to move closer towards Arawn. The figure was dressed in black, and appeared old and haggard, the figure looked up towards Arawn who caught a glimpse of the figure, the old woman with long black thinning hair, black eyes, behind her thin lips was rotting teeth, her long dirty finger clutched her staff, which she used to hold herself up with.

"You are the one, you are Bana-Shea," said Arawn as he looked closer towards the horrid creature that stood before him.

"I have a quest for you, that may be very fruitful, I know you have suffered, and I know of your loss, should you accept my offer, I will ensure, you will never hunger again," said Arawn as he pulled on a chain and dragged a young, frightened wizard into the cave. Bana-Shea looked at the young wizard she did not show any facial expression.

"Your offer is?" said Bana-Shea as she sat down to rest.

Arawn, explained that Bana-Shea was to enter the human world and bring back the soul of a woman, known as Mary Jane, He explained that she was a very powerful and cunning witch, and he believed the only thing that could bring her to Drumtara is another powerful witch.

121

"The wizard is yours and, I can offer you more on return of the human witch," said Arawn as he pulled the young wizard closer to Bana-Shea.

As Arawn left the cave he could hear the cries of the young wizard. A few moments later Bana-Shea appeared from the cave in full strength and reformed to her former beauty.

"We are in an agreement then?" said Arawn as both he and Bana-Shea stepped into the mist and disappeared.

Thomas Roberts stood looking out his small bedroom window, the snow had started fall it was laying on the fields and yard of Hog Hill Farm, Thomas was in an incredibly happy mood and was looking forward to Christmas day.

"Time for bed young man, you and I need to find a Christmas tree, so it an early morning rise for us," said Murrigan as he put a warm bed pan warmer at the bottom of Thomas's bed.

"Can I cut it down this year?" asked Thomas.

"Yes of course you can, make sure you get a good night sleep you will need some muscle power," replied Murrigan.

Thomas climbed into bed with a big smile on his face, Murrigan blew out the candle as he left Thomas bedroom. Thomas looked towards his window he could see, the brightness of the white snow coming through the edge of the curtains. Slowly Thomas drifted off into a deep sleep.

Thomas found himself in the dream again, standing in the middle of the murky pond. He looked down and he could see the face of a man, looking back at him, he recognised the face of the man from the memory stone, it was Tirk, his father. Thomas looked up to see the stone wall, on the wall was the little boy, he knew it was himself, but a younger version, the boy was smiling and laughing. Thomas wondered why he was having these dreams, same place every time with someone on the wall.

"Hello," said Thomas as he waded through the pond until he got to the wall, Thomas sat beside the boy.

"You are me, aren't you?" asked Thomas Roberts to the young boy, who had this big smile on his face.

"Yes, I am you, I am a small part of you, do you know what part I am?" asked the younger Thomas.

"I think you are my happiness," replied Thomas Roberts.

"You are getting good at this, I am your joy, your happiness, look at what makes you happy," said the younger Thomas.

Thomas Roberts looked up and could see, Bella running in a buttercup filled meadow, he then saw Moria, baking cakes and laying them on the kitchen table with a big smile upon her face. The image then changed to Murrigan who was sitting on the grass with Bimbo beside him, he was stroking Bimbo and puffing smoke on his long smoking pipe, he looked so happy and content. The Imaged changed he could see Mary Jane in the kitchen with a smile on her face it was Christmas evening, the Christmas tree was covered in tensile and was glittering in the candlelight of the candles that floated around it. Thomas could see himself as he approached Mary Jane, she put her hands out, Thomas took one and put the other around Mary Jane waisted, they both started to dance the waltz, both smiling and laughing when Thomas stood on Mary Janes feet.

Thomas, sitting on the wall started to laugh when he seen how clumsy a dancer he was, he appeared lost in the image of the dance with his mother, it was a golden moment a happy moment, his heart was filled with joy.

"Such happiness!" said the younger Thomas.

Suddenly, Thomas Roberts could see the image of the dancing pair, catch fire he could see Mary Jane burning, in pain, suffering, screaming. The tranquil, happy dancing had become a nightmare. Suddenly Thomas started to fall, this time in slow motion as Thomas fell, he turned to see the younger Thomas with his hand out as if trying to save him from the fall.

"Don't ever let them take away your happiness, they will only replace it with misery and despair, the long fall is coming soon," shouted the young Thomas.

Suddenly Thomas Roberts could feel himself descending, downwards he was falling fast he braced himself for the impact "BOOM."

Thomas awoke in his bed.

"It was only a dream, just a dream," Thomas said quietly.

Thomas looked at the window sunlight was shining through the gaps of his window; it was the dawn of Christmas Eve and Errol was up singing his head off with the farm's morning wake up call. Thomas Jumped out of bed and opened the window. Errol had cleaned the snow of his singing fence; the countryside was beautiful and white with snow. Bimbo was running about the yard, snapping at the small flurries of snow, the sky was white and there were signs that plenty more snow was on its way.

Thomas got out of bed and got dressed into some warm thermal long johns, it was going to be a cold morning. As he ran down the stairs, he could smell the aroma from the kitchen, Moria was, baking. Thomas opened the door, Mary Jane was sitting in the rocking chair knitting, Pooka was sitting beside her, large horns, and a brass ring in his nose, he was a frightful looking beast. In his hand he had Mary Janes pink wool waiving in and out of his hands and fingers, slowly releasing the wool when Mary Jane required it. Pooka was a big softy who had become a big part of the Roberts family. He looked up at Thomas and gave him a big grinning smile through his horse shaped face.

"Morning everyone," said Thomas with a big smile on his face.

"Good morning, Thomas," was the reply from everyone at once.

Thomas looked at Moria who, was reading the morning paper with a cup of tea on the table. A tablespoon popped up from Moria saucer, it floated across to the sugar bowl and picked up a lump of sugar the spoon floated back over the top of Moria teacup, paused and then dropped the lump into the cup, the teaspoon dived into the cup and began to stir the tea and sugar vigorously, the spoon suddenly stopped stirring, paused, and then jumped out of the cup and landed back on the saucer. Moria did not appear to be doing any baking instead the wooden spoon was stirring on its own, the rolling pin was rolling pastry, the pans were being scrubbed by a magical scrubbing brush, suddenly the oven door opened, and twelve mince pies came flying out and laid to rest on the kitchen table to cool down. The kitchen was truly a magical sight, with drawer's opening and closing, knives chopping, potatoes peeling and the whole time Moria just sat there.

"Morning Moria," said Thomas as he peered over Moria's paper.

"Porridge?" replied Moria.

"Yes please," said Robert.

125

The ladle lifted itself up and jumped into the big pot of porridge, which was simmering on the stove, a bowl flew out of a cupboard which magically opened itself. The bowl hovered over the porridge pot and the ladle rose up from the pot and fill the hovering bowl, with hot steaming porridge. Thomas sat at the table, still staring at the magical activity. The bowl then moved towards Thomas and softly set itself down in front of him, not a drop of porridge was spilt. Thomas looked at the side of the bowl, he was looking for a spoon. Suddenly the cutlery drawer opened, and a steel teaspoon shot out of the draw and was hovering just in front of Thomas face, the spoon then shot across to the sugar bowl.

"No, thank you," said Thomas and the spoon shot back to Thomas and hovered right in front of his nose.

The event happened that fast that it nearly caused Thomas to fall of his chair. Thomas reached out and grabbed the hovering spoon.

"Anyone for a cuppa?" asked Moria as she stood up and poured herself a cup of tea.

Moria looked at Thomas with a concerned look.

"Everything alright?" asked Moria.

"Yes, yes everything is fine," replied Thomas as Moria carried on pouring her tea with a big smile upon her face. Thomas put his head down and eat his porridge.

Thomas pulled on his wellie boots, duffle coat, woolly gloves, hat and scarf before he went out, by order of Mary Jane. *"You don't want to catch the cold,"* she scolded as Thomas stepped out of the kitchen and into the white world of Hog Hill farm.

"Bang, Bang, Bang."

Thomas could hear a banging noise coming from the barn. As he walked towards the barn door, he seen Bimbo's head peeking through a hole at the bottom of the door.

"He's coming," Thomas could hear Bimbo say as his head darted back behind the door. Thomas opened the barn door to see Murrigan standing with a hammer in his hand, which he quickly hid behind his back.

"Morning," said Murrigan with a nervousness to his voice.

"What's that?" asked Thomas.

"What's, what," replied Murrigan.

"That," as Thomas pointed to the object on the floor.

Sat on the floor was a large woven sheet, which appeared to be covering something.

"This is an early Christmas present from me to you," replied Murrigan as he lifted the sheet from the object on the floor.

"It's a Slode," said Murrigan.

"A what!" replied Thomas.

"You know, a Slode, you slide along the snow on it," said Murrigan, looking very chuffed with himself.

"You mean a sledge," laughed Thomas.

"Yes, yes a sledge, that what I meant," laughed Murrigan.

Thomas got closer to the sledge, it looked amazing, the wooding lats that formed the seat were smooth and varnished, the ski's that ran along the bottom were made of smooth wood with smooth tin along the bottom to allow it to glide across the snow. At the front there was a rope to pull the sledge along.

"It's amazing, let's try it out," said Thomas, with excitement.

"Helmet," said Murrigan.

"What you mean helmet?" replied Thomas.

Murrigan pulled a silver centurion style helmet from his side and placed it on Thomas head, The large silver helmet looked heavy, however it was very light on Thomas's head.

"It's too big," stated Thomas just as the helmet shrank to fit his head.

Thomas took hold of the rope, and dragged the sledge into the yard, followed by Murrigan and Bimbo. Just before they left the barn Maisy could be heard saying *"It's going to end in tears,"*

Thomas stood in the middle of the yard looking all around in excitement.

"What are you doing?" asked Murrigan

"I'm looking for the largest hill on the farm," replied Thomas.

"Blue Hill, it is then," shouted Thomas as he grabbed the sledge and started to run through the snow towards Blue Hill, which

had got its name from the blue bells that grew there during the spring. It didn't take Thomas long before his enthusiasm started to lag, Blue Hill was steep, and the snow was deep. After a while Thomas, Murrigan and Bimbo made it to the top of Blue Hill.

"I'm at the front, then Murrigan and you can jump on to Bimbo," as Thomas gave orders on each seating position on the sledge.

"Yes," replied Bimbo in excitement as he started to chase his tail.

"ALL ABOARD," shouted Thomas, he was ready to go, ropes in his hand feet on the ski's and gritting his teeth. Murrigan and Bimbo both got onto the sledge. All three of them sat on the sledge but it didn't move.

"Nudge it," said Thomas.

"Nudge it!" replied Murrigan with a strange look upon his face.

"Nudge forward," as Thomas started to rock back and forth, but the sledge did not move, Murrigan joined in and the sledge started to move very slowly, Bimbo also joined in.

"Someone is going to have to get off and pushhhhhhhh," screamed Thomas as the sledge shot forward and was making its way down Blue Hill. The wind was blowing into Thomas face his cheeks where pushed back from the speed the sledge travelled down the hill, Murrigan and Bimbo where shielding behind Thomas as he took the full force of the wind. The sledge was gaining speed going faster and faster as they reached the steepest part of Blue Hill. Thomas could hear Murrigan and Bimbo laughing out loud.

"Ooooo, no!" shouted Thomas, just as Murrigan and Bimbo looked up and to their front, a large snow drift had built up at the bottom of the hill, the sledge hit it hard and shot up into the air the sledge shot forward and up, but Thomas, Murrigan and Bimbo where no longer on the sledge. Laid in the deep snow was Thomas, he sat up dazed and looked for Murrigan who just sat up with a big grin on his face, a few moments later Bimbo jumped up and started to chase his tail in excitement. Shaking the snow of his fur and shouting *"again, again,"* Thomas and Murrigan sat on the snow laughing so hard.

Murrigan got up from the snow and put out his hand to pick Thomas. Thomas took Murrigan's hand and stood up. He gave Murrigan a big hug.

"Thank you, for the sledge it was a wonderful present," said Thomas.

Murrigan was full of joy, he wiped a small tear from his eye, he had grown very fond of Thomas Roberts, their friendship had become a very special bond.

"Right then young man, that Christmas tree won't cut itself," said Murrigan.

Thomas grabbed the rope attached to the sledge and all three of them started to walk towards the woods on the west side of the farm. Once they got to the woods, they needed to pick the right tree, not to big as the celling of the kitchen was low and not too wide as there was limited space. Murrigan and Thomas argued.

"This one," said Thomas as Murrigan looked at the tree Thomas had picked a tree which was nearly as tall as the small farmhouse.

"This One," said Murrigan, which was almost dead.

"What about this one, its perfect," said Bimbo as he cocked his leg and wee's on the perfect tree.

Murrigan and Thomas started to laugh, it was the perfect tree, it was just going to smell of dog wee. Murrigan pulls the saw out of a bag, it was an old rusty saw not sharp at all and reaches it to Thomas.

"There you go, get on with it," said Murrigan as he reaches the blunt saw to Thomas. Murrigan looks around and finds a log, clears it of snow, he sits down and pulls his pipe out, strikes a match and sits on the log puffing on his pipe as Thomas, starts to saw at the Christmas tree. After fifteen minutes Thomas was getting hot, he took his coat and scarf off and laid it on the ground. Thomas looked towards Murrigan who was still smoking on his pipe, Murrigan took the pipe out of his mouth and gave Thomas a smile and a wave. Thomas picked up the saw and continued to saw the tree. After a further fifteen minutes Thomas hands started to get sore. He looked back at Murrigan who was still puffing on his pipe.

129

"Can we not?" Thomas was interrupted by Murrigan.

"Can we not, what?" Murrigan said sharply.

"Use your sword, one sweep and its cut," replied Thomas.

"Yes, we could, but you see the sword is mine to wield, not yours and you wanted to cut down the Christmas tree this year, so carry on, it will be dark soon," Murrigan replied as he sat down with the smile on his face, puffing on his pipe. Thomas picked up the saw and carried on trying to cut the tree down. He had to take a break every now and then to shake the stiffness from his hands. Thomas had nearly cut the tree down when he looked at Murrigan who had drifted into a sleep with his pipe still in his mouth and smoke pouring from his nose.

"Timber," shouted Thomas as loud as he could, Murrigan looked up as the tip of the tree crashed between his legs, Thomas and Bimbo fell to the ground in laughter.

"Not funny, not funny at all, get the tree on the sledge and let's get back to the house, Moria and your mother will be scolding as to where we are," Thomas dragged the tree onto the sledge and started to pull the tree back to Hog Hill Farm, as they all walked back, Bimbo and Thomas could here Murrigan mutter *"Not funny, not funny at all,"* Thomas and Bimbo could not stop giggling the whole way back to Hog Hill Farm at Murrigan's expense.

*

The kitchen door to Hog Hill Farm opened and in came Thomas, Murrigan and Bimbo, with the Christmas tree in tow. They could feel the warm of the fire and the sweet smell of baking.

"And where do you think you are going?" scolded Moria.

"I'm going to warm my hands," replied Thomas.

"Not you, him!" as Bimbo's head popped from behind Thomas leg, he looked cold and had a frighten look on his face, he knew that Moria would pick up the broom and chase him out, he was well known to sneak in and steal food from the kitchen table when Moria was not looking. However, there were a few occasions when he was caught red handed.

Thomas looked down at Bimbo he had the big sad eyes.

"Can he not stay in for a while, its bitter cold outside the snow is beginning to fall and it is Christmas Eve after all?" Thomas asked in a very compassionate voice.

"I don't want that flee bitten mut in this kitchen," scolded Moria.

"Mum," Thomas looked across to Mary Jane.

"Fine, he can have a few minutes to warm up and a bowl of milky tea," replied Mary Jane.

"Thanks mum," replied Thomas who looked down at Bimbo who had just winked at him.

"Go lay, by the fire that's a good boy," instructed Thomas.

"That's a fine, looking tree," said Mary Jane as Murrigan stood it up in the kitchen.

The tree was a perfect height as Murrigan forced it into a bucket of sand.

"Yes, it is a fine tree, cut it myself and have the blister to go with it," stated Thomas as he showed Mary Janes his hands. Thomas hand where red raw and blistered, *"We will need to soak those in salt water,"* said Mary Jane with a concern look upon her face.

"No, no, its fine," replied Thomas, he knew how much it would sting when his hands would be bathed in salt water, he plucked out his chest.

"I will live, no requirement for salt water,"

Mary Jane and Moria both looked at each other with a smile upon their faces.

"First it's time to get this tree decorated," said Mary Jane as she pulled an old wooden box from the cupboard.

"Stand back!" said Moria as she clicked her fingers, the old wooden box started to open, inside of the box at the top was a paper angel that Thomas had made at school a few years back. Suddenly the angel came to life and flew up from the box, it hovered above the top of the Christmas tree and started to glow in mid-flight lighting up the dark corner where the tree stood, the glow also made the pine's on the tree glow and flicker, it was so magical. Suddenly the tensile in the box stood up straight, it was gold and green, the tensile started to fly through the air towards the Christmas tree and wrap itself perfectly around the tree. There were small reindeers prancing

towards the tree a Santa Clause, clutching his red sack, snowman, toy soldiers and small angels blowing trumpets, figurines that started to dance through the air towards the tree, the angels who were blowing on their trumpets sounded a chorus that was astonishing, filling the room with a festive sound. Each figurine started to attach themselves with small pieces of golden lace that was attached to each figurine. Red, green, silver and gold bobbles jumped up out of the box and started to fly around the kitchen, Mary Jane had to duck as they came flying towards her. They flew around the kitchen once, hovered over the tree and landed softly onto the branches of the tree. Everyone was full of joy, watching the magical entertainment of the tree beginning decorated. From the box came twenty candles they hovered in a circle above the box and one by one they started to light up, the sight was amazing as the candles lit the kitchen up, each candle took its turn and landed on the tree being careful not to ignite any other items on the tree, once all twenty had landed on the tree the sight was magnificent, the lights the sound and the angel hovering above the tree was a sight never to be forgotten.

"Bang, Bang," came the sound from the door the light of the angle disappeared the candles went out and the sound of the trumpets stopped suddenly, the small kitchen had gone dull only the light from the fire and a small oil lantern lit the room, a cold eery feeling had entered the kitchen. Bimbo growled as the room fell into silent.

"Bang, Bang," went the small door. Mary Jane turned and walked towards the door, Murrigan had raised to his feet, hand on his hip ready to defend Mary Jane or attack whatever was at door. As Mary Jane got to the door she reached up and pulled the double-barrelled shotgun off its hooks, it was already loaded and cocked all Mary Jane had to do was point and shoot.

Before she opened the door, she looked round at Murrigan and Moria, Murrigan gave the nod, Moria stepped in front of Thomas, with a saucepan in her hand and at the ready to use it, Bimbo was up from his resting place teeth bare and ready to attack.

"Bang, Bang," once more went the door, Mary Jane grabbed the handle opened the door quickly and stood back, she raised the shogun into both hand with a firm grip, as the door opened to the image that was standing at the door.

Standing at the door was a face of a woman that Mary Jane once knew.

"This is not the way to great your mother-in-law, is it now?" said the voice of the lady standing at the door.

Mary Jane lowered the shotgun and stood at the door with a look of shock upon her face.

"Our you not going to invite me in?" asked the woman.

"Yes, yes please do come in," said Mary Jane in a nervous voice.

The figure at the door stepped inside to the kitchen, Murrigan shivered as he felt a cold shiver run down his spine. The tall figure was that of a lady, in a long black coat which looked too big. Her hair was long jet black and shiny; she was beautiful. Mary Jane starred at the woman, she looked like John Roberts mother but younger.

"Everyone, this is John Roberts mother, my mother-in-law, Thomas Roberts grandmother," said Mary Janes. There was this strange quietness in the kitchen. No one knew this woman except Mary Jane. Thomas Roberts was thirteen years old, never had a birthday card or Christmas present in all these years and here she was after all this time standing in the kitchen of Hog Hill Farm.

"Cup of tea, my dear?" asked Moria.

"No, I'm not staying long, I was just visiting John's grave and thought I would call in," said the grandmother. For some strange reason, the grandmother kept staring at Mary Jane, she would not take her eyes of her.

"Something going off Moria, bit of a bad smell in here?" asked Murrigan. Moria looked at Murrigan they both sensed something was not quite right with this woman. Murrigan

looked at Moria, who has tightened her grip on the saucepan, Murrigan was getting ready for the attack.

"This is your grandson, Thomas Roberts," said Mary Jane as she introduced Thomas to his grandmother.

Thomas placed out his hand, *"Nice to meet you grandmother,"* said Thomas as he went to shake her hand. Suddenly Thomas felt a cold shiver run through his body, his grandmother turned her stare from Mary Jane to Thomas.

"You are not my grandmother, are you?" said Thomas in a quiet voice.

"No, I am not," the woman said back in a stern evil voice.

Suddenly she throw off her coat, which fell to the floor, and raised one hand towards Mary Jane.

Mary Jane stepped back she could feel a tight grip around her neck she was being choked by some kind of magic, controlled by the thing that was in her kitchen. Mary Jane could feel the tightening grip, but no hand grasped her throat.

"Witch!" screamed Moria.

The witch tapped the floor with her staff, all the knives and forks raised in front of Moria's face, ready to attack her if she moved. Murrigan gripped at his sword he almost had it drawn, when he felt his whole body being lifted of the floor and slammed against the ceiling. His sword dropped to the floor; he could not reach it as his body was pinned to the ceiling.

Mary Jane looked at Thomas, she was choking, *"Run Thomas, run,"* she said as she struggled to breath. The witch tapped her staff against the floor Mary Jane lifted of the floor and moved towards the witch.

"Well, well, well your meant to be this all powerful witch, all I see is a weak puny woman, is mian liomsa anan a Choinneail," spoke the witch.

Nothing happened, *"is mian liomsa anan a Choinneail,"* she said again. still nothing happened.

Suddenly the small front door of the kitchen ripped open and the roar from the foot of the doorway blow the witch of her feet and smashed her against the kitchen wall. Thomas reached out and snatched the staff from the witch.

"Keep your hands off her roared the voice," just as Pooka crashed into the kitchen with his steel axe in his hand. Murrigan had fallen to the floor and swiftly picked up his sword ready to attack. The knives and forks witch held Moria hostage had dropped, and her saucepan was at the ready. The spell that choked Mary Jane was released and she could breath, she reached down to pick up the shotgun, all five, Pooka, Murrigan, Moria, Mary Jane and Thomas Roberts with the witches staff in his hand. The witch was surrounded, she had nowhere to go.

"Who are you and what do you want?" asked Mary Jane as she raised the shotgun towards the witch.

"I am Bana-Shea, once queen of the witches and I have been sent on a quest to take the soul of the one call Mary Jane,"

"That quest has failed witch, now you burn," said Moria.

"No, no one burns, here, we let her go," said Mary Jane.

"You cannot let her go, Mary Jane, she will return, she has failed this time, but she will be back," said Murrigan.

"No, no one burns,' Mary Jane looks Bana-Shea in the eye and tells her *'You will go back to Drumtara and tell your lordship or whatever they are, that you have killed me and that there is no harm from me, do you understand?"*

"Yes," replied Bana-Shea.

"My staff," Bana-Shea placed out her hand to claim back her staff from Thomas.

"I don't think so, Thomas has taken it from you, as I recall the law of the witch, takers are keepers," stated Moria.

Bana-Shea, snarled at Moria, showing her razor sharp teeth. Moria raised her saucepan and snarled back.

"Go, go now and never comeback," Mary Jane shouted. Bana-Shea looked at Mary Jane and dissolved into a ghost like figure, she floated towards the door, she paused turned around and stared an evil stare with red, eyes and her jet black hair blowing in the air. She then shot out of the kitchen leaving a deafening scream as she disappeared into the night sky.

"I don't think that's the last we will see of her," said Pooka, as he eyed the sugar lumps sitting on the kitchen table.

"Go on then you have earned them," said Mary Jane with a smile upon her face.

"Let's get this Christmas, started, any one for a glass of me home brew?" Murrigan said with a big smile on his face.

"Why not," replied Mary Jane. Everyone sat in the kitchen sipping on hot chocolate and Murrigan's vile home brew, chatting and laughing. Thomas picked up Bana-Shea's staff and started to examine the black crystal on the end.

"The staff of power, wielded by the Kincorian witches, once used to do good, now they are weapons of chaos," said Murrigan, as he took the staff from Thomas, walked over the broom cupboard and placed it inside.

"There is a lot I can teach you about that staff, but tonight is not that night and tomorrow is a special day, I think it's off to bed for you young man," Murrigan's said as he gave Thomas a big hug. Thomas walked around everyone in the kitchen and bid them all goodnight and gave everyone a hug, including Bimbo who was laid by the stove enjoying the heat before Moria sweep's him out with the broom.

That evening Mary Jane sat in her armchair watching the flames of the fire, Murrigan was puffing on his pipe, Moria was sitting on the rocking chair, humming a gentle tune to herself. Pooka was sat on the floor with his back against the door as if on guard for the night. Bimbo was still laid by the stove, whimpering in his dreamed filled sleep.

That night Mary Jane felt warm and safe in the small kitchen of Hog Hill Farm, she knew that Murrigan, Moria, Pooka and even Bimbo where not just the guardians of Thomas Roberts, they were his family.

Bana-shea has crossed over to the underworld and was standing a short distance from the gates of Creeve as she passed, the keeper of the book he just bowed as if to gesture it's not a permanent stay. As Bana-shea approached the gates they started to screech loudly as they opened an eerie noise that filled the deafening silence of Creeve.

Arawn sat upright on his throne, he had been fast asleep, only the crowing of his raven that sat perched upon his arm startled him and he awoke.

"Your back, I see," said Arawn in a voice that was half asleep.

"Yes, I am back and with good news," replied Bana-Shea.

Arawn sat up on his chair.

"You have my full attention,"

Bana-Shea stepped closer to Arawn, out of the shadows behind Arawn came a shadow demon, a protector of Creeve. Bana-Shea stopped, she had her eyes on Arawn staff, she had lost hers and was defenseless without one. Bana-Shea stopped she knew she was outnumbered and had nowhere to run. She bowed her head and took a step back.

"The one they call Mary Jane, is no more, I have consumed her soul," stated Bana-Shea.

Arawn stood up in a rage, Bana-Shea was nervous as she depended on her lie to save her.

"No, No, No," screamed Arawn *"This was not your order, you were to bring this Mary Jane to me instead you consume her, why?"* Arawn looked at Bana-Shea with pure rage in his eyes. Bana-Shea feared this would be the end of her.

"My Lord," Bana-shea was groveling for her life. *"There was four of them and the fighting was intense, I took down the three guardians. The human witch, was too powerful, I had no choice but to end her, there and then. My lord Arawn, this witch was not safe to have in our lands she was the most powerful being that has crossed my path,"*

Arawn sat back in his throne and started to think hard about his next move, Nicopulas wanted Mary Jane alive. Arawn felt uneasy as he sat on his throne.

"This is what we are going to do. You and I will go to Nicopulas, we will tell him we had planned to get him a special gift from the both of us.

The one they call Mary Jane from the human world, but her powers were overwhelming, and she was not going to come without a fight. We will tell him the battle raged for a long time. In the end you prevailed and had to consume her soul. Do you understand the plan Bana-Shea?" asked Arawn in a stern voice.

"Yes," replied Bana-Shea.

Arawn knew that if this did not go to plan, it was the end of his alliance with Nicopulas. Nicopulas was unpredictable, he was sure that Bana-Shea would burn, at worse he would get the same or end up in the tower. Bana-Shea felt that Arawn was nervous, she had doubts that the plan would work, that she would get found out and burn at the stake by the hands of Nicopulas. She could not run as she was in Arawn's underworld; she could not hide as Nicopulas would hunt her down, she had no choice but to follow Arawn's plan.

Arawn stood up and stepped down from his throne, he tapped his staff on the floor and a mist started to appear in front of him.

"Follow," said Arawn as he walked towards the mist. Bana-Shea held her head up high as she took a deep breath. She watched as Arawn disappeared into the mist, Bana-shea followed, and she also disappeared into the mist.

Arawn walked through the mist shortly followed by Bana-Shea. Arawn looked all around to see the front of the great city of Lantara. The once white walls had been painted in black tar with shards of black glass sticking out from the walls. Creatures loyal to Nicopulas stood guard on top of the walls, points of large arrows sticking out between each mantlet on the city walls, right to the very top, there where hundreds of them.

There were giants, giants had been banished from Drumtara long ago, giant's where war lords and would fight for the army that paid the most. Nasty creatures that tend to eat whatever they killed or captured. It looked like Nicopulas had the giants fighting on his side. The giants could be seen digging up deep trenches with large shovel's, tossing earth hundreds of feet into the air. There was three set of trenches the first had water in it.

Bana-Shea leaned over the side to have a look, she could see mirky water below with something moving about in the water, Woosh, up from the water leapt a Merrow, this creature was half fish half human, as it leapt up it swung a sword at Bana-Shea, she had moved her head back just in time as the blade just missed her face. *"splash,"* the Merrow fell back into the water. Suddenly two more leapt out of the mirky water filled trench, leaping high into the air you could see their magnificent shape of half fish and half human. The two merrows landed feet first, in front of Arawn and Bana-Shea. The merrows where amphibious creatures they lived in the water and on the land. On land they walked amongst other creatures they were fearless and exceptional warriors. Both Merrows had trident spears held in their hands, helmets dawned and looked as if they were ready for battle.

"State your business here?" asked one of the merrows as he pointed the trident spear towards Arawn.

"My business, you wretched fool, I am Arawn, lord of the underworld and if you don't put that thing down and let us pass, you will be my permanent guest at my humble home," snarled Arawn. The two merrow lowered their trident spear and moved aside to let them pass.

As Bana-Shea and Arawn walked towards the doors of the great hall, it was plain to see that Nicopulas was building his defenses, some of the trenches where deep into the ground, large catapults were placed in them, giants where stocking piling arrows and glass bombs, spheres of smooth black glass that exploded in mid-air causing severe injuries and death. As they walked into the courtyard, there was chaos and carnage, black smoke belted into the air from furnaces, the heat from the furnaces was intense. The glass statues that once filled the court yards of the city where being pulled down and melted in large furnaced pots and converted into glass bombs and large shards of glass being used as pickets in the ground.

Nicopulas loyal servants where sharpening swords and prepping arrows, they were dawning armour of black steel and preparing for war.

Arawn was puzzled by what was happening, who was Nicopulas about to invade, was it his underworld? Arawn and Bana-Shea walked towards the door at the great hall of the city. Standing at the door where two deathly looking creatures. Arawn stopped short of the doors and looked at these creatures. As he watched them standing at the door, he thought to himself *'What are these creatures he had never seen there likes before in Drumtara.'* He could not see their faces under the hoods that draped over their heads, they carried no weapons of any kind. Arawn felt a shiver across his body and down through his spine. As he stepped closer, he looked at one of the creature's faces, he seen what looked like his own face, it looked distorted and death like. Bana-Shea stepped closer and also looked, she could also see her image in the face of the other creature that guarded the door.

"Don't look at them," commanded Arawn as he quickly stood back and dropped his gaze from the creatures that guarded the door. Immediately Bana-Shea obeyed Arawn command. As both moved away their faces faded from the creature's glare, the creatures once again became faceless.

"What are these creatures?" asked Ban-Shea.

"If I am not mistaken these creatures are of an ancient world, which has long gone and only live-in myth," replied Arawn.

"They are called, Sleepers," came a voice from behind Arawn and Bana-Shea. They both turned round to see an old man standing in chains, his hands were cuffed in steel bracelets which had chains leading to a neck cuff.

"They will not inflict any pain on you at all, however one touch from a sleeper and you sleep for eternity never to be awoken again. What happens in that eternal sleep no one really knows," said the old man as he walked up to one off the sleeper and put out his hand, the sleeper lent forward, the image of the old man's face was

140

reflected on the face of the sleeper. The sleeper pulled its own hand out from its long sleeves and touched the old man with a long white boney finger, on the center of the old man's palm. The old man dropped to the floor and went into an eternal sleep never to wake again.

Suddenly the doors to the great hall opened, there were three chairs at the bottom of the great hall with three figures sat in them. Arawn and Bana-Shea started to walk slowly down the center of the hall aware of the silence and the watchful eyes in the shadows. As they drew closer to the three figures, Arawn could make out Zoda to the left and Gear-ra to the right. Sat on a throne in the middle was the old man figure of Nicopulas. Arawn was not taken back by the old figure he knew the powers of Nicopulas and knew that he needed to be careful of his words and actions. Bana-shea on the other hand was not.

"Lord Arawn, what brings you too my domain? and with a guest I see," asked Nicopulas in a pleasant tone.

"My lord," replied Arawn as he fell to his knees.

"My lord, I come before you as the bearer of news, the one they call Mary Jane of the human world is gone. After a long hard fight with the guardians and the witch herself, they are no more, consumed by Bana-Shea queen of the witches, who presents herself before you,"

There was a long silent pause, then Nicopulas started to clap his hands, Gear-ra and Zoda followed, hand clapping could be heard all around the great hall as the creatures in the shadows imitated the response from Nicopulas. Nicopulas stopped clapping and the hall fell silent apart from Zoda who strangely continued clapping until Nicopulas glared at him.

"Well, well, Bana-Shea queen of the witches you have done me a great favor by destroying my enemies. Tell me this, what of the boy, the one they call Thomas Roberts?" asked Nicopulas.

"My lord, I watched the boy burn in the flames of white fire, as he cried for his mother," replied Bana-Shea as she bowed her head to Nicopulas.

"You showed no mercy?" asked Nicopulas.

"Non, my lord," replied Bana-Shea.

Nicopulas sat up on his throne with a grin upon his face.

"Well done to you both, my loyal servants, you will be rewarded for your great service to me," Nicopulas clapped his hands and a creature appeared from the shadows, with a chain in his hand, attached to the chain was a link of four chains at the end of the four chains were four young wizards cuffed at the hands and feet in black steel.

"Bana-shea, queen of the witches you will never hunger again, your kind will never suffer under my reign, you have already shown your loyalty. I ask you now to offer your allegiance to me, if you do this, you will go forth and build an army of witches under your command, will you honor me, (There was a silent pause) *What is your reply, Bana-Shea queen of the witches?"*

Bana-Shea was taken back by the request of Nicopulas, she looked up at the young defenseless wizards in chain, she was feeling the hunger and weakness. She lifted her head and looked at Nicopulas.

"You have my allegiance, my lord," replied Bana-Shea.

"Good, very good," replied Nicopulas with an evil grin upon his face.

Bana-Shea knew it was time for her to leave, she grabbed the chain from the creature and lead the young wizards from the great hall across the court yards and out of the gates where the two sleepers stood guard. She could see the edge of the woods in the distance and started to make her way directly to the cover of the woods. She knew she had to get as far away from the city of Lantara as far away as possible. She knew, that if Arawn or Nicopulas knew what had happened back at Hog Hill Farm she would be finished.

Bana-Shea walked deep into the woods, until she could no longer see the city or hear the noise of chaos form the preparation of war. She was feeling tired and weak. She commanded the young wizard to sit, and they obeyed her command. As she looked at one of them, she knew it was time to get her strength back. She wrapped the chain around a tree to secure the young wizards. She then released one of them and ordered him to follow her. She led him away from the others so that they would not see what she had in store for all of them.

She took the young wizard by the hand, and placed the other on his face, she appeared to be kind and gentle with the young wizard, she leans forward and kissed him gently on the lip and muttered the words.

"Is mian liomsa anan a Choinneail,"

Bana-Shea and the young wizard started to raise into the air as she consumed his soul and strength. When she let go of the young wizard he fell to the ground, all that was left was an old man of skin and bone. Bana-Shea had drained him of all life he had. The young wizard who was once young, lay on the ground weeping, so weak he was unable to move. Bana-Shea was glowing, her strength and her beauty had returned. Suddenly she stopped and sniffed the forest air, she knew this smell, she turned around to see a young witch looking at her.

"Don't be afraid my child, come here, I will not harm you," said Bana-Shea. The young witch stepped closer to Bana-shea; the young face reminded her of her daughter taken from her a long time ago.

"Where is your coven?" Bana-Shea asked.

"They are all gone, the hunger and madness got to them, are you, witch?" asked the young witch.

"Yes, I am, and my name is Bana-Shea," the young witch fell to her knees.

"Please, forgive me my queen," cried to young witch.

"Stand child, what is your name?"

"U-san, my name is U-san," replied the young witch.

"Well U-san, would you like to join me in the Covenant of Bana-Shea,"

"Yes, my queen I would, can I ask you where is your staff?" asked U-san.

"That's a long story, that I would rather forget,"

"I have spare staffs they were left behind, when my coven turned on each other, I can give you one,"

"Yes, us witches need our staffs, first let's get you some strength, I have something you will enjoy," replied Bana-Shea.

"*Torm*" Nicopulas called out as he sat on his throne in deep thought.

"*Yes, my lord,*" came the reply from the shadows as Torm presented herself in front of Nicopulas.

"*I need you to go to this place in the human world and confirm the destruction of the guardians the witch and her son, this Thomas Roberts,*"

"*My Lord,*" replied Torm as a set of wings appeared from behind her, she shot up into the sky light in the great hall.

Torm landed quietly on top of the big barn across from the farmhouse, she was invisible to the eyes of others, she sat there just watching for some time and observing each member of the little farmhouse. Torm first spotted, Murrigan in the yard puffing on a pipe and chopping firewood. Then Moria as she tended to feeding the chickens and collecting eggs. Mary Jane was seen in the back garden hanging out the washing. Torm then spotted Thomas Roberts on the top field practicing with his arrows. Torm thought, this was an opportunity to attack Thomas, however she noted that Pooka was not far watching over him. Torm noted how accurate he was with the Arrows of Lantara. Torm decided she had seen enough, and it was time to report back to Nicopulas. '*Whoosh,*' Torm wings had expanded, and she shot into the air.

Murrigan had heard the strange noise and felt the wind on his face, he looked up curiously to the roof of the barn, he then turned his gaze towards Thomas just to make sure he was there and unharmed. He knew Pooka was closed by, but Murrigan also knew it was dangerous times for all of them.

Torm landed outside the gate of the great hall, the doors opened, and she started the long walk to Nicopulas throne. There was a gathering around the throne with lots of cheering and shouting. As Torm got closer she could see two Lepz fighting each other with sticks in each hand, beating each other up in a wager fight. Lepz were odd creatures of the forest, who looked after the other forest creatures and tended to the tree's, now they were under the control of Nicopulas and fighting each other for his pleasure.

Nicopulas sat on his throne watching his entertainment. Torm could not get through, so she walked around the crowed until she was behind Nicopulas, with all the noise she leaned forward towards Nicopulas left ear.

"You have been betrayed, my lord," whispered Torm into his ear.

Nicopulas stood up, stretched his arms out to his side, at the same time, there was rage in his eyes, and his face was distorted with fury, Gear-ra and Zoda raised into the air as Nicopulas, drained them of their strength after a few moments both Zoda and Gear-ra fell to the floor as lifeless corpses. The crowed had gone quiet with fear as Nicopulas stood in front of them eyes black his muscle pounding in his rage, his fist clinched in front of him, suddenly he flicked his fingers, *'BOOM'* the crowed that had gathered to watch the fight had been blown away and were bouncing of the wall at the far end of the great hall.

Torm fell to her knee, she knew the wrath of Nicopulas anger and that he showed no mercy not even to his trusted servants.

Nicopulas screamed aloud *"TRAITORS,"*

"Sleepers," he screamed. From out of the shadow walked four sleepers. They stood a few feet apart from each other and stood in silence in front of Nicopulas.

"Torm," he screamed.

"My Lord" came the sound of Torm who was on her knees face down on the floor and trembling with fear.

"Go to the underworld and bring me that traitor in chains,"

"Yes, my lord," replied Torm, she raised to her feet quickly, a mist appeared in front of her. Torm and the four sleepers disappeared into the mist with the quest to place Arawn in chains and present him to Nicopulas.

Nicopulas fell to his knees crying.

"My children, my beautiful children, look what they have made me do, they will pay, they will pay with eternal pain," cried Nicopulas as he sat on the floor stroking the head of the corpse of Zoda and Gear-ra.

"Clink!" Arawn woke as black steel cuffs were placed on his wrist feet and neck.

"What are you doing," shouted Arawn.

"Guards" commanded Arawn. Two creatures appeared from the shadows.

"Stop, if you want to sleep forever, I can arrange this," said Torm as the guards were just about to draw their swords.

"Go back to the pit you came from, or you can join him," Torm stated as she stared at Arawn.

Both guards slowly walked backwards into the shadows and disappeared.

"You, my lord Arawn are about to have consultation with the whip," smeared Torm.

The sleepers held a chain each, which were connected to the cuffs on Arawn neck, wrist and ankles. As Torm walked back into the mist, the sleepers followed, Arawn was dragged of his throne, his raven squawked and flew off. Arawn hit the floor hard unable to break his fall with his hands. He was dragged along the ground and into the mist.

On the other side Torm passed over first she was standing outside the doors of the great hall. Then came the sleepers dragging Arawn behind them. The doors of the great hall opened, inside was a large gathering of giants, Lepz and creatures of Nicopulas army. There was a silence in the great hall, all eyes were on Arawn. Without warning they attacked him, a great roar came from the crowd as the endless beating began. They punched, kicked and stripped him. No mercy was shown or given. Blow after blow rained down on Arawn. Arawn showed no pain, he did not flinch, he felt the pain but showed no sign of it. Arawn was hurting from humiliation more than anything he knew nothing of why he had ended up in this moment, he was helpless all he could do was endure.

After the long drag along the floor, up the foot of Nicopulas throne, Arawn reorientated to get his bearing of where he was. He stood up only to have his chains pulled hard, he fell hard smashing his face on the floor. Five Lepz jumped on him and started to saw of his horns. They danced around him with his horns in their hand, in celebration of their achievement. Arawn was defeated, he did not try to get back on his feet, he was too weak.

"Look at me," said a powerful voice. Arawn lifted his head, his black blood was running down his face from where his horns had been amputated, he struggled to see who it was, he did not have to see, he knew. It was all mighty Nicopulas.

"You lord Arawn, now lord of nothing, have betrayed me," scolded Nicopulas.

Nicopulas, reached down to his side and pulled a large cat whip, he rolled the whip into his hands.

"You told me they were destroyed," just as Nicopulas flicked the whip into the air it caught fire, it was blazing in white fire. "LASH," as the first strike of the whip struck deep into Arawn back. This time he gritted his blood-soaked teeth and growled in pain.

"No, No, No," cried Arawn.

"You told me the witch was dead," "LASH" the second blow struck his back.

"You told me the guardians were dead," "LASH"

"You told me the boy was dead," "LASH" this time Arawn reached up and grabbed the whip, which was burning, into his hand. He pulled hard and Nicopulas was dragged close to Arawn.

"I did not betray you, Bana-Shea betrayed us both," stated Arawn, he let go of the whip and fell forward.

Nicopulas screamed out in rage *"Take him to the tower,"*

"Torm, go seek out this Bana-Shea, tell her I need her council," stated Nicopulas.

Torm, opened her wings and flew towards the sky light in the great hall once more. She flew across the land in search for Bana-Shea which took some time. Finally, she did find her deep in the dark forest.

"My lady, lord Nicopulas wishes to speak to you in person in regard to the army of witches and your progress," said Torm.

147

Bana-Shea was unaware of what had happened to Arawn or what was to become of her. She felt nervous, she had no trust for Arawn or Nicopulas.

"Yes, I will follow shortly," replied Bana-Shea.

"My lord has asked that I escort you back to Lantara, my lady,"

Bana-Shea could sense that something was not right, however she needed to play along with what was about to unfold.

"U-san, I need to go and consult with lord Nicopulas, you are in command in my absents, continue with our plans," Bana-Shea commanded.

"Yes, my lady," replied U-san.

U-san picked up Bana-Shea staff and handed it to her. U-san sensed the tension in Bana-Shea as Bana-Shea took her staff in hand she notes that Torm had placed her hand over the top of her sword. Bana-Shea seen this as a hostile action and knew that her fate was sealed.

Bana-Shea leaned towards U-San and kissed her on the cheek.

"Leave now, I will find you," Bana-Shea whispered to U-san.

Torm and Bana-shea both shoot into the air and flew back to Lantara. The doors of the great hall opened. There were no chanting crowds to meet them, only the silence and the things that lurked in the shadows of the great hall. Torm and Bana-Shea walked toward the three thrones at the far end of the hall. As Bana-Shea got closer, she could see the creature sat up right in the middle throne. Paled skin, jet black hair, with horns and eyes of black. On either side of the center throne sat the bodies of Zoda and Gear-ra lifeless and cold.

Torm approached, the throne and fell to her knees.

"My lord, I present, Bana-Shea queen of the witches,"

Bana-shea stepped closer as she did, Nicopulas stretched out his hand, Bana-Shea's staff flew from her hand into the hand of Nicopulas, his long white fingers with black glassed, razor sharp nails on the ends of each finger snapped the staff in two, just like a twig.

Bana-Shea knew at this stage she was in trouble, she knew that Nicopulas had gained the information that Thomas Robert's and Mary Jane were alive.

"How's my army of witches coming along?" asked Nicopulas in a cold calm voice.

"Very well," replied Bana-shea, she was trembling, her lips were quivering as she spoke.

"Very well, my lord," replied Nicopulas in a sarcastic voice.

"Do you not respect me, witch, am I not your lord and master, do you not bow before me?" Nicopulas held his left hand slightly in front of him. Bana-Shea felt the grip on the back of her neck, as if someone's hand was squeezing it, she felt her head being pushed down as she looked towards Nicopulas she could see he was pushing his hand down, tightening his grip. He was using a spell to force Bana-Shea to the floor. Bana-shea was in pain as the grip tightened. She resisted but Nicopulas was too powerful. As she fell to her knees, she raised her head and looked at Nicopulas.

Bana-Shea snarled and hissed like a wild cat. *"I bow to no warlock,"* she growled.

Nicopulas, laughed as he pushed her face into the dirty floor.

"Chains," he commanded.

Out of the shadows came four foul looking creatures, they began with her hands and feet followed by a tight black steel cuff around Bana-Shea's neck. Bana-Shea was defeated, she was weak and powerless against the might of Nicopulas.

"Torm, my loyal servant, you have done well, go to the covenant of the witches, take a legion, KILL THEM ALL," he commanded.

"Yes, my lord," replied Torm as she splayed her wing and few up to the sky light.

Bana-Shea and Nicopulas where alone in the great hall, as Bana-Shea laid on the floor in chains. Nicopulas sat there for a few moments and stared at her.

"We could have been great together, you by my side queen of the witches, queen of Lantara, mother of my children," as he looked left and right to the cold bodies of Zoda and Gear-ra.

"But you betrayed me, you lie and deceived me and, that's made me so very emotional," Nicopulas got up from his Throne, He was tall and powerful, Bana-shea could make out the wings that clung to his back. He was like no other warlock she had ever seen

149

before. As he walked around her, she could see he was in deep thought. She feared him, he was unpredictable and angry.

"Do you know where, Arawn is at this moment in time?" asked Nicopulas.

"No, I don't know where he is, and I don't really care," replied Bana-Shea as she tried to pull free from the chains that bound her.

"Well then, let me tell you. He was dragged up the center of the great hall in chains and beaten, every inch of the way by the cruelest of creatures, until he got to me,"

Nicopulas got down onto his knees and pulled Bana-Shea, by the hair he looked at her with his dead stare in his black glazed eyes. Bana-Shea could see her own reflection in his eyes, and she knew her time was at an end.

"I ordered his horns be ripped from his skull, he was stripped and lashed by the whip of white fire, and yes it did hurt," said Nicopulas with great pleasure in his voice.

Nicopulas loosened his grip on Bana-Shea's hair, her head fell forward as she laid on the dirty floor staring into the dust and dried black blood on the floor. Nicopulas slowly walked back to his throne and sat down.

"What am I going to do with you?" stated Nicopulas as laughter started to echo from the shadows through the great hall.

"Your pain, your suffering will be tenfold," said Nicopulas as he lifted his head and took a deep breath.

"There is nothing you can do that will every hurt me, do what you must, I will laugh in the face of your infliction," said Bana-Shea in defiance as she rose to her feet standing tall and proud in front of Nicopulas.

Nicopulas sat on his throne watching Bana-Shea. He raised his hand into the air. From behind him Bana-Shea could see the figure of two sleepers moving slowly forward, she could hear the sound of chains scraping along the floor. As the sleepers moved further forward, they were holding chains. Attached to the chains was a figured, in dirty rags as clothing, long dirty hair, long thin finger with long nails, the creature was filthy and there was a foul smell that was coming from the creature.

The creature was placed beside Nicopulas, by the side of his throne. The creature just stood still; it did not speak. Nicopulas lifted his long thin fingers and pulled the long dirty hair to one side of the creature's face. The creature's eyes were closed. He then placed his finger under the creature's chin and lifted its head up.

Nicopulas then turned his head towards Bana-Shea, with an evil look upon his face.

"I think it's time that mother and daughter are reacquainted," snarled Nicopulas.

Bana-Shea could not believe her eyes, her knees trembled, and she fell to her knees.

"That's more like it," stated Nicopulas in a triumphant voice.

"Respect, my lady that's all I command, respect"

"Nuska," cried Bana-Shea.

Nuska opened her eyes they were glazed over in white, Nuska had been a captive of Nicopulas for a long, long time locked away in the darkness of the towers. Her sight had blended with the darkness, and she was blind and could not see.

"Mother is that you or another demon who has come to hunt me?" weeped Nuska.

"It's me Nuska, it's really me," cried Bana-Shea as her emotions went wild. Here was her daughter, who she thought to be dead long ago.

"This is just beautiful, long lost mother meets long lost daughter, take this thing back to the tower," screamed Nicopulas.

Slowly the sleepers, walked back into the shadows pulling Nuska behind them.

"My lord, Nicopulas, what would you have me do. I will do what you command me," begged Bana-Shea.

"There is nothing you can do for me; your betrayal is an insult. Know this you and your daughter will spend eternity in my towers, you will be tormented by the devious of demons and tormented by each other's scream. Take her away," commanded Nicopulas.

From the shadows returned the sleepers, they gripped hold of the chains that bound Bana-Shea and dragged her, kicking and screaming to the towers.

Murrigan stood by the kitchen sink and looking out of the small window, slurping on a cup of warm tea. As he looked out the window, he noticed Thomas Roberts running past the window being chased by a stick of some kind. Chasing the stick which was floating after Thomas was Bimbo. Murrigan looked down at his morning tea. *'Had Moria put some of her strange herb into his tea,'* he looked up and out the window to see the exact same actions only in the opposite direction.

Murrigan walked towards the small kitchen door he grabbed his coat and peak hat, which he placed on his head, he put on his coat, buttoned it up and pulled his pipe out of his coat pocket, followed by a tin of smoking tobacco. He filled his pipe with the tobacco and pulled a small box of matches out.
"Don't you dare light that up in here," scowled Moria, from behind a paper, while the cloths were being wash in a big pot of boiling water over the stove with a large wooden spoon magically stirring the cloths as they boiled.
Murrigan opened the door, he looked up, he could see what he thought he had seen, Thomas was being chased, by Bana-Shea's staff and Bimbo was chasing the staff, barking as he ran after it. Murrigan leaned against the fence where Errol was perched upon, also staring at what was going on. Murrigan lit his pipe and stood watching his morning entertainment.

"Boy, what are you doing?" shouted Murrigan, by this time Bimbo had the staff in his mouth and was hanging onto it as it chased after Thomas, Bimbo was literally flying attached to the staff.
Thomas ran past Murrigan, he stretched his hand out and caught the staff with Bimbo still attached.
"You can stop running now and explain what you are doing," said Murrigan.
"Well, I picked the staff out of the closet and went outside with it, Bimbo came over and said 'if you throw it, I will chase it. However, in my head I was thinking, I don't want you to chase it, go away or I will smack you

153

with it, I was only thinking it, I wasn't really going to smack him. Suddenly the sick jumped out of my hand and walloped me across the back, not once, but twice, as I moved away it chased me around the yard. I really don't understand what I have done," replied Thomas.

"Right, lad let's get one thing clear this thing is not a toy," said Murrigan in a stern voice.

"I agree, it's a stick, you throw it, I chase it and fetch it back," said Bimbo as he wagged his tail in excitement and ready to chase the stick.

"No, it a staff of power, the instrument of power and magic used by wizards, witches and warlocks. It can be used for good or bad, this one belonged to a very powerful witch, who we have all met. Now it belongs to you Thomas," stated Murrigan as he stood holding the staff in his hand.

"I don't think it really likes me," replied Thomas.

"I don't think that is the case. You must connect with the staff, it has to trust you and you it, I recall your father, Tirk was always losing his staff, he had this trick that no matter where he was his staff would always come to him. Now let me think, the word he used," Murrigan was thinking and chattering to himself *"mar, mer, MEAR"* he shouted.

Murrigan placed the staff on the ground and walked a few paces away. "MEAR" suddenly the staff jumped up and flew to Murrigan, who took the staff in his hand.

"Woo, that was amazing," said Thomas with excitement in his voice.

"Yes, it was, now it's your turn, try to connect with the staff, feel for it."

Murrigan placed the staff back on the ground a few paces from Thomas. Concentration was all over Thomas face as he stared at the staff "MEAR" he said in a firm and loud voice, but the staff did not move, he looked at Murrigan with a nervous look, Murrigan gave him a nod of approval. "MEAR" but the staff did not move. "MEAR, MEAR, MEAR" Thomas kept repeating, suddenly the staff jumped up and hovered a few paces away from Thomas. There was a smile on his face as he looked at Murrigan who was also looking in anticipation as was Bimbo.

Suddenly the staff shot off in a completely different direction, it disappeared behind the chicken coup, followed by Bimbo, who shouted *"I will fetch it,"* as he also disappeared behind the chicken coup.

Murrigan looked at Thomas who has a disappointing look upon his face. *"Not to worry these things can take time, tomorrow is another day,"* said Murrigan.

The following morning, Murrigan had poured a cup of fresh tea from the pot, Mary Jane was cleaning out the fireplace. While Moria was sowing the holes in socks, while she was holding the morning paper.

"You're abusing your powers," stated Murrigan as the needle magically sowed the socks overlooked by Moria.

"Use it or lose it, I cannot help it if I am gifted and can multitask," replied Moria. Mary Jane started to laugh at Moria reply. Murrigan stood by the small window looking out at the yard to see Thomas Roberts, teaching Bimbo to sit at his command, he also noticed the staff on the floor in front of Thomas.

"He has been up since first light, with that dog and that staff," said Mary Jane.

"You better be careful with that staff, it could turn on him, don't forget who owned it," stated Moria.

"He will be fine, he may need it one day, will do him no harm to learn to use it to its full potential," replied Murrigan as he looked out the window, he could see the staff hovering about five paces from Thomas, As Thomas put out his hand the staff came towards him.

"That's my boy," said Murrigan with a smile upon his face. Murrigan grabbed his coat hat and pipe and left the warmth of the kitchen to the bitter chill of a cold February morning.

"Your mother tells me you have been at it all morning," said Murrigan as he lit his pipe and took a puff.

"Yes, I have been, I think I have mastered it now," replied Thomas.

"MEAR" commanded Murrigan and the staff that was in Thomas's hand shot out of his hand and was now in Murrigan hand.

"Mastered what? you know a simple trick, but this staff does not belong to you. It does not feel your present, you do not command this staff, therefore you can be easily disarmed," replied Murrigan.

"How do I get the connection? I have been trying hard all morning," said Thomas with despair on his face.

"Closes your eyes, take a deep breath and relax your thoughts. Now think of the one thing you desire most in your life, hold that thought," said Murrigan in a very calm hypnotic voice. Thomas did exactly what Murrigan requested.

"Hold it, keep that one thought locked inside you, now command the staff to come to you," Murrigan said softly.

Murrigan was holding the staff in his hand tightly.

"MEAR" Thomas said quietly with his eyes still closed, the staff ripped from Murrigan grip and flew directly to Thomas with eyes still closed, Thomas placed out his hand *"Boom"* a shock wave occurred from the moment the staff touched Thomas hand. The energy wave made Murrigan stubble backwards and knocked his hat off his head.

"You, alright," asked Thomas who appeared oblivious to what has just happened.

"Yes, I'm alright" replied Murrigan as he collected his peak hat from the floor brushed it down and placed it back on his head.

"Isn't that something,"

"Isn't what something," replied Thomas.

"Bimbo, Bimbo where are you dog?" shouted Murrigan.

"I'm here," came the reply from behind Murrigan.

Bimbo was standing behind Murrigan tail thrashing from side to side, tongue hanging out the side of his mouth.

"Were going to play a game," stated Murrigan.

"Yes," shouted Bimbo *"I love games,"* Bimbo then started to chase his own tail round and round in a circle when he couldn't catch in, he started to chase it in another direction.

"Stop, you're making me dizzy," shouted Murrigan.

Bimbo stopped chasing his tail and started to listen carefully to what Murrigan had to say.

"Bimbo take the staff, hide it, Thomas and I will turn our back, so we don't see which direction you go, come back and tell us when you have hidden it," explained Murrigan.

Bimbo took the staff in his mouth and off he went, it was not long before he had returned.

"Ready or not go find it," shouted Bimbo.

"Are you ready, Thomas?"

"Are you ready, Murrigan?" replied Thomas, with a big grin on his face.

At the same time Thomas and Murrigan shouted "MEAR"

With a few second the staff came flying over the top of the big barn and flew straight to Thomas. With a big smile Thomas turned to look at Murrigan. Murrigan gave a slight bow of his head in respect for Thomas and his newfound powers.

"Again, again," shouted Bimbo full of excitement and loving the new game of hide the stick.

Murrigan and Thomas were laughing at Bimbo's excitement.

"OK, we will have another go," said Thomas.

Bimbo took the staff in his mouth, and off he went, Murrigan and Thomas turned around so they couldn't see what direction Bimbo had gone. Only this time Bimbo was gone for some time.

"Where has that dog gone?" Thomas asked Murrigan.

"Probably ran into town." they both laughed.

"Finders keepers," came the noise from behind them, Bimbo had returned.

"Where have you been?" asked Thomas as he turned around, he could see a dog completely covered in wet mud.

"Bimbo, what have you done?" scolded Murrigan.

Thomas shouted out "MEAR", but no staff appeared, he repeated himself numerous times, "Mear, Mear, Mear" the staff did not appear.

"Bimbo where is the staff?" shouted Murrigan.

"No, I'm not telling, this is not how the game works," snarled Bimbo.

Murrigan and Thomas walked all round the farm, with Bimbo following and still the staff did not show itself.

"Enough of this, Bimbo no supper for you ever again, where is the staff?" shouted Murrigan.

Bimbo dropped his head and walked to the edge of a large piece of swamp land.

Bimbo lifted his head and looked over the swamp.

"No, you didn't," said Thomas.

Bimbo has taken the staff out into the middle of the swamp and buried it deep in the soft ground.

"Right, you, get out there and find that staff or I mean it no supper for you tonight," Murrigan said starring at Bimbo. Bimbo shot into the swampy field, while Thomas and Murrigan watched. Muck and swamp weed where flying into the air. This stopped and began in a different area of the swamp.

Thomas looked at Murrigan *"I guess we need the shovels,"* said Thomas as he started to walk towards the barn. They spent the rest of the day digging up parts of the swamp until, finally the staff was found by Bimbo, who was showing his excitement while Thomas and Murrigan were covered from head to toe in stinking swamp mud.

The next morning Thomas got up early, cleaned his teeth got dressed and ran down the stairs. He opened the broom cupboard and grabbed the staff.

"No, you don't young man, put that stick back and sit at this table," said the voice from behind the morning paper" Moria laid the paper down and was looking directly at Thomas.

Thomas placed the staff back into the broom cupboard and walked towards the table the chair moved back itself to allow Thomas to sit on it. The chair then started to bounce forward while Thomas sat on it until he was seated at the table.

"I have some fresh fruit scones just about ready, nice with a blob of butter and a drop of fresh strawberry Jam," stated Moria.

"O' YES Please," replied Thomas with a big smile upon his face.

158

The oven door opened, and the freshly baked scones started to fly out, the aroma from the baking was amazing. The scones landed on a plate building themselves into a pyramid shape. Thomas reached out to grab one. *"Och, their hot,"* he said sticking his burning finger into his mouth.

Just them Mary Jane came down the stairs and into the kitchen.

"Morning," she said as she passed Thomas, she ruffled his thick black hair.

"Morning mum," replied Thomas.

"Tea," replied Moria

"That'll be lovely," Mary Jane replied.

"Moria, can I ask you something," said Thomas in a low tone voice.

"It depends on what you want to ask" replied Moria

"How come you know so much magic?" asked Thomas.

"There is a time and place for magic and it's not at the kitchen table, now eat up an get on with your chores," said Moria with a frown upon her face. Just then the front door opened and Murrigan was standing there.

"What's this, you not out training with your staff this morning, hurry up boy, you got a hard lesson this morning," stated Murrigan.

Thomas jumped up from the chair, still munching on his scone and ran to the broom cupboards while mumbling a reply to Murrigan. He opened the door grabbed the staff and ran outside to meet Murrigan.

Moria sat at the table and sighed.

"Are you alright this morning Moria, you seem a little distance?" asked Mary Jane.

"He reminds me of his father, full of exploration and eagerness to learn," said Moria.

"That's not a bad thing, is it?" asked Mary Jane.

"I believe it was the undoing of his father, his intention where to do good, the outcome was destruction, the line was crossed that should not have been crossed. I worry for the boy, learning witchcraft and wizardry is not the best option for him," Moria said.

"*Bad things have happened to us Moria, these creatures from another world want Thomas and I dead. Don't you think we should defend ourselves with everything we have, what will he do if we are gone? who will defend him then? We must give Thomas Roberts every opportunity to survive and if that means learning witchcraft then so be it, I do wonder Moria who's side you are on,*" Mary Jane said in anger, she grabbed her coat and stormed out.

Moria sat at the table with her head bowed, she knew what Mary Jane had said made sense. She was feeling bad for upsetting Mary Jane. She had been good to her over the years and their friendship was solid. Now was not the time for it to crumble.

Thomas Roberts was standing outside in the yard, there was a light drizzle of rain wisping around him. "*Murrigan*" Thomas called out, he could feel a breeze coming from behind him, where Murrigan landed behind him. Thomas slowly turned around to see Murrigan. He had transformed into his true self. Murrigan stood staring at Thomas with his piercing blue eyes, he smiled at Thomas.

"*Do you want to learn to fly?*" said Murrigan in a quiet voice.

"*Yes please,*" replied Thomas in a quiet voice almost whispering,

"*How? and why are we whispering?*" Thomas asked.

"*Let's go to the barn,*" said Murrigan as he started to usher Thomas to the barn and looking at the farmhouse to see, Moria looking out the small kitchen window directly at them. Just as they went into the barn, Murrigan smacked his head of the doorframe, after all he was seven feet tall.

"*Right, this is the plan, you must not tell your mother or Moria, I am teaching you to fly they will kill me,*" said Murrigan in serious voice.

"*Kill you,*" laughed Thomas.

"*Yes,*" replied Murrigan.

"*I'd really like to see them try,*" Thomas was looking Murrigan up and down, here was this seven-foot-tall guardian a Drumtarian warrior, scared of Mary Jane and Moria.

"*Moria can be emotional when she is angry,*" said Murrigan.

"Seriously, this is our secret Thomas Roberts, and you swear never to tell I soul," demanded Murrigan.

"Cross my heart and hope to die, stick a needle in my eye," replied Thomas.

"WHAT!" replied Murrigan all confused with what Thomas had just said.

"I SWEAR, I won't tell anyone," Thomas replied.

"I'm going to tell Mary Jane, you're putting that boy's life at risk, he's too young to fly, what you think he is a bird, or a bee, he can't fly, he's not got wings, I never heard anything so ridiculous in all my cow years, boys can't fly, yee all gone mad," said this voice from behind Thomas and Murrigan.

"Looks like where having steak for dinner tonight," said Murrigan as he turned around and drew out his sword.

"I won't say a word, a won't says a thing to anyone, matter o fact, I will move over here and keep a look out, my moo is sealed" stated Maisy, the farm cow, who had been standing in the shadow of the barn listening to every word that was spoken. Murrigan starred at Maisy with his piercing blue eyes.

Maisy wonder of to the back of the barn to keep an eye out for anyone approaching the barn. Murrigan turned to look back at Thomas.

"You need to focus, really carefully now, I want you to connect with the staff, take it in your left hand and hold it horizontal," Instructed Murrigan. Thomas took the staff into his left hand and had a straight face full of concentration.

"When I say so, I want you to say 'e-i-tilt,'"

Thomas repeated *"e-i-tilt,"* suddenly the staff slammed into the barn floor and Thomas bounced off the floor with it.

"O, that hurt," said Thomas as he got back up onto his feet.

"Are you sure that those are the correct words?" asked Thomas.

"Yes, they are, if you let me finish before you said them, you must state them to the staff, without actually saying the words aloud, you must connect with the staff," replied Murrigan.

"Right, I'm ready," said Thomas as he closed his eyes, he spoke the words quietly without any sound. Murrigan could see his

lips moving. Slowly the staff started to rise, slowly Thomas legs raised behind him he hovered above the barn floor horizontal with the staff in his hand.

"Good, now I want you to stay connected to the staff, command it to move forward, slowly," said Murrigan. Thomas and the staff floated through the air.

"Stop," shouted Murrigan as Thomas was about to hit a wooden support beam, that was holding the roof up, Thomas and the staff both stopped just in time.

"You're getting to grips with this flying," Murrigan said as he was looking up at Thomas who was about eight feet of the ground.

"Move backwards now, that's it you're doing good and stop," Thomas stopped and looked down at Murrigan, Thomas had a big smile upon his face as he looked down.

"One more thing you need to learn, when you need to land the word, you require is "Sio's, are you ready?" asked Murrigan, who appeared a little nervous.

"Yes, I'm ready," Thomas dropped eight feet and slammed into the barn floor.

"May be that was the wrong word required, yes it's the wrong word 'Sio's' means drop, not land the word you require is, Talamh," stated Murrigan.

"Talamh, it sounds nothing like Sio's are you trying to get me killed, Murrigan?" shouted Thomas as pulled himself up from the floor.

"You're ready," said Murrigan.

"Ready for what?" replied Thomas.

"Your solo flight,"

"I'm I," said Thomas with nervous, excitement, Thomas didn't have the same confidence as Murrigan, Murrigan opened the barn door and had a good look around.

"You ready, straight out, straight up, no one can see you, low clouds will give you some cover,"

"Woosh," Thomas shot out the barn door and headed into the sky. He felt a little nervous to start, he held the staff in his hands with a tight grip, his legs wrapped around the staff and

leaning forward, he could see the black crystal at the top of the hawthorn staff, there was a small white glow in the center of the stone. Thomas flew up into the low cloud, and paused in the air, he felt free and excited. Coming up from the low clouds he could hear the beating of wings and through the swirl of the low clouds came Murrigan. Thomas was amazed he was in the air with Murrigan, Murrigan was hoovering like a kite, floating in the breeze of the air, directly in front of him, his wings outstretched, he looked amazing, as if he was standing in mid-air. Thomas was breathless at the spectacular sight of Murrigan the guardian floating in front of him.

"You ready for some fun?" asked Murrigan, Thomas just smiled and nodded his head. *"Whoosh,"* Murrigan rose higher and higher, Thomas followed, way up above the clouds and into the blue clear sky. Thomas could feel the warmth of the sun on his face. Murrigan twisted in the air, paused and then started to dive, Thomas followed they were diving fast through the higher clouds and into the low-level clouds as they both pierced the cloud's, they could see the wonderful land scape below. The farm was all but a dot in the vast landscape. Murrigan leveled out and Thomas followed as they shot through the air, The lakes and forest below blended into the green fields, rivers twisted through the land scape. Thomas never felt so happy, his sense of freedom was overwhelming. Thomas hit some air turbulence, he lost his grip of the staff, he started to fall. Thomas was falling fast through the air, he did not scream or shout for help, strangely he felt relaxed, in control. Thomas had de ja vu, he had been here before as if it was another of his dreams. Thomas realized that it was not in his dreams, as he fell, in a soft voice he spoke, "MEAR," within a few seconds his staff was in front of him. Thomas reached out and held the staff, he stopped falling, taking the staff in both hands and mounting it, he started to fly up towards Murrigan who had stopped.

"Your very slow," stated Murrigan.

"Slow, I will show you slow," Thomas flashed past Murrigan causing his feathers on his wings to ruffle and his helmet to slip of his head. Murrigan straightened his helmet and flew after Thomas as hard as he could. Thomas was going faster and faster, Murrigan was struggling to keep up. Thomas hit some low-level cloud that obstructed his vision for a moment, as he pierced through the cloud, he suddenly stopped, Murrigan was close on his tail and had to divert off to the left to prevent a collision.

Thomas sat on his staff looking out cross a blanket of blue sea. Murrigan straightened himself up and glided to where Thomas stopped.

"Isn't that something?" said Murrigan in a quiet voice.

"I've never seen the sea before, it is truly amazing," Thomas replied. Murrigan looked at Thomas with a big grin upon his face.

"Not many folk will ever see it from where your siting, let's get the sea on our feet and the sand between our toes," laughed Murrigan.

Thomas and Murrigan landed in the high sand dunes, they were careful not to be seen by anyone. They sat down, Murrigan, transformed into the farm hand cap and pipe present.

"Socks and shoes off and I will race you to the sea," commanded Murrigan.

Thomas already had his off, he was rolling up his trouser legs and started to run over the sand dunes towards the sea. Murrigan quickly took his socks and shoes off and started to chase Thomas, Murrigan noted that his short legs where not moving as fast as he would have liked them. When they reached the water, they ran in and started to splash each other. Thomas and Murrigan had become awfully close, and the bond of friendship was unbreakable. After all the excitement, Thomas and Murrigan went for a stroll along the beach, talking and laughing with each other.

"Will you teach me everything you know about magic?" asked Thomas.

"I'm not the magical one, I'm more off the warrior, arrow and sword are my preferred tools, now Moria, she is the one with the witch's wisdom. She used to belong to a covenant,"

"You mean Convent?" asked Thomas with a puzzled look upon his face.

"No, they called it a covenant or coven, like a school for witches," replied Murrigan.

"Moria, could tell you a spell or two, she would be the best to teach you,"

"I don't think she would' she gets very up tight when I ask her a question and the only thing, she does is read the papers and bake very good cakes and even then, she uses magic," laughed Thomas.

"Speaking of cake, it's getting late and I' m hungry," said Murrigan as a large rumble came from his stomach. Thomas and Murrigan paused as the sun slowly started to drop behind the costal bays.

"We better get a move on, night flying can be left for now," said Murrigan.

*

Thomas walked into the kitchen and could see the sunlight beam through the small kitchen window. He sat at the kitchen table where Moria was sat, reading, yesterday morning paper.

"I have some fresh bread, just baked and fresh pot of black berry Jam," stated Moria from behind her paper.

"Sound's......," before Thomas could finish his sentence the fresh loaf of baked bread was being cut, the butter knife was scraping the butter and the jam knife was digging the jam out of the jar. The bread was no sooner cut and landed on Thomas plate which also had just landed in front of him. The butter knife scrapped the butter onto the bread and the Jam knife slapped the jam onto the bead with half of the jam landing on the table and splatting onto Thomas grey jumper.

Thomas picked up the bread and started to eat slowly, looking at the paper Moria was reading.

"Well then?" came Moria's voice from behind the paper.

"Sorry," replied Thomas.

"You're staring at me," came the voice from behind the paper.

"No. I'm not,"

165

"Yes, you are," as Moria dropped the paper and stared at Thomas.

"Well then?" Moria said in a stern voice staring directly at Thomas.

Thomas appeared nervous and as he spoke, he got his bread and jam stuck in his throat. After he cleared his throat, and his face went from bright red, back to its natural color.

"Will you teach me some magic?" asked Thomas in a nervous voice.

"No, I will not teach you," replied Moria,

Thomas dropped his head in disappointment.

"I will not teach, but you will learn," said Moria.

Thomas looked at Moria, *"I don't understand!"*

"Magic is for the learner, it is an overwhelming desire, deep inside and as the knowledge grow the desire grows, I can teach you many magical spells and potions, the question is will you learn them? if you don't have the deep desire, then you will never learn," said Moria.

"I do have the desire, Murrigan has taught me so much and I have learnt so much already and I want to learn more," replied Thomas.

"Murrigan!" laughed Moria, *"Murrigan don't know much, all sword and no brain,"* scolded Moria.

"He did say you would be better than him in the teaching of magic," said Murrigan.

Moria's expression changed, she had a little smile on her face.

"And he be right," said Moria in a proud voice.

"Right then, we start at the beginning," Moria placed her hand into the front pocket of her very clean apron. *"Here it is,"* Moria pulled something small out of the pocket, Thomas could not quite see. Moria throw the item onto the table.

Thomas looked down at the item and then looked back at Moria. The Item was the smallest book he had ever seen it was about two inches wide and two inches long, it looked to be made of leather, with brown stitching on the book edges.

"Is it a book?" asked Thomas.

"Yes, it's a book, but not just any book. This is the cornicles of Witchcraft and Wizardry, the book of spells and magic, look after it, keep

it, safe and learn from it. Now get on and get you chores done," scolded Moria as she picked her paper up and started to read it.

Thomas slowly picked up the book, in his hand and wrapped his finger around it. He put his coat on and turned to look a Moria just before he walked out. Moria had not moved. from behind the paper, Moria had a big smile on her face, personally she was happy that Thomas has come to her to seek her knowledge of Magic.

That evening Thomas was laid in bed, beside him, candlelight lit up his reading space. Thomas held the small book in his hand. He couldn't make out the writing on the front cover. Thomas leaned under his bed to find an old wooden box, inside the box were balls of string, stick men, old handkerchief, and a magnifying glass. Thomas took the glass out and put the box back under his bed. He picked the glass up, took the book in his hand, he placed the glass over the top of the book. unexpectantly a face jumped out of the book and through the magnifying glass, the face screamed at him. Thomas jumped back, crashing his head of his thick wooden headboard, the magnifying glass and the book flow up into the air and landed at the bottom of the bed.

Thomas gathered himself together, rubbing his head, he looked at the bottom of his bed and quickly snatched out picking up the magnifying glass. He got out of bed and slowly walked round to the bottom of the bed. Laid on the bed, on top of his light brown blanket was the small book, Thomas felt nervous, and anticipated that if he used the magnifying glass again the horrid face would jump out again. Thomas gathered his courage and leaned over the book, he held the magnifying glass close to his eye, but the book was blurred and unreadable, he slowly moved the magnifying glass closer and closer until he read the writing engraved in gold. *"The Cornicles of Witchcraft and Wizardry"* below the title in smaller writing was the name of the author Thomas had to read it twice *"By Moria-Sham,"* Thomas was amazed that Moria was the writer of this book. Thomas could see smaller writing at the bottom of the book, he held the magnifying glass closer. The small print read *"Only the wisdom of the wise may cast these spells,"*

Thomas sat on the edge of his bed looking at the small book in the palm of his hand.

"Only the wisdom of the wise may cast these spells!" he said to himself aloud.

He grabbed the magnifying glass and looked at the front cover, he was amazed to see a dragon on the front cover a fire breathing dragon, the imaged changed this time he seen Moria's face she was smiling, the imaged changed again, it was the image of a man with the horrid face, he growled and disappeared, the next image was of a great city.

"Lantara," Thomas quietly whispered.

Thomas opened the front cover of the book, inside the front cover was a content list, but he could not make out the letters, they were so small. Thomas thought to himself, *'If only I could make this stupid book bigger.'* Just as he thought this, the words just appeared; he could read the words! The words read *"Enlargement Spells, page 9998,"*

"Page 9998," Thomas said aloud, suddenly the small book started to magical flick through the pages and stopped. As the book laid open on Thomas bed he held the magnifying glass in his hand, he leaned forward and used the magnifying glass to read the words that just started to appear on the pages.

Thomas read *"To read this book, state (MEADU)"* Thomas lifted his head away from the book he was curious, he said out loud *"Meadu, what does that mean?"* As Thomas looked down, to his astonishment the book of spell started to grow and grow. Laid on top of his bed was this magnificent book. Thomas could read the words as clear as day. Thomas was amazed that he had worked it out.

Thomas tried to move the book; however, it was large, thick and very heavy. He now needed to find a spell to make it smaller. Thomas opened the book at the index on the first page. He was thinking small spells. The word started to magically appear on the page. *"Shrinking spell Page 21,"* suddenly the book flicked through the pages to page 21. The word *"To make this book smaller stated the word (CRAPADH),"* slowly, the book got smaller and back to its original size.

"Yes," shouted Thomas as he realized, he should be in bed asleep. He heard a creaking of the floorboards outside his door, he quickly, jumped into bed and pretended he was asleep, he then realized his beside candle was still lit, he quickly sat up and blew it out. From under his door, he could see the faint light, what he didn't know was that Moria was standing outside his bedroom door, listening to his activities. Moria, had a big smile upon her face as she walked away from Thomas Roberts bedroom, The light slowly faded from under the door and Thomas fell into a deep sleep.

-Chapter 14-
The Seven

Nicopulas sat on his throne in the image of the old man, watching his unborn children dual with each other in combat training. Gear-ra was dressed in black Armour which clung to her tall thin body. In her hand was a black shield with sharp spikes and a long black glass sword. Zoda was wearing chunky Iron on his chest, in his hands were an axe of steel and a large heavy hammer in the other hand. They were fighting hard and with intent to hurt each other, both Zoda and Gear-ra had black blood pouring from wounds they had inflicted on each other.

"Enough," shouted Nicopulas as the souls of Zoda and Gear-ra left them and re-entered the body of the old man of Nicopulas, he was now transformed into the mighty Nicopulas.

"CRASH," went the bodies of Zoda and Gear-ra as their lifeless bodies hit the floor. Nicopulas stood up, turned and walk into the darkness of the great hall.

Nicopulas stood in front to two wooden doors, he lifts his hand and the doors opened as he walked into the large room the doors slammed shut behind him. He looked down at the floor, to see the crest of Drumtara engraved into the stone floor. He walked around the floor looking at the crest, as he stared at the crest of the fish, tree, the bird like creature and the skull, he growled. Nicopulas stamped his foot down hard on the crest, the ground shook and a rumble of thunder could be heard through the kingdom of Lantara. The crest began to crack and crumble, as Nicopulas stood on it the floor it gave way and collapsed from below him. Nicopulas disappeared as he fell into the opening in the floor. Up from the hole in the floor the wings of Nicopulas, could be heard beating, he rose above the opening of the hole into the air, he held his position for a few seconds then tucked his wing into his back and dropped rapidly down the long dark hole that went deep into the ground.

Nicopulas fell for some time, deep into the dark tunnel that kept going down and down. Suddenly the deep tunnel was no more. Nicopulas opened his wings and broke his fall. He was in a large underground cavern, it was a doomed shape cavern, below where pits of fire which lit up the cavern on the wall were painting of ancient demons of war, fighting the great ancient wars in a time before Drumtara's existence.

Nicopulas landed on a floor of clear thick glass, below he could see, creatures entrapped in the glass, as if frozen in time. He looked around, the floor and could see hundreds of these creatures. He knew exactly what the where. Die-a-naut the ancient army of the underworld. Commanded only by the seven. Die-a-naut have not been seen or heard of for an eternity, some had said they were ancient myths of stories long ago and here was Nicopulas standing on an army of them perfectly preserved in their glass prison. Nicopulas got down on one knee and touched the glass, he could see a Die-a-naut looking straight at him.

"What could I do with an Army like this," he said with an evil smile upon his face.

Nicopulas looked up to see a figure glide towards him floating just above the glass floor. The creature was tall and thin, she wore a long white robe, her face was pale her lips cherry red and the most piercing green eyes. Nicopulas stared at her beauty, and she stared back. Nicopulas felt peculiar, her beauty had him in a trance. He quickly broke her gaze as he knew she was a charmling, a creature of great beauty, who can charm the soul of any creature and trick them to obey their every command. Charmlings were known to suck the soul out of a creature and then feed on their flesh.

"My lord Nicopulas, they are waiting for you," said the charmling, her voice was mesmerizing in Nicopulas head, he knew that her voice was enchanting, he quick returned his reply, to break the charm of her voice.

"Lead the way." he commanded, the charmling turned around and started to glide back from the direction she came from, Nicopulas followed. Nicopulas and the charmling came to a set of large glass doors.

"Wait here," said the Charmling. Instead of opening the large glass doors the Charmling just pasted through them. Nicopulas

stood looking at the glass doors, imbedded into them where two Die-a-naut, they stood tall inside the glass doors as if they were standing guard. Nicopulas could see these Die-a-naut very clearly standing in the glass. What he was looking at was a creature that looked like him, a pale white demon with black glazed eye, jet black hair with two black horns coming from its head. Both Die-a-naut had large spears in their hands, Nicopulas could see the tips of their wings coming up over the top of their muscular shoulders. Nicopulas smiled at both the Die-a-naut.

Suddenly the two large doors started to open, the Charmling was standing in front of Nicopulas.

"They are ready to see you now, my lord," said the Charmling, as she passed by Nicopulas she looked across at him, she spoke but her lips did not more, was she playing mind games with Nicopulas, he paused as she passed.

"Do not trust them," the voice said.

Nicopulas walked into the large room, the room was round and was lit up by torches of fire placed all around the room. Nicopulas entered the room he walked to the center of the round room he knelt down on one knee and bowed his head. Inside the room were seven thrones on each of those seven thrones sat seven kings. These were the ancient kings of Drumtara all seven wore crowns upon their heads the crowns were made of heavy steel, no jewels or gold. Each king appeared different from each other according to which chair they sat upon. Each throne had the name of the king engraved into the thrones, that they sat upon, just above their heads.

The first king of the seven was younger than the other six, he sat tall in his throne. His name was Brod, the king of pride. The second king was slightly older, he had gold and jewels surrounding him, he had a gold coin in his right hand, which he was flicking back and forth through his fingers and a gold dagger in his left hand. His name was Saint. The third king was older than the second king. He was well dressed and had two maidens by his feet, with their arms wrapped around his legs, his name was Lust. The fourth king was looking much older than the first three. He sat with his hands on his knees, his palms of his hands faced up and black blood was pouring from the center of his hands. His name was Ead, the king of death. The fifth king was extremely fat he was so big he could not sit on his throne properly. He was surrounded with luxurious foods; his clothing was filthy with food and vomit stains. His name was Gluttony. The sixth king was old and frail, he sat with a shield at his feet and an axe in his hand, he looked like he had fought many battles. His name was Fearg the king of wrath. The seventh king was almost skin and bone a death like creature, he sat on his throne gulping for breath. His name was sloth.

"My kings," stated Nicopulas.

The seven kings sat quietly on their thrones, they just sat there staring at him.

The seventh king, king Sloth lifted his body up onto his chair.

"Lord Nicopulas, please tell of the kingdoms above us and the kingdoms beyond our reach. My little ones tell me you prepare for a great war, which war do you prepare for, as the prophecies tell of no war?" asked king Sloth.

"My kings, the son of Tirk, lives and grows powerful in a kingdom beyond your reach. I have seen the prophecy upon the walls where the boy will fall for eternity, but I have also seen he will fall to our kingdom and he my kings is the rightful heir to the kingdom above and below," said Nicopulas still knelling on the floor.

"The only kings that rule the kingdoms are the seven you serve. You are weak Nicopulas, I smell your fear of this child, you reek of it, you are not worthy of our presence," said Fearg as he stood up in a rage.

"Enough of this bickering, tell me lord Nicopulas, how have you come to know of these prophecies, who has foretold these omens?" asked king Sloth.

"I have seen the walls behind your thrones in my nightmares, I know what you hide, your deepest darkest secrets. I know what you will have me become, tonight I will burn your souls and bathe in your blood," said Nicopulas in a calm voice.

Nicopulas stood up and throw seven chains onto the floor, one chain landed in front of each throne. Nicopulas lifted his hand and clinched his fist. The chains came to life and started to wrap themselves around the seven kings' throats choking them as Nicopulas clinched his fist harder and tighter. Suddenly the kings started to transform into dragons their chains broke lose. Nicopulas looked at the seven vicious dragons who were circling around him ready to destroy him.

Nicopulas stood in the middle of the circling dragons and started to laugh. Nicopulas also transformed into a magnificent dragon, he was pure white with black horns and piercing black eyes he was three times bigger than any of the seven. He grabbed the first dragon and smashed him through the glass doors, he lay on the floor lifeless. The dragon fight had spread into the great cavern. Nicopulas had spread his white wing and had taken flight. One of the seven took fight at the same time, breathing fire at Nicopulas the fire had no effect. Nicopulas took a deep breath and exhaled, white fire hit the attacking dragon and crystallized him into black glass. In slow motion the black glass dragon fell hitting the floor below smashing into millions of little pieces.

Nicopulas looked down to see the five dragons who remained.

"Listen to me, you will not and cannot defeat me, I will spare you on the terms that I am your king and I only, defy me and I will spare you not," came the roar of Nicopulas.

One by one the dragon changed back to themselves and fell to their knees, before the mighty sight of Nicopulas.

"Go now, and when the time is right, I will call upon you," demanded Nicopulas.

The five kings got up to their feet and walked into the darkness of the cavern. Nicopulas transformed from dragon to himself in midflight he landed on his feet and started to walk back to the throne room. He lifted his hands and six of the seven thrones crumbled into dust. He lifted his hand again and the name of Fearg changed to Nicopulas.

Behind Nicopulas throne was a red curtain, he walked towards it and ripped it down. On the wall was the prophecy, the pictures drawn onto the wall that had been there for eternity. Nicopulas could see the image of the falling boy, the image of the great war to come and the boy upon the throne. Nicopulas took his long black nails on his hands and dug them into the image of the boy on the throne, scraping down he ripped the rock and image off the wall. He then turned walked out of the throne room and shot into the sky towards the tunnel back to Drumtara.

Nicopulas sat upon his throne in the great hall of Lantara. He was in deep thought, Thomas Roberts was a great worry to him, the prophecy could not come true. Nicopulas was about to hatch a plan to rid his thoughts of Thomas Roberts and his guardians.

"Sleeper," Nicopulas called out in a calm voice.

From the shadows came two sleepers, they stood in front of Nicopulas, these tall, hooded creatures, stood quietly in front of Nicopulas, they never spoke as Nicopulas just sat there looking at them. After a few minutes Nicopulas pulled and old rusty steel key attached to his side.

"Bring me that traitor, Arawn," as he reached the key to one of the sleepers, the sleeper moved forward and reached out to take the key. There was no flesh or bone on the hand of the sleeper only the hand of a ghost like spirit. The sleeper took the key in his hand which disappeared under his long dark cloak, the sleeper bowed his head to acknowledge Nicopulas command. The sleeper disappeared into the shadows behind Nicopulas.

After some time, the sound of heavy chains could be heard, the sound of dragging heavy chains being dragged along the ground, slowly with pauses, getting louder the closer they got to Nicopulas. From the shadows returned the two sleepers, from behind them came the defeated, bruised and hornless Arawn. As he slowly made his way past the throne on which Nicopulas sat upon, dragging his heavy burden chain. Once he got to the front of the throne, he dropped the large metal ball with was attached to the heavy chain. Its thud as it hit the ground echoed like thunder in the great hall. Arawn fell to his knees and bowed his head.

"The great Arawn, lord of the underworld, what a sorry looking sight you are," said Nicopulas in a calm almost caring voice.

"What am I to do with you?" he questioned.

Nicopulas sat on his throne staring at Arawn.

"Would you like to go home?" asked Nicopulas.

Arawn nodded his head in a gesture of yes.

"Sorry, I never quite heard, my lord," replied Nicopulas in a sarcastic voice.

"Yes, my lord," replied Arawn.

"I can make that happen, but you must pledge your loyalty to me, this minor punishment you have received it nothing compared to what I can bestow upon you," said Nicopulas.

"My lord, I did not betray you, the witch deceived us both," replied Arawn.

"Yes, yes, I believe you to be right, she did betray us both, that's why I have a quest for you both, you my friend are to be my eyes and ears as I send you to kill the boy and his faithful guardians, do you think you can do this for me?"

"Yes, my lord, I will do what you command," replied Arawn.

Nicopulas lifted his hand and the shackles fell from Arawn's hands, ankles, and neck.

"You are free to go back you your homeland, get well, get strong for there is a battle that awaits you. I will call upon you when the time is right," said Nicopulas.

Arawn bowed his head and rubbed his wrist that were now free from his chains. He turned slowly around to see the two-sleeper standing behind him. They both parted and Arawn started to walk through the gap they had created. Arawn could see the large doors at the bottom of the hall. It was a long way off and he feared that the creatures in the shadows were watching him and that Nicopulas was using him for his wicked entertainment. Arawn kept walking when he made it to the large doors they open, he walked through them and into a mist taking him home to his underworld.

Nicopulas sat back on his throne, he looked at the two sleepers.

"Bring me the witch," he commanded.

The sleepers moved of once again to the towers to bring Bana-Shea, before Nicopulas. It wasn't long before Nicopulas could hear the sound of chains being dragged across the floor of the great hall. Bana-Shea stood before Nicopulas. She was weak, and filthy her once beautiful long black hair had been shaven off, her once, sparkling green eyes were dull and weary her body was thin and fragile. Nicopulas sat there looking at her.

"Look at me," he commanded.

Bana-Shea lifted her head and looked at him. Nicopulas sat forward on his throne to have a good look at her face, Nicopulas could see that she was broken, he knew, now was the time to offer her the opportunity to redeem herself.

"Your daughter lies rotten only a few yards from where you lay, you are both helpless to each other, and the torment of those demons that dwell in those towers, I have no doubt they hunt your every hour, thoughtless creatures they are. Do you know who those demons are that lurk in the shadows? They are the ones who thought they could defeat me, betray me, they will dwell in their own insanity for eternity. Tell me Bana-Shea, is that what you want for your daughter?" asked Nicopulas in a concerning voice.

"No, my lord," replied Bana-Shea as she tried to speak, her throat was dry and her lips almost raw.

"Speak up, I cannot hear you," replied Nicopulas.

Bana-shea had to clear her voice as she struggled to speak.

"No, my lord," she said aloud.

"My lord, yes Bana-Shea, I believe I now command your respect, would you like a drink to quench that agonizing thirst?" asked Nicopulas, there was almost kindness in his words.

"Yes, my lord," replied Bana-Shea.

Nicopulas raised his hand, from the shadows came one of Nicopulas servants with a metal chalice in one hand and a large clay jug in the other. The servant reached Bana-Shea the cup and filled it with dirty water. Bana-Shea put the chalice to her lips and slowly sipped the dirty water. The water was soothing and cooled the dry burning of thirst at the back of her throat.

"That feels better, do's it not?" asked Nicopulas.

"Yes, my lord, I thank you," replied Bana-Shea.

Nicopulas sat back on his throne, with a smile on his face, he raised his hand and the metal cuffs on Bana-Shea's wrist, ankles and neck opened and fell off.

"Take those things away we will not be needing them," commanded Nicopulas.

The sleepers moved away dragging the heavy chains behind them as they moved into the shadows of the great hall and disappeared.

"My lady, do I have your loyalty, your devotion, your respect?" asked Nicopulas.

"You do my lord," replied Bana-Shea.

"I have a proposition for you, which will no doubt be rewarding for us both,"

Bana-Shea lifted her head up to listen to the proposition.

"Five days from now, Arawn and yourself will go to the human world, you will command my assassins and you will wipe this witch and her son of the face of existence. In return I offer you your freedom and that of your daughters, betray me and you both will burn, do we have an agreement?" asked Nicopulas.

Bana-Shea bowed her head, *"We do my lord,"* was her reply.

Nicopulas, throw Bana-shea's staff in front of her, she looked down at her staff and then over her shoulder to see the two sleepers had return, the thought for a split moment crossed her mind to strike down Nicopulas. She knew she was weak and with two sleepers in his defense and his strength she would not be victorious.

"Go now my lady, rest recover in five days from now, you go to war," commanded Nicopulas.

Bana-Shea took her staff in her hand and used it to pull herself back onto her feet, she turned around to see the two sleepers, who had parted to let her take the long walk to the doors of the great hall. She made her way slowly with the sleepers following her to the doors. The doors opened and

Bana-Shea step outside into the light of the day. Her eyes were unfocused from the brightness of the sun that was high in the sky. Once she was focused and could see, she gripped her staff and flew off into the sky.

Back a Hog Hill Farm, Moria and Thomas Roberts where chatting in excitement at the kitchen table about the book of spells. Moria was teaching Thomas the importance shrinking objects and how to conceal them. She made Thomas take the staff of power and shrink it to almost the size of a matchstick, he then took his arrows and shrank them.

"You learn fast young man," said Moria with a big smile.

"Bang, Bang," went the door.

Moria looked at Mary Jane who was sitting by the fire reading a book.

"Pooka, is that you?" shouted Mary Jane, but no answer came. Mary Jane got up of her chair and moved towards the door. Murrigan had gone into town about twenty minutes ago to buy tobacco, it was not him and she knew he would just walk in. She reached above the door and slowly lifted the shotgun of its resting place; she quietly broke the shoot gun to confirm the two cartridges were still there.

"Pooka," she called, but there was no reply. It had been drizzling with rain outside all day and there was very little sunlight. Mary Jane looked down and could see a shadow at the bottom of the door which was blocking any the light coming through. Someone was there but they had not responded to Mary Janes call. Moria stood Thomas up and pushed her behind him, she picked up the rolling pin that was on the kitchen work bench to her right. She gave Mary Jane the nod, Mary Jane quickly swung the door open and pulled the shotgun into her shoulder tightly, Moria had the rolling pin raised ready to attack.

"I come in peace," came a voice from the rain soaked image standing at the door, they had raised their hands in front of

them to show they had no weapons in them. Mary Jane lowered her shotgun, she kept a tight grip of it, still pointing in the direction of the image of what appeared to be an old homeless woman, her wet hair was filthy, and her clothes were rags, there was also an unpleasant smell.

"What can we do for you?" asked Mary Jane. The old woman was shaking with fear. She pulled her wet hair from her face. Mary Jane raised her shot gun.

"I know you, you're that witch that came to kill me," said Mary Jane as she gripped the shotgun even tighter ready to pull the trigger if necessary.

"My lady, I come in peace, I mean you no harm, I have come to warn you of the great danger you and your boy are in. I am Bana-Shea, and we have met before, forgive me for past wrongs against you. I swear upon my daughter soul, I mean you no harm."

Mary Jane stood for a moment; she was not sure what to make of what was happening, was it a trap? She looked over her shoulder to Moria who shrugged her shoulders. She looked across the yard and up onto the meadow where Pooka would be, suddenly Pooka jumped over the stone wall in his horse image in midflight of the jump he transformed into the mighty Pooka and came running towards Bana-Shea and Mary Jane with his large axe held above his head ready to attack Bana-Shea. Just as he was ready to drop the axe Mary Jane screamed "STOP"

Bana-Shea fell to her knees, Mary Jane leaned over her to protect her from the falling axe. The axe stopped just inches from the back of Mary Janes head. She looked up at Pooka who was just staring back at her.

"What are you doing?" she scolded.

"I, I, I, I was protecting you, my lady," replied Pooka who now had a big nervous grin on his face. Pooka pulled his axe away *"Sorry,"*

"Stay outside the door stay alert," ordered Mary Jane.

Mary Jane took Bana-Shea by the hand and picked her off the floor. Bana-Shea looked at Mary Jane. Mary Jane could not help but notice the sadness in her eyes, she could tell that she had gone through a hard time.

"Moria, get the water on, hot tea is required, heat up some of that broth. Thomas, blankets and some clean clothes." ordered Mary Jane. Thomas and Moria got on with the tasked given to them by Mary Jane. Mary Jane led Bana-Shea to the kitchen table and sat her down. She poured her a cup of hot tea added milk and two sugar lumps. Moria set a large bowl of steaming broth down in front on Bana-Shea, who picked it up and drank the whole lot in one go.

Moria and Mary Jane gave Bana-Shea a bath and Moria burnt the old smelly clothes that Bana-Shea was wearing. After Bana-Shea was cleaned up and had been fed. Mary Jane notices a small sparkle in Bana-Shea's eyes. Mary Jane brushed Bana-Shea long black hair with magical dried and shone in the candlelight.

"What a difference a nice hot bath and some home cooking can make," Mary Jane said as she notices that Bana-Shea was radiant.

"Thank you for your kindness, I feel slightly strange," said Bana-Shea.

"You don't feel ill?" asked Thomas.

"No, not at all, I feel warm inside, I have never felt this feeling before." replied Bana-Shea.

They all began to sit round the kitchen table, just as the door opened and Murrigan walked in, he paused when he seen Bana-Shea.

"Pooka told me," said Murrigan as he took off his cap, coat and hug them up behind the door.

"You'd better tell Pooka to come in," said Mary Jane as she sat at the table.

They were all sat round the table, staring at Bana-Shea, when they heard a crunching noise, they all turned to look a Pooka who had a mouth full of sugar lumps in his mouth and was munching away at them.

"Sorry," he replied as he tried to munch them quietly.

Bana-Shea started to speak.

"On the going down of the sun, five days from now, Nicopulas will send his company of assassins into your world, and will destroy all that is dear to you," Bana-shea was looking direct at Mary Jane.

"Why?" replied Mary Jane.

"The answer to your question, I do not know, all I know is that he is obsessed that your son must die, and he will do whatever it takes."

"Why have you come to tell, us this, are you not one of his?" demanded Murrigan.

"Yes, I am his servant, but I do not obey him, he has my daughter" replied Bana-Shea as she lowered her head.

"What do you mean he has you daughter?" asked Thomas.

Bana-Shea began to tell the story of when she had thought her daughter had been taken by the witches in the covenant who had gone mad and that she presumed her daughter to be long gone. Bana-Shea explained that she lied to Nicopulas, that she told him Mary Jane was no longer and that there had been a great battle to destroy Mary Jane. When Nicopulas found out that Mary Jane still lived, he locked her in his towers. Before she was locked in the tower, she was reunited with her long-lost daughter who is also a prisoner held in the towers.

"That still does not explain you being here!" said Murrigan.

"My daughter, is all I have left, knowing she is alive has rekindled my soul, there is a light in me that tells me I must do the right thing this time. I need to save my daughter, if I save your son, I believe you will save my daughter, I don't know how, but this feeling is beyond my knowledge. Your strength, your power is strong, I know it will prevail." replied Bana-Shea.

"How can we help; your daughter is in Drumtara, and we are here?" asked Mary Jane.

"You must prepare for the battle; on the fifth night I will lead the assassins along with Arawn lord of the underworld. I will protect your son and fight on your side. You will have the element of surprise as you know they are coming, prepare your defenses and have a battle plan in place," said Bana-Shea.

"I will destroy the portal," said Murrigan.

"No, you must not do that, they will know they have been betrayed and my daughter will be destroyed," begged Bana-Shea.

"That's it then, we will fight, you have done us a great service and taken a great risk by coming here, we will prepare, I think you for your courage and we will do whatever we can to save your daughter from this Nicopulas," said Mary Jane.

"Thank you, my lady, I will return on the fifth day from now, may you be victorious. I must leave now," said Bana-Shea as she stood up from the kitchen table and walked towards the small kitchen door. Mary Jane and Thomas got up and followed her. As they stood at the door. Bana-Shea looked down at Thomas Roberts and smiled. She then looked at Mary Jane and smiled. Bana-Shea took Mary Jane by the hand.

"For our children," said Bana-Shea.

"For our Children," replied to Mary Jane.

Bana Shea pulled her staff from the inside of her cloak and shot into the sky.

Mary Jane looked down at Thomas.

"I think it's your bedtime young man, we have a big day tomorrow," said Mary Jane.

Thomas walked back into the kitchen and hugged, Pooka, Moria and then gave Murrigan a long hug.

"Off you go now lad," said Murrigan in a nervous voice, he had grown very fond of Thomas, he knew that in five days' time that their world could be very different place.

Thomas left the small kitchen and stood behind the door that led to the bedrooms upstairs.

"Right then, we will convene, tomorrow morning first light for a war council," said Moria in a very commanding voice

"And you, young man, get to bed," she shouted. Thomas sprinted up the stairs and into his bedroom.

Chapter 15

Battle Plan

"Thomas, Thomas, wake up," came the voice inside Thomas's head, as he opened his eye, he was startled to see Murrigan, leaning over him. *"Get up, get dressed we gather in the barn in fifteen minutes,"* said Murrigan in a prompt commanding voice.

Thomas closed his eyes just for a moment, when he opened them Murrigan was gone. Thomas gave a big stretch and rolled out of bed. He walked towards his small bedroom window, dressed in his red and white striped pajamas, he opened the small curtains, he could see the tip of the sun rise over the top of the hill. The sky was blue but the there was something strange going on. No morning call from Errol, no sheep in the fields, no Bella or Pooka in the meadow as he opened the window, he could not hear a sound. Thomas quickly grabbed his clothes and got dressed. He ran down the stairs and into the kitchen, there was no Moria, no Mary Jane the kitchen that was the heart of the farm was lifeless. Thomas felt a cold eerie feeling come over him. He grabbed his coat and ran into the farmyard.

Thomas stood in the middle of the yard he had a good look round, there was no one or no animal to be seen. Thomas could her strange noise coming from the barn, chattering, voices. He remembered Murrigan's voice, *"Gather, barn, and fifteen minutes,"* it wasn't a dream after all. Thomas made his way to the barn door the chattering of voices got louder, he opened the door and stepped inside the chattering stopped. Thomas slowly closed the door behind him aware of the presents of something behind him in the barn, there was a strange aroma in the air. As he turned around Thomas could see hundreds of animals, they just sat there, staring at him. The barn was like a colosseum from the floor to the roof there were bales of hay, straw and wool sat upon them was the spectacular sight of every animal that lived on or near the farm. Thomas looked down at his feet to see two otters, they both nodded at him, Thomas nodded back in acknowledgement. He looked up to see birds of prey, owls, kites perched on the beams of the barn. There were swallows, swifts, king fishers, He looked all around him to see badgers, fox's hedgehogs and mice. Thomas could not believe his eyes.

"You managed to get here, sleepy head and it's not a dream," said the voice in the middle of the barn.

"Sorry, Murrigan," replied Thomas as he looked at Murrigan who was standing in the middle of the barn in his full guardian glory.

"Take a seat lad, we have lot to plan, and time is short,"

Thomas could see Mary Jane she had reserved a place beside her for him to sit on, as he sat down, he realized that Moria was standing beside him, however she wasn't the kitchen maid with her cooking apron. She looked magnificent, Thomas could not help but stare at her beauty, her long silver, white plaited hair hung over her muscular shoulder, her white wings were tucked neatly into her long back. Thomas was taken back by her height she was tall and elegant. Thomas had caught her eye as he sat beside Mary Jane. She turned to look at him, he couldn't help but notice her beautiful blue eyes, full of kindness. As Moria looked down Thomas gave her a shy smiled. Moria gave a big smile back, to his shock she had beautiful white teeth, however they were pointed and sharp, he had no doubt that they could give a ferocious bite. Thomas felt safe in Moria's and Murrigan's present after all they were his family.

Murrigan raised his hand, the chattering from the birds and animals stopped.

"Thank you all for your attendance at this war council, in four days from now we will face a foe that has only one desire, that is to destroy all that is dear to us," said Murrigan as he looked over his shoulder and glanced at Thomas and Mary Jane.

"We the guardians will do all in our power to prevent this, I have drawn up our battle plans for which every single one of us will play our part," said Murrigan as he lifted a blanked from the ground. Under this blanket was the perfect model of Hog Hill farm, the pond, stone walls, trees and hills. Murrigan had a long stick in his hand which he used to point out each location and what actions where to be take. He started off by pointing to a large

rock which sat on the top of the highest hill that overlooked Hog Hill Farm.

"Here is the portal, the door from which are enemy will enter," said Murrigan as he pointed to the large rock on his model.

"The enemy have advantage with the high ground, rabbit, moles," Murrigan was looking directly at the rabbits and moles, one rabbits was so excited he couldn't stop his paw from tapping the ground very fast and hard. The tapping only stopped when a fat rabbit sat on his paw.

"Your mission is very important, you will dig long deep burrows into the ground at the foot of the large rock, they must be very deep and many. When our foe step into this area the ground will give way, they will fall into your pits and get stuck in the mud. Do you understand your mission?" commanded Murrigan.

"Yes, we do, sir," replied all the rabbits and moles while nodding to each other.

Murrigan looked up to the birds perched on the roof beams.

"There will be witches and demons that will take to the air once they are through the portal, birds your mission is to disrupt them in flight, witches will have staffs that that have the power of flight and white fire. Disarm them and we will have air superiority," stated the Murrigan.

The birds responded in the squawk's and song, which filled the barn with the sound of triumph. Murrigan raised his hands again and the barn fell silent.

"The remainder of you will attack in the barley field, they must pass through the barley to get to the farmhouse, use the field as cover and ambush them, you must be quick and swift in your attack. Do you all understand?" asked Murrigan.

"Yes, yes," came the reply along with loud cheers. Murrigan raised his hand once more and the barn fell silent.

"When they breach our first lines of defense, our enemy will focus the attack on the farm. This is where we make our stand, we defend and fight to the end." Murrigan looked at all the farm animals, the sheep, Maisy, Errol and Bimbo, Murrigan looked at his friends and smiled.

"My friends, go now and prepare yourself, we are united, and we will be victorious" shouted Murrigan in his triumphant voice.

All the creatures in the barn gave a loud cheer, they had their orders and now they prepared for the battle. As the animals left the barn, Murrigan, Moria, Mary Jane and Thomas Roberts thanked each and every one of them. When all the animal had gone there was only the four of them.

"Do you, really think we will win the battle?" asked Thomas.

"Yes, we will, we have something these foul creatures don't have that makes us unbeatable." replied Moria.

"What that?" asked Thomas.

"Each other," replied Moria as she placed her hand on Thomas shoulder and smiled at him. Thomas felt reassured that they would defeat the creatures that came through the portal. Thomas looked down at his mother, he could tell that she was unsure.

"Let's go get some breakfast young man," said Moria as she turned back into the house maid, taking Thomas by the hand and leading him out of the barn, leaving Murrigan and Mary Jane alone in the barn.

"Do you believe that we can win this battle?" asked Mary Jane.

"If I didn't believe, my lady, we would be running by now, but we would only run for so long and they would catch up on us. You ask if I believe, yes, I believe, this battle will be fought and won not by our size of our army, but by the size of our hearts. I know you understand that."

"I do," replied Mary Jane with a halfhearted smile one he faces.

"I have gift for you," said Murrigan as he tried to change the tone of the conversation.

"A gift for me!" replied Mary Jane who seemed to be flattered by Murrigan's charm.

From and old sack which lay on the floor Murrigan pulled out a shotgun, not just any shotgun this was made of sliver it was half the length, with a short double barrel.

"It's a shotgun," stated Mary Jane, who had deflated from the flattery.

"Yes, I made this one for you, it will only work for you, no one else can fire it," said Murrigan in and exited voice. Mary Jane took the short barrel shotgun in her hand.

"My goodness, it's so light,"

"Yes, it made of a precious sand, called silver sand, I forged it myself, I have cartridges." Murrigan reached Mary Jane six cartridges.

"They won't last long in a battle," said Mary Jane as she took the cartridges in her hand. The cartridges were green, red and orange.

"These are not just any old shotgun cartridges these are repeaters, when you fire one, take it out put it back in and fire it again and again," replied Murrigan as he stated to get even more exited.

"Right then, why are there six with three different colors?" asked Mary Jane.

Murrigan picked up the green cartridges and held it up to sunlight that was coming through the cracks in the barn door, he placed it in front of Marry Janes face, Mary Janes looked intensely at the green cartridge, she could see something moving about inside the cartridge.

"Is there something inside this cartridge?" asked Mary Jane who appeared very puzzled looking.

"Yes, they are CRITs, nasty little miters, all you have to do is point, shoot whatever they hit they eat, once they eaten that they eat each other, nasty, here have a go," said Murrigan as he loaded Mary Janes new shotgun with the green cartridge. He was looking about the barn for something Mary Jane could shoot.

"Shoot the sack of potatoes, in the corner,"

Mary Jane lifted the shotgun into her shoulder and took aim at the large sack of potatoes which sat in the corner of the barn, 'BOOM' the noise was deafening, however there was no kick from the gun, out of the barrel flew hundreds of little green balls about the size of small garden peas. As the tiny green ball flew forward, they started to grow to the size of a small ball that would fit into the palm of your hand. The balls stuck to the sack of potatoes and suddenly started to sprout arms and legs followed by eyes, and mouth with little razor-sharp white teeth. Within a few second the little green balls had eaten the full sack of potatoes, then they eat each other until there was one left. The little green ball just stood on a bag of wool looking at Mary Jane and Murrigan 'PUFF' the last green ball just exploded into a puff of green smoke.

"whoooo!" said Mary Jane in amazement.

"Isn't that something," replied Murrigan who was just as amazed as Mary Jane.

"Right then, let's try the orange one," Murrigan took the shot gun broke it open and removed the green cartridge and handed them back to Mary Jane. As she looked at the green cartridge she could see the movement inside from the little green balls, the cartridge had looked as if it had never been fired.

Murrigan handed the shotgun back to Mary Jane, Mary Jane took the gun in her shoulder and aimed it at the sacks of wool sitting in the barn. *'Click,'* Mary Jane had pulled the trigger, there was no bang just the *'Click'* Mary Jane paused and looked over the barrel at Murrigan.

"Wait for it, wait," Murrigan was looking at the end of the barrel in anticipation. From the end of the barrel Murrigan and Mary Jane could see four small metal balls, connected by, what looked like sewing thread. *WHOOSH*, the four small ball shot forward as they did, they got larger and the thread that connected them extended in a large net. Within seconds the metal balls had wrapped themselves around the sack of wool and covered it in a net.

"Now, try getting out of that in a hurry," said Murrigan as he walked towards the sack of wool and started to unwrap the net for the sack. Mary Jane had snapped open the shot gun and took the perfect orange cartridge out, she then continued to load the red cartridge, she pulled the shotgun to her shoulder *'BOOM'* Murrigan turned round to look at the small fire ball floating in the air directly in front of the shotgun barrel.

"Mary Jane, what where you are aiming at?" asked Murrigan very softly, as the small fireball began to get bigger and bigger it was about the size of a football, it suddenly began to spin very fast.

"I aimed........" Mary Jane didn't get time to reply the fireball shot forward, Murrigan ducted just in time as the fire ball crashed through the wooden barn wall leaving scorch mark where it had punched through the wall.

"Run," screamed Murrigan as he smashed through the barn door followed by Mary Jane followed by the fireball, Murrigan

opened his wings and flew into the air, as the fireball whizzed, past Mary Jane and began to chase after Murrigan, who had now started to dive very fast *'SPLASH'* Murrigan had dived from a great height into the pond, there was a large splash as he hit the water in the pond, followed by a second large splash as the fire ball hit the water and created a large puff of steam high into the sky. Mary Jane ran towards the pond to see Murrigan crawl out. Mary Jane gave him her hand and help him back to his feet.

"I'm so sorry, I was aiming at the sack," said Mary Jane with concern that she may have hurt Murrigan.

"I guess we will have to work on your aim," Murrigan smiled, Mary Jane began to laugh, both walked back to the farmhouse arm in arm and having a good laugh about the mornings adventure.

Back in the great hall of the city of Lantara, Nicopulas, Gearra and Zoda stood round a large table that had a model of Hog Hill Farm and the surrounding areas. Nicopulas was old and weak and was using his staff to hold himself up.

"Torm," Nicopulas commanded.

From out of the shadows came the tall, elegant figure of Torm.

"Yes, my lord," she replied as she bowed her head.

"Go forth my loyal servant and assemble my assassins, with haste," Ordered Nicopulas.

Torm opened her wings wide and flew up. Her first visit was to Bana-Shea and then to Arawn, she then visited the woods of Ballie where she spoke to a cluster of Lepz in the darkest part of the woods and a covenant of witches who were loyal to Nicopulas. Over a short period, the gathering was taken place, the great hall had fifty of the vilest creatures in Drumtara, many were once peaceful now they were under the command of Nicopulas who commanded his bidding.

"My loyal subjects, welcome to Lantara, you're gathering here in this great hall is a momentous and historical occasion on the eve of battle with our greatest enemy, to that end our battle plan is ready to be executed," stated Nicopulas in a triumphant voice.

The assassins stamped their feet and shouted in acknowledgment of Nicopulas speech. He raised his hand and the hall fell quiet. As he sat down Gear-ra got to her feet, in her hand was a long pointing stick, which she used to identify key areas of attack on the model.

"Before us on the table is the layout of the land, here is our entry and exit point to the human world, The witches will enter first and take to the sky's Bana-Shea will lead the attack formation. Arawn will lead the ground assault, surprise is paramount use this field and the surrounding wall as cover, be aware Pooka the horse lord roams these fields, he is powerful and a fierce warrior. There are two guardians that protect this area of the small dwellings, then there is the witch they call Mary Jane, we know that she is powerful, do not look or speak with her, do not let her touch you, she can spell bound on the touch of her hand, kill her swiftly and without hesitation. Once we have this area under control the boy will be easily destroyed." said Gear-ra.

Gear-ra sat down and Nicopulas stood back up.

"My friends go now rest and prepare for battle for tomorrow we will go forth into victory," another great roar and the stamping of feet could be heard echoing through the great hall.

"Bana-Shea, Arawn, grace me with your presence," said Nicopulas as both Bana-Shea and Arawn were about to leave. They both turned around and moved back towards the throne that Nicopulas was sat upon, as they approached Zoda, growled at them.

"Be calm my son," Nicopulas said to Zoda who quietly sat back and remained quiet.

Arawn and Bana-Shea where both nervous they knew that Nicopulas was unpredictable and very cruel.

"This plan cannot fail, your role is simple destroy everything, burn them all," He commanded as he lifted his hand the model of Hog Hill Farm on the table started to catch fire and burn.

Arawn and Bana-Shea bowed their heads in fear.

"We will not fail you may lord," replied Arawn.

"Be gone," commanded Nicopulas.

Arawn and Bana-Shea turned and walked into the shadows.

Nicopulas sat on his throne and watched the small farmhouse on the table burn.

"Come forth," commanded Nicopulas

"Are you ready to sit at the side of your lord and ruler are you ready to do my Bidding?" asked Nicopulas as a figure came from the shadows.

"Yes, my lord, I Fearg King of wrath am ready, what do you ask of me?" said the figure of fearg one of the seven kings of the dark underworld.

"My orders for you are simple, go with my assassins, through the portal and ensure that everything burns nothing survives," said Nicopulas.

"It will be done," replied Fearg, he bowed his head and walked into the shadows of the great hall.

Nicopulas sat back on his throne, with a big smile upon his face, he looked at Gear-ra and then Zoda with a kind smile as he took both of their hands in his.

Standing in the great hall on the eve of the battle was the army of Nicopulas, there was all kinds of creatures in the hall to wish Nicopulas assassins victory over his enemies. The noise was deafening as the war drums sounded inside the hall. At the end of the hall was Nicopulas who was walking amongst his assassins, looking frail and week and supported by Zoda and Gear-ra as he stopped to talk. He was helped back to his throne where he stood for a moment to overlook his army with great pride. He raised his hand and the great hall fell silent.

"My loyal servants, I welcome you to my kingdom. Tonight, we stand united, tonight we go forth to smite our foe of the face of existence, pay homage to our warriors who will face our enemy on this night. Go now and destroy them all," shouted Nicopulas in a triumphant voice.

The drums started to beat, the army to cheer, and the assassins started to march towards the doors at the other end of the great hall. The crowd applauded and cheered until they had marched to the large doors which opened. They marched out of the building into the court yards which had thousands of spectators cheering and beating drums, an escort had joined the front of the assassins they had a giant banner with two large poles and tassels held by giants who were leading the parade of assassins, they waved the giant banner to-and-frow. The banner had an image of Nicopulas who was standing in fire, his wings spread looking magnificent. The gathering of Nicopulas army spread out of the city wall, there were many who had come to celebrate the start of the battle. Large fires were lit along the pathway, the assassins started to hum a somber tune, at first it was hummed quietly by the assassins, it spread slowly through the gathering of the army "O wee O, Way O, O wee O, Way O, the tune got louder and louder. The tune was chanted the entire way up to the foot of the door that would lead them to their battle ground at Hog Hill Farm.

Thomas opened his eyes to find himself standing in the shallow pond, he knew he was dreaming, he had been in the same dream many times before. This dream was different, he looked down to find himself ankle deep in blood. He looked up to see the wall, it seemed far away from him, Thomas started to walk towards the wall as he got closer her could see a figure standing in front of the wall. It was his mother, Mary Jane, she was smiling at him, he smiled back and picked up his pace to reach her. As he got closer, he noticed her face had become distorted, Thomas could see she was in pain.

"Mother are you ok?" he asked.

From over Mary Janes shoulder came the grinning face of Arawn.

"Let her go," shouted Thomas.

Mary Jane slumped to her knees, Arawn was gone, he had just disappeared from behind Mary Jane. Thomas moved fast and held Mary Jane in his arms.

"Mother what's wrong?" Thomas asked frantically as Mary Jane fell into Thomas arms, he placed his arms around her to stop her from falling forward face first into the pond of blood. Thomas could feel something warm and wet he pulled one of his hands away from Mary Jane to have a look. It was blood, Mary Janes blood and there were lots of it, Arawn had hurt Mary Jane, he had stuck his blade into her back.

193

Thomas realised that Mary Jane was he trouble, he shouted for help, but no help came, he tried to pick her up, but she was too heavy.

"Mother, please, please don't die," said Thomas as he looked his mother in the eyes as her life started to leave her. Thomas could hear a rumbling noise like distant thunder, his surrounding stated to shake, the wall in front of him started crumble and fall. Thomas was holding his mother tight.

"Wake, up, wake up sleepy head," suddenly Thomas woke up to see Mary Jane who had been lightly shaking him and telling him to wake up.

"Mother!" said Thomas Roberts with a sound of relief in his voice.

"You need to get up, Murrigan wants to go through some final points," said Mary Jane as she opened the small curtains in Thomas room, she looked across the farm, it looked beautiful and full of life, she wonders what the days end would bring.

"Our you afraid?" asked Thomas.

"A little," Mary Jane replied.

"I'm not afraid, I just don't want any of us to get hurt or worse killed." said Thomas.

"None of us will get hurt and definitely no one is going to get killed, so get up and get going," replied Mary Jane.

Mary Jane stood in the small staircase as Thomas got quickly got dressed, she was petrified of today's outcome, but she knew she had to draw all the courage she could to get her through today.

The Hog Hill Farm final battle preparations were being put in place. Murrigan was standing in the farmyard with Moria and Mary Jane at his side.

"We have a few hours of sunlight, I will go and check our guardians and ensure they are in place," stated Murrigan, he opened his wings and flew up into the sky.

Thomas Roberts has just come out of the kitchen doors, his sheaf of arrows in his hands.

"Where do you want me?" asked Thomas looking at Mary Jane and Moria.

Moria looked at Mary Jane and smiled, *"I will go rally up the farm animals,"* said Moria.

"My young warrior, I need you to be brave and hide down the dry well," said Mary Jane.

"No, no, no, I need to help you, Murrigan and Moria, I need to do this mother, I'm not a child anymore, I'm thirteen now." replied Thomas.

"Fine, here's the plan you stay near the house and protect it from any attack," replied Mary Jane. She was informed by Murrigan that the fighting would be contained in the open ground and that they would never reach the farmhouse. This information gave her some comfort, if Thomas was near the farmhouse, then he was at less risk.

"You must promise me something, if the battle gets too intense and we are overrun you must run hard and fast far away from here. Do you understand me, Thomas Roberts?" asked Mary Jane with a stern look upon her face.

"Yes mother, I understand," replied Thomas.

Murrigan had returned from the frontline and Moria had finished with her speeches to the farm animals. All four stood in the middle of the farmyard, there was a silence amongst them, they all knew that this could be the last time they would all ever be together.

In the distance the sky was darkening, not from the going down of the sun, but a storm moving in over the horizon, the flashing of lighting could be seen lighting up the darkening sky, followed by a distance rumble of thunder.

"There is a storm coming," stated Mary Jane.

"There certainly is," replied Murrigan.

"Right then, who's for cream cake and tea?" asked Moria in an upbeat voice.

Murrigan gave Errol a glance and a nod, Errol was to give the warning call to alert the farm of the assassins coming through the hidden door at the top of hill. The light of the day started to fade, and the rain started to get heavy.

"Cock-a- doodle- do, Cock-a-doodle do," screamed Errol.

"This is it," said Murrigan as he stood up and transformed into a Drumtarian Guardian.

Mary Jane grabbed Thomas and gave him a gripping hug, she was trembling with fear, *"Remember what I said?"* she whispered into his ear.

They all ran out the door of the little farmhouse weapons at the ready and prepared to fight to the end.

-Chapter 16-
The Battle Of Hog Hill

The rain was falling hard and heavy, the storm was just above the farm, the rumbles of thunder where loud and deafening and the flashes of the lighting filled the dark sky.

Murrigan and Moria looked at each other, both smiled and their head touched.

"In this life or the next," said Murrigan.

"In this life or the next," replied Moria.

Murrigan moved towards Mary Jane, he stood over her, they both stood for a moment, he placed his forehead on hers.

"In this life or the next,"

"In this life or the next," Mary Jane replied.

Murrigan moved across to Thomas Roberts, he got down on one knee and looked Thomas in the eyes, Murrigan bright blue eyes where as clear as the blues sea.

"Our you afraid?" asked Murrigan as he looked Thomas is the eyes.

"No sir I am not." replied Thomas.

Murrigan placed his forehead against Thomas's forehead.

"In this life or the next, we will all meet again, do you believe?" asked Murrigan.

"I believe, In this life or the next," replied Thomas Roberts.

"Let's fight, Errol what have we got?" commanded Murrigan.

"Fifteen in the air, with forty to fifty on the ground," replied Errol.

Murrigan silver lace shoot from his right hand and laced a silver arrow from Murrigan's sheaf, which hung over his right thigh, as the arrow came up from the sheaf, Murrigan caught it, in his right hand he drew the arrow over his shoulder and was ready to fire the arrow, before he did, he blew lightly onto the silver arrowhead. The arrowhead caught fire and was burning a bright blue flame. Murrigan launched the arrow into the dark sky as it flew the flame got bigger and brighter, BOOM, the arrow hit the barley field and suddenly a ring of fire spread around the field entrapping the creatures from Drumtara in the ring of fire.

"Moria, Mary Jane, take down the witches, Thomas Roberts guard this farm with your life." shouted Murrigan

Murrigan opened his wings he shot into the sky a few moments later he landed in the middle of the barley field, ready to fight. Moria opened her wings and few into the night sky, Mary Jane cocked both barrel of her shot gun and placed the butt into her shoulder, pointing towards the skies. Thomas already had a silver arrow in his right hand his ring shield in his left ready to defend the farm.

Moria flew into the wind and the rain, she could hear the howls and the screams of the witches war cries, crack, flash the lighting just struck as a witch came flying towards her, the witch had her staff in one hand and a large dagger in the other, Moria seen her coming and drew her long sword, swish, Moria cut the end of the witches staff severing the magic crystal that gave it its magic powers and ability to fly. The witch that had attacked Moria, suddenly found herself falling from a great height.

The witch hit the ground with a thump about ten meters from Mary Jane, the witch got up looked up and screamed.

"Quiet please," said Mary Jane as she lifted her new magic shot gun and pointed in the direction of the fallen witch. BOOM went the shot gun out from the barrel came the small green balls, hundreds of them, hit the witch all over, she looked as if she a small green spot on her face. The witch laughed at Mary Jane.

"You're laughing now, wait for it, wait," said Mary Jane.

Suddenly the little green critters started to grow first their little arms and legs then the razor-sharp teeth, they started to bite into the witch who was frantic, she ran off into the darkness, shouting *"Get them of me,"* a few moments later there was a puff of green smoke and there was silence from the witch. Mary Jane could hear step coming from behind her. *"Woosh"* a silver arrow few past her head, just missing it. *'thud'* there was a sound of something hitting the ground. Mary Jane looks around to see a witch laid on the ground with a large silver arrow sticking out of her. The witch crumpled up on the ground and turned to ash. Mary Jane watched for a moment as the heavy rain washed the ash away.

"You alright, Mother?" she knew that voice, it was Thomas magic shield and an arrow in his hand. *"Great shot,"* said Mary Jane.

"I think Moria, is in trouble there is to many of them," said Thomas as he looked into the sky, there was flashes of lighting, white fire, sparks from blades, it looked like a night time firework display.

"Let give her some help then," said Mary Jane.

Moria was frantically fighting in the air with witches and winged creatures. There was a witch hovering just above Moria, who was about to jump on her. When out of nowhere came the birds, a kestrel hit the witch and unbalanced her a large barn owl hit the witch and knocked her of her staff. The witch was hanging onto her staff in midflight when a large kite ripped the staff from her hands and flew away with it, the witches and creatures where now in battle with the birds and Moria the fight for the skies was getting intense. The witches that fell to the ground were taken out by Mary Jane and Thomas.

Mary Jane looked up and could see a large, winged beast, he was about ten feet from Moria, the creature started to spue out small metal balls from his mouth they were hitting Moria hard, blue blood was pouring from wounds that Moria was receiving from these thousands of small metal ball that where hitting.

Mary Jane realized Moria was in trouble, Mary Jane raised her shotgun into the sky and took aim at the beast, CLICK the gun went off and four small ball, that started to get larger as they flew through the air. The net hit the creature hard wrapping the steel balls around the winged creature. Mary Jane followed the first shot with a second, 'BOOM' this time the small fire ball, floated out of the end of the barrel it floated for a few seconds, suddenly it shot up into the air, getting bigger and bigger, 'BOOM it hit the winged beast, which incinerated on impact.

Moria landed beside Mary Jane and Thomas.

"There retreating to the barley field, to join forces with the ground force, we have forced them out of the sky, we must go and support, Murrigan and our ground force." commanded Moria.

Mary Jane and Thomas could see that Moria had fought hard, she was battered and bleeding, but she look strong and courageous.

"Your hurt," said Thomas.

"Let's sort those wound out, first," said Mary Jane.

"No time we must win this battle, or we will be lost, I will meet you at the opening at the bottom of the field," replied Moria as she shot up into the air.

"Stay here, Thomas protect the farm," commanded Mary Jane.

"Yes, I will,"

Mary Jane started to run towards the barley field that was now burning, from white fire that was coming from the witches staffs. Mary Jane knew that Thomas has some safety being in the area of the farm. As she ran towards the barley field she paused to look round, to see Thomas run into the barn.

As Mary Jane got to the bottom of the barley field, she could see the ferocity of the battle. Creatures from Drumtara had stormed the fields, farm animals and wild animals were engaged in the fight. Mary Jane looked across the field to see the large oak, picking up a large creature and tossed it high into the sky. Mary Jane was overwhelmed at the sight of the battlefield. She could see witches attack the great oak, with white fire, the oak was burning intensely, however it managed to sweep the attacking witches of the ground and smash their bodies together.

Moria landed beside Mary Jane.

"Are you ready?" shouted Moria.

"Born ready," replied Mary Jane.

Moria, drew her sword and her shield appeared from her ring.

"Let's go," said Moria.

Murrigan and Pooka where in the middle of the barley field surrounded by witches and creatures, the fighting was intense, with witches firing bolts of fire at them, beasts with six arms with blades and pikes. As some of the creatures moved closer, they were unaware of what lurked in the long barley. One witch came screaming towards Pooka, Pooka had a small hatchet in his hand, he was about to raise the hatchet and throw it at the witch, when she vanished into the long barley. What lurked in the barley was many wild animals. The witch had been tripped up by a large badger and was now being attacked by foxes, rabbits, and rats, even the farm cat was doing her bit.

Maisy and Bella came running up the field bulldozing and kicking witches and creatures as they ran through the battleground. Moria and Mary Jane caught up with Murrigan and Pooka, the battle raged on.

Thomas was in the barn when a creature walked through the yard, the beast was small, with hoofed feet, small beady white eyes and had two short black pointy horns. The creature was sniffing the air as if hunting its prey. The creature suddenly looked towards the barn its beady white eyes enlarged as it looked towards the barn door. The creature caught a glimpse of Thomas Roberts eye through the crack in the barn door. Thomas stepped back when both their eyes met. Thomas knew the creature had seen him. Thomas stepped back and kicked an empty bucket. The noise was deafening inside the empty barn, Thomas knew that the creature had seen and heard him. Thomas ran and hid at the back of the barn. It was only a short matter of time before the creature would enter the barn.

The creature drew a dagger from his sheaf and walked towards the barn Before he got to the barn, the creature made a clucking sound, two more of these creatures moved over the top of the barn roof. Thomas looked up he could see the dust shimmer to the ground and hear the creaking of the wooden planks that covered the roof.

Thomas could see the shadow of the creature at the barn door. Thomas moved his hand that was by his side close to the sheaf where he had twelve Drumtarian arrows, his silver lace appeared shining under his skin, the lace moved slowly, silently and slid along his fingertips, the lace slide from the tip of his fingers and started to caress the feathers of the arrows. 'SMASH' the door was kicked in by the creature he was screaming a deafening scream at Thomas. 'WHOOSH' the creature hit the floor with a thud the arrow hit the creature in the center of the chest, the impact was so powerful it lifted the creature of it feet and slammed it to the floor. Within a few seconds the creature had turned to dust.

Thomas knew that there were some creatures on the roof, he could hear them banging on the roof, Thomas looked up to see a small hole appearing in the roof. He then noticed that something had been dropped from the hole and landed in the stable. Thomas moved closer to the stable to get a better look at what had been dropped. Thomas could hear the creatures laughing from the roof, as he got closer Thomas looked down to see a cute looking face looking up at him, it was some kind of bug with a cute face and smiling at him. Thomas put out a hand to touch the funny looking bug. Suddenly a trump sound came from behind the bug and a flame shot out of its back end. The flame hit some straw and it caught fire.

"No, No, don't do that," said Thomas in a concern voice.

Thomas opened the gate to the stable, in doing so he startled the bug who let of another *'THRUMPH'* a bigger flame shot out from the bugs backside. More straw caught fire Thomas realized that the creatures on the roof had dropped a fire bug into the barn to burn Thomas out. Thomas managed to pick the bug up, but not before it had another pump. Thomas picked the bug up and placed it inside a horse nose bag, he then placed the bag over his shoulder.

"I think it's time we got out of here," said Thomas.

Thomas knew he would be ambushed as he ran out of the barn door, he also knew he had no other option. As he ran out of the smashed barn door his silver lace lifted the arrow that laid on the ground where the creature he had slain fell. He ran out turned around to see two creatures staring down at him. Both clucked at each other and then launched an arrow each a Thomas. Thomas raised his shield which was invisible to the creatures, both arrows bounced of the shield and fell to the ground. Both creatures looked at each other, clucked and then went to draw another arrow each.

Thomas was ready, by the time the creatures reached for their arrows, Thomas had returned two arrows both striking the creatures, as they fell from the barn roof, they both turned to dust. Thomas was nervous he had another arrow in his hand. The barn was burning intensely, Thomas could feel the heat on his back from the burning barn. Thomas looked towards the farmhouse. There was a strange noise coming from the house he couldn't make the noise out due to the noise of the burning barn behind him the wind had changed, and he was engulfed in the smoke from the barn. The strange noise was getting louder and louder. Thomas could feel a breeze on his face that was also getting stronger, the smoke that once engulfed him had cleared. Thomas coughed to clear the smoke from his lungs. Thomas lifted his head, the strange noise, that was sounding on the breeze was the beating of wings large wings of a blue scaled dragon, The dragon was five times bigger that the small farmhouse. Thomas was breathless, he had never seen anything like it, and he knew that this dragon was not friendly.

As the dragon hovered over the top of the farmhouse, it breathed in deeply and breathed out a blue fire flame deep from within it lungs. Thomas fell to his knees and raised his ring shield to protect himself, the flames bounced of the shield, splintering into shards of blue glass as the flames cooled.

The dragon stopped breathing blue fire and landed on the roof of the small farmhouse, digging its sharp claws into the thatched roof.

"Such a clever thing you are, with your shield and your puny arrows, do you think you can defeat the strength of Fearg, surrender to me and they will live, don't and I will burn all that you hold dear," said Fearg.

Nicopulas had his own plan, Arawn and Bana-shea where not aware of this plan. He had discussed his own battle plan with Fearg. Fearg was promised a throne by Nicopulas side on the agreement Thomas Roberts was destroyed.

203

"I'm not afraid and I will not give into the likes of you," Thomas shouted at Fearg.

"So be it," replied Fearg, just as one of Thomas silver arrows hit Fearg on the chest, as the arrow hit the blue scales, on impact turned to blue glass and the arrow simply bounced off and landed on the ground. The glass scales then turned back into blue scales. Fearg opened his wings gave a loud laugh as he started to flap his long expanded blue wings, he flew above the farmhouse.

Mary Jane looked round when she heard the loud laughter echo through the night sky.

"Murrigan!" she screamed.

Murrigan looked round, the barn was burning, and he could see the image of Thomas standing in the middle of the farmyard and the image of the giant blue dragon flying just over the top of the farmhouse. From the dragon came the blue flame the small farmhouse was burning in the intense heat of fearg's blue flame.

Murrigan realized that Thomas was in trouble. Murrigan open his wings and had just lifted of when something hit him hard, It was a creature, Murrigan had taken his eye of the fight, the dragon and Thomas has distracted him. Murrigan found himself rolling about the ground wrestling the creature another creature joined in. Murrigan was frantically fighting of creatures, no sooner had he defeated one another had joined in.

Fearg took a long deep breath this time he didn't aim his blue flame at Thomas, the flame hit the smaller building around the farmyard, within seconds the whole yard was engulfed in flames. Fearg then continued to deliver his flame encircling Thomas, he had created a ring of fire. Thomas looked around to see that every farm building was in flames. Fearg landed back onto the roof of the burning farmhouse, this time it crashed to the ground, the small farmhouse crumbled under the weight of fearg and the destruction of the blue flames.

Mary Jane had started to run back to the burning farmhouse, she needed to save Thomas, Pooka followed along with Moria, Murrigan was still in a fight with a number of creatures. Once he had shook them off, he shot into the air. The objectives had now changed for everyone, They needed to save Thomas Roberts from the dragon. Murrigan and Moria could not fly into the farm the heat was so intense from the flames. Pooka and Mary Jane could not get through the ring of fire.

Fearg stepped through the flames to face Thomas.

"They cannot save you now, boy, the prophecy of the boy that fell ends here,"

Fearg, took another deep breath and shot out his blue, flame, this time directed at Thomas at close range. Thomas dropped to his knees and raised his shield once again to protect himself. The force of the of the flames was so strong that Thomas found himself being pushed backwards. The shield was doing its job in protecting him from the flames, Thomas had doubts that he had the strength to hold the shield, and the force that was being used against him.

Thomas looked at his hand the silver lace was coiling along his arms down his wrist and flickering on the end of his fingers. Suddenly Thomas has a magical idea. The silver lace moved from his fingertips and wrapped itself round one of the arrows. Thomas flicked the arrow up, just as Fearg stopped breathing fire on him.

Thomas lowered his shield and stood up facing the dragon.

"You are hard to kill, boy, I commend you for your courage," said Fearg.

"I don't fear you, you puny little dragon." replied Thomas.

"I think your courage has changed to stupidity," replied Fearg.

"Go on then, give it all you got, give us a big flame the biggest you ever done," requested Thomas.

Fearg grinned, but his grin was a nervous one, *'what trick was this boy about to conjure,'* Fearg thought.

"We end this now, boy," Fearg roared as he opened is wings and started to flap, the force of fearg's wing nearly forced Thomas of his feet. The force created dust and ash to be lifted into the air and swirl, for a moment Thomas could not see fearg. As the ash settled, he caught a glimpse of him, his head held high as he took a deep breath, Fearg was going to wipe Thomas Roberts of the face of the farm.

Thomas held the arrow by his side, when the time was right, he lifted the arrow above his head and over his shoulder. Thomas could see Fearg he was just about to let loose the blue flame. Thomas flung his Drumtarian arrow just as he released the arrow Thomas screamed out.

"MEADU" the arrow was now flying in the direction of Fearg. The target was the center of fearg's expanded chest. The arrow was getting bigger and bigger as it flew towards its target. Thomas had cast a spell he had been working on to enlarge objects, he used the magic spell to make the arrow bigger. Fearg glanced to see the large arrow hit him directly in the chest. The arrow penetrated the thick blue scales, the arrow buried deep into Fears, chest, first he felt the shock of the arrows impact followed by the intense pain. Fearg fell to the ground smashing into the ruins of the destroyed farmhouse. Thomas paused, he was shaking with fear and excitement. Had he destroyed fearg? Out of the flames, Thomas heard a loud roar, he could see Fearg rise up out of the burning flames wings expanded and flapping, this time there was no flight, Fearg was wounded, blue fire was fanatically released from fearg's closed jaws, the flames poured out like a molting volcano, fearg was rolling his large head back and forth the blue molting fluids fell onto his body and started to burn him after a few moments fearg fell back and was consumed by his own flames.

Thomas sighed in relief, he had destroyed the dragon single handedly, Thomas could see Mary Jane, and Pooka, they both had that look of relief on their faces. Murrigan and Moria Managed to get through the flames and had landed beside Thomas.

"Are you hurt?" asked Moria.

206

"No, I, m ok," replied Thomas.

"Well done lad, but this battle is not over yet," said Murrigan.

A witch flew hard at Pooka she hit him from behind and he tumbled forward, through the ring of flames, that had reduced, but still too dangerous for Mary Jane to jump through. Pooka got back to his feet. He looked directly back at Mary Jane, Thomas, Murrigan and Moria were also staring in her direction standing behind Mary Jane was the powerful figure of Arawn. He slowly stepped closer to her. Mary Jane was unaware of his presents. Thomas looked directly at Mary Jane; he knew she was in trouble.

Mary Jane was, in pain, Murrigan, Moria, Pooka and Thomas where frozen with shock and fear. Mary Jane just continued to stare back. Arawn had stabbed Mary Jane in her back he stabbed hard and deep forcing his dagger deeper into Mary Janes lower back. Arawn rested his head onto Mary Janes shoulder he was looking directly at Thomas Roberts at the same time he spoke to Mary Jane in a calm voice.

"Your time has come, I wait for you at the gates of Creeve, where your soul will be mine," he spoke, with a smile on his face never lifting his gaze from Thomas Roberts. Arawn withdrew his blade and was ready to stab Mary Jane once more. Suddenly, Bimbo had jumped onto Arawn's back biting him hard. Arawn could feel the sharp pain as Bimbo had locked his teeth into his dark flesh. Arawn fought hard to get Bimbo of his back, he swung to his left then his right, hoping that he would loosen Bimbo's grip. Arawn stopped what he was doing, standing still he reached his hand over his shoulder and grab Bimbo by the neck. Arawn gripped Bimbo hard, Bimbo gave a whimper, Arawn swung Bimbo over his head and slammed his body into the ground, Bimbo gave another whimper and laid lifeless on the ground.

The ring of flames was dying down, Arawn was aware of the flames getting lower and at any time Thomas, Murrigan, Moria and Pooka would be ready to attack, Arawn glanced down at Mary Jane who was laid on the ground, he knew she was fatally injured.

"Retreat, retreat," Arawn shouted as he ran away towards the gateway at the top of the hill. One by one Arawn's army started to retreat back through the gateway, back to Drumtara.

Mary Jane laid on the ground bleeding badly and in immense pain, Bana-Shea had landed beside her.

"Forgive me my lady, I did what I could to help you and your child," said Bana-Shea as she held Mary Janes hand.

"Go now, save your daughter and I thank you for all your help," replied Mary Jane as she laid on the ground with her life slowly drawing to an end. Bana-Shea shot into the air with her staff in her hand and landed at the gateway. She took one look back to see the figures of Mary Janes loved ones surrounding her as she lay dying. She glanced around to see the destruction and chaos that had been caused in the heat of battle. Bana-Shea went through the door in the large rock, and it closed behind her leaving a dark cold rock face.

Thomas walked towards Mary Jane followed by Murrigan, Moria and Pooka. Thomas had knelt down beside his mother; he could see she was badly injured.

"We must help her," Thomas shouted as he looked back at Murrigan and Moria. Pooka had fallen to his knees and was sobbing. Moria knelt down beside Mary Jane and held her blood-soaked hand. Moria could feel that her life was drawn to an end, Moria looked up at Murrigan and shook her head *"Sorry,"* Moria said as she stared at Mary Jane.

"What does that mean?" Thomas asked when he seen the reaction from Moria.

"It's fine son, do not trouble yourself," said Mary Jane as she took his hand.

"We did good, they are gone, and you are safe, that all that I need to know," Mary Jane said to Thomas, Mary Jane was in a lot of pain, she was hiding it well.

"I think it's time to say our goodbye's, Murrigan come closer," said Mary Jane. Moria stepped out of the way as Murrigan took her place, he knelt down beside Mary Jane and took her hand. Murrigan looked Mary Jane in the eyes as a blue tear rolled

from his eyes. Murrigan knew also that Mary Janes life was fading.

"Come closer," said Mary Jane, as Murrigan got close Mary Janes whispered something to him, Murrigan listened intensely. As he pulled his head back Murrigan placed his forehead onto Mary Janes forehead and softly spoke.

"In this world or the next," he said.

Mary Jane smiled a smile of content.

Mary Jane looked back at Thomas she smiled, she opens her hands which held the box of requirement, keep this safe its special, Mary Jane closed her eyes and passed away.

"We must act quickly, Pooka and I will take her, you stay with Thomas Roberts." commanded Moria.

"What are you talking about, take her where," cried Thomas.

"Pooka get up, pick up Mary Jane, you need to help Moria." said Murrigan as he reached out a hand and pulled Pooka up of the ground and onto his feet.

A glowing light appeared from Mary Janes body her soul lifted from her; the transparent image of Mary Jane stood over her lifeless body laid on the ground. The soul of Mary Jane looked lost with a dead look in her eyes.

Moria went towards the transparent image and took Mary Janes soul by the hand.

"We must go to the gate way now!" shouted Moria.

Pooka picked up Mary Janes lifeless body, Moria had Mary Janes spirit by the hand, and they started to move up the hill, towards the large rock at the top of hill.

Thomas looked around to see the bodies of the farm animals laid dead on the ground, small white lights started to rise from the dead animal bodies that lay on the ground the souls of the animal started to follow them up the hill. Thomas could see the light image of Bimbo jumping over rocks and tuffs of grass, he looked back, and he could see, Maisy and Errol who had all perished in the battle. As they got to the large rock Moria stopped.

"The Key, we need the key Thomas," said Moria as she glared at Thomas.

"Key, I don't have a key!" said Thomas with a voice of confusion.

Thomas looked at the box in his hand he could see the glow of light coming from the edge. Thomas looked at the box and opened it. He was surprised to see a small rusty key sitting in the middle of the box. Thomas took the key out and reached the key to Moria.

Moria looked at Thomas with a caring smile.

"We must leave you now, Murrigan will stay with you," said Moria.

"No, I don't understand, go where, why, Mother," replied Thomas dazed and confused.

Moria stepped close to the confused Thomas and placed her forehead onto Thomas forehead.

"In this world or the next we will meet again, you will meet Mary Jane, we must save her soul from the damnation of Creeve, her soul must never fall into the hand of Arawn," said Moria.

Moria looked at Murrigan.

"Take care of him," their heads touched for the last time.

"In this world or the next," They both said together.

Moria turned toward the gate way, with Mary Janes soul, Pooka holding her lifeless body and they walked into the gate way, a few moments later all the souls of the farm animal followed. Once they had all went through the gateway closed.

Murrigan picked up a witches staff that lay near him, pointed at the large rock face and uttered the words.

"Sruthan," white fire shot out of the staff and hit the gateway, the white fire melted the rock sealing the gateway shut forever.

The silence was deafening that hung over Hog Hill Farm, the flames that had engulfed the whole area of the farm were simmering out and the dawn was just about to break.

"We need to leave, this place," said Murrigan as Thomas sat on the grass lost in a daze of what had just happened.

"Go where? this is our home," replied Thomas in a quiet tone.

"Our home is gone, stand up lad have a look around, all is lost here," Murrigan said as he reached out his hand for Thomas to take.

Thomas took Murrigan's hand and looked over the farm, Murrigan was right all was gone destroyed in the wrath of the battle.

"Where will we go?" asked Thomas.

"As far away from here, as we can go," said Murrigan.

"What will happen to mother and Moria." asked Thomas.

"All is not lost, take comfort and know this, your mother will be saved but not in this world, in Drumtara the soul can be reborn and live for eternity, as Moria said we will meet again in another time and place."

Bana-shea and Arawn lead the remaining warriors down the mountain path, there was no parade, nor chanting crowd of Drumtarian creatures to greet them. They marched down the path, battle-worn and holding each other up many had wounds and fell on the path. No-one stopped to help them to their feet, and they perished where they laid. There was a strange quietness that made Bana-Shea weary of what was before her. Arawn had a skip to his step, head held high as the slayer of the earthly witch.

They marched until they reached the doors of the great hall. The doors opened and inside they could see the legions of Nicopulas army all staring directly at them. The crowd broke into a cheer of celebration. Bana-Shea and Arawn stepped into the great hall followed by the remaining warriors. Drinks were handed to them, pats on the shoulders, drums beating in triumph and glory of a well-fought battle. Arawn was enjoying his fame with a big smile on his face he raised his fist to the sky, this stirred the crowd and a loud cheer bellowed across the great hall. They continued to walk the long walk to the throne on Nicopulas.

"Welcome home my faithful and victorious," said Nicopulas as the crowd fell silent to listen to what Nicopulas had to say.

"Tell me, were we victorious?" commanded Nicopulas.

Bana-Shea and Arawn and all the warriors fell to their knees and bowed their heads in respect and fear of Nicopulas.

"My lord, we fought long and hard, both sides lost many brave warriors. I bring you news you desire, the powerful one, this Mary Jane, the human witch is no more, slain by my very hand, her blood still wet upon my blade," said Arawn as he drew his dagger, stained with Mary Janes blood.

"Arawn, lord of the underworld, my faithful servant, you have redeemed yourself magnificently, go to your world collect the soul of this witch and bring it to me," demanded Nicopulas.

"Yes, my lord it will be done," replied Arawn, Arawn stood up and started to walk back towards the doors of the great hall. He

knew that Mary Janes flesh and soul would cross the gates of Creeve, Arawn was eager to be the one to greet Mary Jane.

"My lady of the covenant of witches what news of the victory do you bring?" Nicopulas asked Bana-Shea

"My lord we fought long and hard in your honour, the dragon was a surprise element to the battle the dragon was not victorious, it hindered our battle plans, the boy slew the dragon with a single arrow and was allowed to escape," replied Bana-Shea.

"Dragons never trusted such creatures, so the boy lives on, we will endeavour to reap his soul," replied Nicopulas as he raised his hand into the air, from the shadows the sound of chains could be heard dragging along the floor. Two sleepers emerged from the shadows followed by the ragged clothed creature with long filthy black hair. It was Nuska the daughter of Bana-Shea.

Bana-Shea was nervous with excitement, Nicopulas was about to reward her for her battle effort, Nuska was standing a short distance with her head bowed.

"Bring the child to me," requested Nicopulas.

The Two sleepers lead Nuska to Nicopulas Thorne where she stood beside him. Nicopulas parted her long black hair which covered Nuska's face. Bana-Shea excitement was getting the better of her and her body started to quiver with the sight of her daughters face. Nuska stood with her eyes shut, the light of the fires and candles were too much for her eyes, even if she could open them, she had been in the darkness of the towers for so long she had gone shadow blind.

"Open your eyes, my child," commanded Nicopulas. Nuska lifted her head and open her eyes, her eyes were white, a dull white, they stared out into the great hall where Bana-Shea stood but she could not see her mother.

"Nuska," Bana-Shea said in a low voice. Nuska recognised the voice, she only flinched, she remained silenced.

Nicopulas ran his fingers over Nuska's face, her eyes changed from white to emerald green. Nuska took a deep breath, this was the first time she had seen with her own eyes for such a long time. Nuska stared at the image of her mother standing in front.

"Nuska, it's I, your mother," said Bana-Shea with the hope that her daughter would recognise her.

"Mother," came the hoarse voice of Nuska, as she grasped her throat as it burned, her voice had not uttered a word for such a long time it was painful to speak.

"Yes, My child, It mother, come to me," replied Bana-Shea.

Nicopulas took a deep breath and smelt the air, he had an evil smile upon his face.

"Fear, I adore the smell of fear, such a content smell, don't you think?" as he growled and stared direct at Bana-Shea.

From the shadows, Torm appeared and stood beside Nicopulas. He put out his hand and touched Torms hand.

"A little demon tells me that you have lost your way, my little demon tells me you have betrayed me.

Unexpectedly Bana-Shea draws her staff from under her cloak, just as she is about to utter a spell, Nicopulas raised his hand and the staff flew into the grip of Nicopulas, his long white fingers with razor-sharp nails took a firm grip of Bana-Shea's staff.

"Know this Bana-Shea queen of the witch, your daughter will watch you burn, the image will hunt her for eternity as her soul lays wasted in my towers," screeched, Nicopulas in a rage.

Nicopulas pointed the staff at Bana-Shea and uttered the words *"Struthan,"* white fire bellowed from the staff hitting Bana-Shea, she did not flinch, she did not scream. Bana-Shea stood tall and proud staring at Nuska, who stood staring back, Nuska did not flinch she did not cry out, she stood there watching her mother burn and turn to ash in the heat of the white fire.

Nicopulas sat on his throne and laughed an evil laugh that echoed through the great hall, He stopped laughing, and looked directly at Nuska.

"My child, you will spend eternity with me in my towers," he ran his hand over Nuka's face her eyes turned white and lifeless and she slipped back into the nightmare of her demons and darkness.

Arawn sat upon his throne with his raven perched upon his arm, in his hand a gold gauntlet with red jewels embedded into the rim. He was looking out at the gates watching the bookkeeper and the table which held the book of souls. Arawn could see figures walking towards the gate, an old man holding the hand of his soul, he walked up the book of souls. The bookkeeper pointed his boney finger at the book *"Make your mark,"* spoke the bookkeeper. One of the old men took the quill and wrote his name. The bookkeeper looked on as the old man put the quill down, *"Walk on,"* said the deathly looking bookkeeper as he pointed to the gates. The two old men walked up to the gates which opened to let them in.

"Well come two Creeve," said Arawn as he greeted the old man and his identical soul.

"You have signed the line, now pay the way," stated Arawn.

The identical soul image of the old man passed into Arawn, and the body of the old man keep walking into Creeve. Time passed and many passed the gates and signed the book. Arawn was getting frustrated. He got up from his throne throwing his raven into the air. Arawn walked up to the gates, and they opened he walked fast to the book of souls and the bookkeeper.

The bookkeeper pointed at the book with his boney finger *"Make your mark,"* said the deathly creature to Arawn.

"Get out of my way you imbecilic," scolded Arawn.

Arawn looked at the book and started to move his long black fingernail along the lines reading the names.

"Where is she, did I miss her, her name has to be here," Arawn was speaking out aloud, there was panic in his voice.

"No, no, no, she lives, she survived, not possible," shouted Arawn, as he looked around to his throne, he caught the glimpse of two sleepers who had come to collect Mary Jane.

"Walk on!" said the bookkeeper as his boney finger pointed to the gates where the sleepers stood.

Thomas and Murrigan had left Hog Hill Farm, knowing they would never return, for days they had moved between towns and villages, looking for farm work. They were strangers and were not welcomed in many of the small farming villages. Thomas and Murrigan never went hungry as the box of requirements would always provide a shilling to buy food. Thomas was going distant and Murrigan was concerned, he didn't have the same abilities as Mary Jane or Moria to deal with Thomas emotions. Murrigan was suffering also he missed the farm; he missed the companionship. Murrigan knew that he was all the family that Thomas had left, and he had vowed to protect and honour Mary Janes last wish.

Thomas and Murrigan had just entered a small village, Thomas stopped at the sign *'Swale,'* the village was named Swale, after the river that ran through it. Thomas and Murrigan crossed the bridge into the village and could see the main street. The street was busy with people walking up and down chatting to each other. There were young men in olive green uniforms, black boots and peak hats they were soldiers, young men from the village, off to join the local regiment and fight in a great war. Thomas was startled by the hustle of the small village alive and bustling in the early summer morning of August 1915.

"Do you smell that? that smells like bacon sandwich to me," said Murrigan as he started to walk further into the village. Thomas passed the post office window, Murrigan was hurrying in front of him on the scent of a bacon sandwich.

"YOU BOY," came a loud voice as Thomas passed the window of the village post office. Thomas turned around, to find no one standing behind him. Thomas peered at the window of the post office to see a poster of a soldier, the top of the poster

stated, '*Your Country Needs You,*' suddenly the image of the soldier started to move.

"*You my lad, your young, fit and healthy and we need you to join the army and fight for king and country, the village hall across the road is recruiting today.*"

Thomas looked over his shoulder to see a young man come out with a beaming smile and wearing a smart army uniform, Thomas looked back at the image on the poster and the soldier winked at him. Thomas turned around and started to walk towards the red doors of the village hall. Murrigan was waffling on about his bacon sandwich when he realised that Thomas was no longer behind him. Murrigan swung around quickly, Thomas was gone, he glances across the road and the back of Thomas caught his attention. Murrigan moved quickly to catch up with Thomas who was now standing at the closed red doors of the village hall.

"*What's on your mind?*" asked Murrigan in a quiet voice. Thomas turned and looked at Murrigan.

"*We need to do something; I can't bear this moving around from town to town,*" replied Thomas

Murrigan knew what Thomas had on his mind, he was seeking acknowledgement and hoped that Thomas was only imagining what it was like to join the army during a war. Thomas reached the door handle of the red doors, Murrigan placed his hand on the door to prevent Thomas from opening the door.

"*You're too young to join the army, they won't let you join,*" said Murrigan, there was tension in his voice, he didn't want Thomas to join the army.

"*Was I too young to watch my mother die?*" asked Thomas he paused and looked at Murrigan who released the pressure from the door Thomas opened the door and walked in, Murrigan followed. Halfway down the corridor of the village hall was a table with a well-dressed soldier, he was sitting upright looking proud, he had three white stripes on each arm and a red sash which hung over his shoulder and ran across his chest. He was cleaned shaven apart from the thick bushy moustache on his upper lip, well-groomed, waxed with a point at either end.

"Come here lads", said the soldier behind the desk.

"My name is Sergeant O'Neill, I assume you both want to join up and serve your country, you have come to the right place, right then lad, you first, what your name?" asked Sergeant O'Neill.

"My name is Thomas Roberts," replied Thomas as he stood tall in front of the Sergeant.

"I require your address and your date of birth and next of kin," requested the Sergeant.

Thomas noticed something strange about Sergeant O'Neill's face it had swollen and become quite red. Thomas notice he also became more aggressive.

"Hurry it up boy we don't have all day, there is a war to win," he snapped at Thomas.

"Yes sir, my address is Hog Hill Farm of the town of Trim my, next of kin," Thomas paused.

"My next of kin, I don't have any my parents are dead," Thomas replied.

"Date of birth, lad?"

"My date of birth is 13th October 1902" replied Thomas.

Sergeant O'Neill put down the quill pen in his hand and looked up at Thomas.

"Lad you need to go outside and have two birthdays, do you know what I mean?" asked the Sergeant

"Yes sir, I understand,"

Thomas turned to walk out the door, Murrigan was standing at the desk, the Sergeant, stared at Murrigan he was angry looking and red-faced.

"You, you need to grow at least another twelve inches, you're too short," said the Sergeant with an evil grin on his face. Murrigan turned and ran out the door to find Thomas standing there.

"How strange, when he asked who my next of kin were, I realised that I have no one, no parents," said Thomas, Murrigan could see the sadness in his face.

"We don't need to do this Thomas, we can find a nice farm, even buy one, crops, animals, even a couple of good horses to ride," said Murrigan as he tried to convince Thomas to walk away from the village hall.

"Sounds good, but I need to do this," replied Thomas as he turned and walked in through the red doors. Thomas walked up to the desk.

"My date of birth, sir is 13th October 1900," said Thomas, as he claimed he was nearly fifteen, Thomas had not yet turned fourteen and lied about his age.

"Good lad, sign here and walk towards the main hall through those blue doors, the corporals will issue you your uniform and give you direction to your billets," smiled the Sergeant.

Murrigan was standing behind Thomas, he strangely had found the twelve inches the Sergeant had requested.

"Where do I sign?" asked Murrigan as Sergeant O'Neill glared at Murrigan, confused that he was a lot taller than he was when he first met him.

"Here," replied the Sergeant. Murrigan signed the papers and ran to catch up on Thomas.

"He's a strange one, we will need to keep an eye on him," Murrigan said to Thomas.

Thomas turned to look at Sergeant O'Neill who had stood up and was looking directly at Thomas and Murrigan.

"Yes, strange," replied Thomas as he opened the blue double doors into the village hall. Inside the hall were several tables.

"Over here you crow's," shouted the fat corporal standing at the first table. Thomas and Murrigan walked over to the first table. Laid on the table was large olive green sausage bags, the corporal picked two up and threw one each at Thomas and Murrigan. Thomas managed to catch his Murrigans, bounced off his chest and landed on the floor.

"Next table, crows," shouted the corporal as he moved to the next table.

"Four pairs of socks," he shouted throwing them very fast at Thomas and Murrigan, they landed on the floor as they bent down to pick them up two pairs of boots came flying over the table, followed by trousers, shirts, jackets and long johns. The floor of the hall was covered with army uniforms.

"Bag it you crow's," screamed the corporal. Thomas and Murrigan picked up the uniform as quickly as they could and ran out of the green doors that the corporal was pointing at.

"Hello, I'm private McGinn and I'm private Mc'Bee, I take it you have had your introduction to corporal, Fat Mat McKendry?" asked private McGinn, standing in front of Thomas and Murrigan where two young fresh-faced soldiers smartly dressed in their army uniforms.

"Yes, we have had the pleasure," replied Thomas.

Both soldiers laughed, private McGinn placed out his hand and shook Thomas hand firmly.

"They call me badger," private McGinn said as he shook Murrigans hand.

"Badger!" replied Thomas with a curious look. Badger removed his army cap he had a short back and side haircut, with longer hair on top, he placed his hand on his head and showed Thomas and Murrigan a white strip that ran across the side of his head. The black hair and white strip looked like the marking of a badger. Thomas smiled to acknowledge the markings on badgers hair, he never asked why he had this white stripe of hair.

"I'm Thomas and this is Murrigan," replied Thomas.

"Jim's the name, and it good to meet you both," replied private Mc'Bee as they all shook hands and got acquainted with each other.

"We will take you to our billets, you will be joining us in Swale Company 586, most of us are from the village or nearby farms. There are three platoons in swale company we are three platoon. Sgt O'Neill is our platoon Sgt. He is a nasty piece of work; you'd be best to stay in his good books," said Badger. The four newly aquatinted friends walked through the town chatting and laughing. Thomas felt a sense of belonging with his new friends. He looked back at Murrigan who looked less than impressed that he had just joined the army. Thomas looked at him and smiled, he was also happy that Murrigan would be by his side.

"Here we are," shouted Jim, as they entered a large field with hundreds of half doomed nissen huts. Small gravel paths lead to the front door of the nissen huts, two blacked-out windows

one on either side of the door. Thomas and Murrigan followed Jim and Badger, who were now marching in step with their arms swinging.

"We need to march while in camp, if your caught, not marching you roll the dice," said Badger

"Roll the dice!" replied Murrigan.

"Sgt O'Neill has two dice in his pocket, mess up and he makes you roll the dice for extra guard duties, get a double your unlucky you get to roll again, nasty piece of work is Sgt O'Neill," said Jim.

They continued to walk deeper into the camp. Until Jim shouted *"HALT"* Jim and badger stopped suddenly slamming their left foot into the ground.

"Look to your left the large white nissen hut with the red cross is the medical centre, beside it is our mess hall, bad food and beer that tastes like......," badger never got to finish his statement.

"What are you crows doing?" came a roaring scream from behind them, Thomas recognised the voice of Sgt O'Neill, he could see Badger and Jim shaking.

"These two men are showing us to our billets and giving us a tour of the camp," replied Thomas in a confident voice.

Sgt O'Neill stared directly at Thomas, there was a nervous twitch at the corner of Sgt O'Neill mouth, his face was turning red with anger and the twitch got faster. Sgt O'Neill moved swift and fast as if he glided across the ground, he was standing directly in front of Thomas the peak of his cap almost touching Thomas on the forehead, He was staring Thomas directly in the eyes. Thomas did not flinch he stood his ground and stared back. Thomas could smell a foul scent on the Sgt breath, he had smelt it before a nasty smell, he could not recall where he had smelt this awful smell before.

"Sergeant," growled Sgt O'Neill.

"My apologies Sgt O'Neill, day one Sgt, won't happen again Sgt," grovelled Thomas.

Murrigan could see the two dice in the Sgt right hand, he was rolling them very fast through his finger, so fast that Murrigan thought that it was not normal, Murrigan stepped forward, Thomas caught Murrigans movement out of the corner of his eye, Thomas raised his hand slightly to indicate that Murrigan should not get involved.

"Very well, carry on men," said Sgt O'Neill in a very calm voice he turned and walked away. A large sigh of relief came from Badger and Jim.

"Bloody hell, you were as cool as a cucumber, I think I wee'd myself," said Jim.

There was a moment of silence, then all four bursts into fits of laughter. Jim and Badger continued introducing Thomas and Murrigan to the camp, explaining rules, regulations, dress codes, and the correct manner to respond to ranking soldiers. They finally got to their billet, above the door was the company name *'Swale Company 586,"*

"Let find you two bunks," said Badger as they entered into the nissen hut. The first thing that hit Thomas and Murrigan was the heat inside and the smell of sweaty feet.

"It gets awfully hot and stuffy in here," said Jim.

"It will be cold in the wintertime," replied Badger.

"You won't be here in the wintertime, we march on France in eight weeks," came a voice from an older man sitting on his bunk.

Thomas and Murrigan found a bunk bed beside, Jim and Badger.

"I'll take the top," said Murrigan, Thomas just smiled and threw his sausage bag onto the bottom bunk.

"It will soon be dinner time, you two better get into uniform," said Badger.

Thomas grabbed his uniform and started to get dressed, Murrigan did the same, however, nothing seemed to fit, his trousers were too short, his sleeves on his shirt too long and his cap was so big, which kept falling off his head.

Thomas stood beside Murrigan.

"You look smart, your mother would be proud of you," said Murrigan with a look of pride.

"You don't look quite right in that uniform," laughed Thomas.

Murrigan muttered a few words, suddenly the hat shrunk to fit his head perfectly, the sleeves grow to fit his arms and the trouser legs grow to fit his legs. To finish it off his boots had such a dazzling shine he could see his face in them.

"*No, no, no, you can't use magic here,*" said Thomas as he looked around to see if anyone had seen what had happened. Murrigan stood tall and proud with a big grin on his face. Thomas glared at Murrigan.

"*And thats cheating,*" scolded Thomas as he looked down at the amazing shine on Murrigans boots.

"*Grubs up,*" came a shout from the door, suddenly the loud sound of clanging and clattering could be heard ringing through the nissen hut. Then everyone in the hut swarmed towards the door. Jim and Badger were one of the first to jump off their bunks and make the dash for the door. Murrigan and Thomas looked at each other for a moment.

"*food!*" shouted Murrigan and made a mad dash for the already crowded doorway, Thomas was not far behind him.

In the mess hall there were long queues of well-dressed smart-looking soldiers, all wearing brand new uniforms. They queued quietly and all that was heard was the squeaking of new boots as they shuffled along in the queue to gather their dinner. The queue moved quickly, and it was Thomas and Murrigan turn to get their food.

"*Mess tins,*" said the chef behind the counter.

"Mess tins?" asked Thomas looking at Murrigan

"Mess tins!" replied Murrigan with a curious look upon his face.

"*Yes, you clown's mess tins you put your food in them,*" shouted the impatient chef.

Suddenly the whole mess hall burst into fits of laughter, everyone had small steel tins, with folding steel handles, these were mess tins, they could be used for cooking and heating water over a fire. Thomas and Murrigan didn't bring theirs to the mess hall.

"*Where's your KFS and cup?*" asked the chef who was standing with his arms folded with his ladle dripping gravy onto his white apron.

"KFS!" replied Murrigan.

"Knife, Fork and Spoon, get out of my mess hall before I make you wear this stew," screamed the chef.

Murrigan grabbed Thomas and they both left the mess hall as quickly as they entered it. Standing outside the late summer sun was getting lower in the sky.

"I'm hungry," said Murrigan.

"Me too," replied Thomas.

"Fish and Chips," smiled Murrigan.

"Yeah" replied Thomas with a big smile.

Murrigan and Thomas started to march down the gravel path in the direction of the town when Sgt O'Neill stepped out in front of them.

"And where do you two think you are going on this fine evening?" asked Sgt O'Neill with a grin and a twitch on his lips.

"Into town Sgt for some fish and chips, your welcome to join us Sgt," replied Murrigan.

"I'm afraid not," said Sgt O'Neill.

"That's a shame, Sgt," replied Murrigan as he tried to walk past Sgt O'Neill. Sgt O'Neill placed his hand on Murrigan shoulder.

"You see lad, I can have fish and chips any time I want, you are grounded, all recruits while in basic training are confined to camp, so turn yourself around and march back to your barracks. Before I have you shot for desertion," said Sgt O'Neill with an evil glare and a twitch from his mouth.

"Come on Murrigan, we have boots to polish," said Thomas as he turned and walked back to his billets. Thomas and Murrigan both went to bed very hungry, the rumbling of Murrigan belly was echoed through the whole of the nissen hut keeping everyone awake. Thomas was tired and soon drifted off into a restful night's sleep.

The next morning Murrigan and Thomas were up before everyone else, they gathered their mess tins, KFS and their big metal mugs. They were standing outside the mess hall not just first in the queue, they were the only ones in the queue. Sgt O'Neill walked past them and into the mess hall.

"Morning Sgt O'Neill," said Thomas as he passed, Sgt O'Neill did not acknowledge them, he didn't even look at them.

"Odd Ball," scolded Murrigan.

Thomas and Murrigan waited for over an hour the queue had grown, suddenly the doors open, and the feeding line began.

"Bacon, eggs, sausage, fried bread, a mug of tea, what more could you possibly need," said Murrigan with a satisfied look upon his face. Just as Murrigan and Thomas took their first mouthful the front door of the mess hall opened, standing in the light coming from the doors was Sgt O'Neill. Wearing a pair of very short dark blue shorts and a very tight red v neck T-shirt, with his bushy chest hair protruding through the V.

"Look at the state of you all, I am expected to take you to war, fight for king and country and you cannot follow a simple order, ten seconds late for my parade. Ten miles you owe me, one mile for every second you were all late. Or we can roll the dice, boys". Sgt O'Neill sneered.

"We will take the ten Sgt," came a voice from the ranks.

"Ten it is, to the tower and back," shouted Sgt O'Neill.

The platoon ran out of the mess hall and formed three ranks facing the mess hall, *"Left turn,"* shouted Sgt O'Neill, the three rows of men turned to the left on the command of a left turn. Murrigan who was still munching on a sausage did not turn, until Thomas physically, had to turn him to face the right direction. *"Break into quick time,"* shouted Sgt O'Neill. The men started to run together as a large squad, keeping in step as they ran.

"What's the tower?" Thomas asked Badger.

"Do you see that very high hill, on top of it is a water tower, you run up and around it, five miles up, five miles down, knee-deep in mud," replied Badger.

Thomas was starting to feel his energy drain, it was a long five miles up, the mud was thick and wet, it was harder coming down as there was little grip in the slippery mud. Murrigan looked at Thomas, he could see he was struggling, tired, weak and hungry. Thomas slipped on the way down the hill and landed hard on his face. Murrigan reached down and pulled Thomas to his feet.

225

"We can go right now, leave this place, just say the words and we can go," said Murrigan.

"No, who would I really be, If I ran away every time something gets difficult. I will see this out, I hope you will be by my side," replied Thomas as he gathered his strength and continued to keep running.

"Always," said Murrigan as he watched Thomas determined to complete the task.

Each day in basic training was full of surprises, Sgt O'Neill was determined to break the minds and souls of every man in his platoon. Over time the platoon became closer, friendships were made, letters written and exchanged promises made and sworn upon, this made them stronger for the war that lay ahead.

"Pack you, gear lads were off to France," said Sgt O'Neill, who was standing at the front door of Swale Company 586 Nissen hut.

"This is it, we go to war today," said Jim.

"We will do a short farewell parade through the town, look your best lads all the girls will be there, to wish you luck and you never know steal a kiss," said Badger, with a smug grin.

Everyone was trying to be upbeat; Thomas knew what was to come, the loss, the grief and the pain. Both Thomas and Murrigan were packed and ready to go.

"Fall in Swale Company 586," came the shout from outside. Each man picked up his kit and rifle and made their way outside. There was no scramble to the door, there was an eerie calm and each man from Swale company got into line and walked out of the nissen hut for the last time.

"Fall in three ranks, stand easy," shouted Mr. O'Leary,

Mr. O'Leary was Swale Companies ranking officer, he held the rank of Lieutenant, He spent very little time with Swale Company and would occasionally hold an inspection parade and speak to the men in each platoon. Thomas and Murrigan had spoken to Mr. O'Leary a few times, he was polite and well-spoken, he was from an upper-class family in the town. A figurehead, tall, handsome and wore his uniform with pride.

As Mr. O'Leary stood in front of Swale Company 586, Thomas could see he was shaking.

"He's shaking," Thomas said in a low voice.

"So am I," said Jim

"Me too," replied Badger.

Thomas looked at Murrigan, he was not shaken, *'why am I not shaking, I' don't feel scared,'* Thomas thought to himself.

"Swale Company, attention," shouted Mr. O'Leary the whole company stood rigid and tall slamming the right heel into the ground beside their left foot. The noise of 100 men coming to attention all at once was a magnificent sound.

"Shoulder arms," every soldier grasped their rifle and raised them resting the barrel and stock on their right shoulders and grasping the butt of the rifle at the same time. This was a drill that Swale company had practised for hours and hours, the drill was carried out to perfection by every man in the company.

"Left turn," came the command from Mr. O'Leary, all at once every man swivelled on their left foot to point in a left direction followed by the right foot lifted and slammed into the ground to meet the left foot, every man in the company was facing in the same direction, ready for the march into town. Thomas could see the other companies there were fifteen hundred men ready to march to war. The shaking had stopped, and the sense of pride swept over the men.

"By the front, quick, march," shouted Mr. O'Leary at the same time the beat of the regimental bands bass drum started.

Boom, boom, boom, boom followed by the pipers and the drummer's boys. The sound was sensational. Each man stepped to the beat of the bass drum.

"Left, right, left, right, left right," Mr. O'Leary shouted with every beat of the bass drum and every man following his every command. As they marched through the entrance of the barrack. Sgt O'Neill who was marching at the side of three platoon shouted out.

"Heads high three platoon," heads were lifted arms straight and extended. For the first time in a long time, Thomas felt proud

227

and alive. As the men marched into the town, they could see banners and hear the crowds cheers. Thomas suddenly felt a strange cold sensation, he knew that no one was watching him, no one was going to wish him luck or kiss him goodbye, No one in this town knew his name, Thomas was feeling lonely, he felt his handshaking and a sense of fear came over him.

The noise from the crowd got louder, Mother's, wife's daughter's, aunt's and grandmothers were running into the companies and hugging their sons', husbands, and boyfriends. No one came to Thomas, no family no friends. As Thomas marched on his thoughts turned to his mother Mary Jane, he was missing her more than ever.

"Thomas, Thomas Roberts," came a shout from the crowd. Thomas looked towards the crowds of people, so many faces that he did not recognise. He knew the voice but could not see the face that fitted.

"Thomas, Thomas Roberts," The voice was louder.

"Mother," Thomas spoke out but not loud, Thomas looks around frantically, *'where is she'* he thought, Thomas stepped out of the ranks and stood looking around for Mary Jane. Thomas was spinning and felt that he had entered a strange dream. Suddenly he stopped standing in front of him was his mother, Mary Jane.

"Look at you, all grown up," said Mary Jane as she placed, her hands on Thomas's chest.

"I miss you so much," replied Thomas as tears streamed down his face as he stood there looking at Mary Jane.

Mary Jane smiled.

"Be brave my boy, I'm here always here," Mary Jane laid her hand on Thomas's chest.

"Get back in line," came a loud voice, Thomas realised Sgt O'Neill was screaming at him to get back in line. Thomas looked at Mary Janes, she had gone.

"Yes Sgt," replied Thomas as he was making his way back to three platoons. Thomas soon caught up, he noticed that

Murrigan had a big smile on his face and was humming a tune along with the bagpipes.

"What you are so happy about?" asked Thomas as they both marched together.

"I think your starting to understand" smiled Murrigan.

"Understand what?" replied Thomas a little confused by Murrigan riddles.

"In this world or the next we will meet again," whispered Murrigan, just loud enough for Thomas to hear.

"Yes, yes I do," replied Thomas.

Swale Company 586 marched through the town and into the valley towards the coast where a ship waited, to take them to France. The band played on until the bass drum faded to a rumble of thunder in the distance.

THE END
TO BE CONTINUED
The Wolfbeing And The Blood Moon Curse

Printed in Great Britain
by Amazon

82367358R00132